Rare Earth

JM BAYLISS

jmbayliss.com

Rare Earth

March 2022. This book is a work of fiction. Unless otherwise stated names, characters and incidents are the product of the author's imagination and any resemblance to actual people living or dead or any historical event is entirely by coincidence.

ISBN 978-1-7397245-0-4

Mark's debut novel 'The Lucidity Programme', is a paranormal mystery, and best-seller, reaching #33 in its Amazon category in 2021.

His short story 'Taste the Darkness', won the Henshaw International Short Story Competition in December 2019 and can be found in his anthology of short stories 'Valley Noir - Valley Blanc'. A mixture of mysterious, dark, and fun short stories, inspired by Wales.

In memory of my grandmother
Augusta 'Gussie' Carter 1905-1928

Fact

Rare Earth Minerals, Metals, and Coal Fields.

The most valuable metals mentioned in this story *do* exist. Today they *are* worth more than gold. The periodic table classifies them as 'Noble metals', categorised somewhere between rare earth metals and precious metals such as silver, gold and platinum. Coalfield spoils around the world, similar to those in Blaenavon, *are* known to contain such valuable metal particles, but usually, though not always, in smaller PPM (parts per million) than suggested in this book. Large global corporations *are* already identifying and targeting old coalfields.

The particles are minuscule. So please don't waste your time and rush out with a carrier bag and a metal detector!

Original Artwork produced by Michael Blackmore
Copyright of Blaenavon World Heritage Site Partnership.
With thanks to V Gopalan

Chapter Index

Chapter 1

Cold Heart

Blaenavon, Wales - February 1973

"It's getting dark, I wanna go home now Jason. I've had enough, my hands hurt, please, *please*, I wanna stop and go home. I want my mam."

Rhys could barely feel the warmth of the tears as they streamed over his taut rosy cheeks and mingled with the snot dribbling from his runny nose.

Irritated by the annoying outburst Jason swooped, plucked the wet red bobble hat off his little brother's head, and flung it across the frozen pond. "Yeah, well I'm off, you can go home on your own. You'd better fetch that first though."

At the end of a harsh winter week, the high and exposed Keeper's Pond endured an incessant, biting north-easterly. The centuries-old irregular-shaped pond, about the size of three large football pitches, once served a long gone mining community as a reservoir. That week the expanse of deep water transformed into a shimmering pane, surrounded for miles around by the ethereal topography of *talc dusted* heather mounds, with not a single tree in sight. It looked like a moonscape – with sheep.

Late on a quiet Saturday afternoon, the two young Price step-brothers played at the pond, two miles over the mountain moors from their home in the Welsh coal-mining town of Blaenavon. The boys wore wellies, bread bags over socks for extra warmth, knitted woollen gloves - frozen rigid, and parkas with rabbit-pelt brims and rubber-lined pockets.

The eldest, eleven-year-old Jason tormented and bullied eight-year-old Rhys relentlessly, the same as he did most days. As a toddler, Rhys suffered brief spells in a hospital due to his asthma. A misguided Jason always felt devoid of a fair share of affection and attention growing up, often taking things out on his little brother. The vindictive, disturbing cycle perpetuated, as Jason's volatile step-father and vicious leather belt responded to Jason's behaviour with great regularity. No amount of whining from his wet, and cold brother would resonate with him that day at the *Keepers.*

Rhys wailed even louder, trudged off the snow-laden bank, and gingerly shuffled his way across the ice towards the awaiting bobble hat, to a spot where they played earlier. They had practised jumps and attempted 360-degree mid-air spins, neither landing them with any success, ending up with wet backsides and even colder hands. As he shuffled, he rubbed behind his left ear where the bendy wire arm of his steamed up NHS glasses kept digging in. The ear rubbing discomfort always became more noticeable when something or someone, usually Jason, upset him.

When Rhys bent down to pick up the hat, Jason yelled from behind him, "Hey Rhys!"

Rhys turned and spotted a large chunk of rock, the weight of a bag of sugar, looping through the air. It must have taken every ounce of Jason's strength to hurl the heavy rock as high and far as it went, landing with a hefty thud at Rhys's feet. The boys had thrown dozens of smaller, similar-shaped rocks earlier, which all landed, and chattered along the ice with the hint of an echo. Not on that occasion. The sharp-edged rock became embedded in the ice as cold mountain water oozed upwards all around it. Straight after the initial thud came a groaning and creaking noise, followed by the sharp sudden snap of wellies penetrating vulnerable thin ice. A splash, and another shocking splash. Rhys's terrified screams echoed all around the pond, but with the frosty surrounding area deserted, no one else could hear him. Only his brother.

Standing motionless on a nearby heather mound, Jason peered out from his parka hood. He kept his hands in his pockets as he observed his sibling's distress, fascinated, amused - and pleased. Always a spiteful child, not a muscle moved as Jason stared expressionless at his brother's desperate grasps. His useless woollen gloves made frantic clawing motions, polishing the hard shiny surface before he disappeared from view.

Rhys's wellies, parka hood and rubber-lined pockets filled with water. The rest of his clothes sponged up more pints, all combining to drag him under the freezing water. He emerged for a moment, gasping from the surprise and frigid shock, yet somehow his lungs helped produce a desperate scream for help. Rhys summoned up all the strength and energy his tiny body could muster. Instinctively kicking his legs, his wellies dropped away under the surface, giving him the impetus to place an elbow then a knee on the ice. He appeared to have rescued himself. But once again the ice snapped, and he lost his energy-sapping battle to gravity for a second and final time.

Three yards to the side of the vacant ice hole, a bare hand pressed upwards against the underside of the frozen barrier. Then a face. Then nothing. Jason Price never saw the face of his little brother again after that moment.

Within a year of the tragic *accidental* event, the Price family moved away from Blaenavon, without ever uncovering the truth about what happened to their youngest son. After Rhys's funeral, amidst speculation and local tongues wagging, moving away became the only option for them to put the past behind them.

~

Jason Price's next visit to the Keepers Pond came forty-nine years later. He passed by in his Range

Rover, his responsibility for the dreadful incident and his poor brother's screams for help barely registered, erased, as he stared impassively across the moors. He gave a cursory sideways glance towards the expanse of water, more interested in admiring the mountain ponies and scenic views stretching out towards Crickhowell and Brecon than recollecting Rhys's last gasps of life.

Price had more important things on his mind than a younger brother wiped from his memory five decades ago.

Chapter 2

The Olive's Evidence

Cardiff, Wales - November 2021

Sorry Lauren, I don't understand, is there something wrong with the Zoom connection? Or could it be because I'm on Australian time and half asleep? Did you say they fired you for eating an olive? Darling, you work in a pizza parlour. How can they fire anyone for eating an olive for God's sake?"

"Mum, it's complicated. And it wasn't even a whole olive, just half of one. I could hardly keep my eyes open, and my stomach wouldn't stop rumbling. I did a shift at the bakery in town last night, got four hours sleep, went to Uni for one early rubbish lecture and then started a lunch shift at Luigi's. To make matters worse my one-to-one at Uni made me late, and Luigi's is in Cardiff Bay, so I needed a taxi to make it over there in time. Today's been crap. End of."

"I'm worried about you, you're overdoing it. You know we can wire you some more money if you need it, you only have to ask. How much do you need?"

"Mum I'm fine for money, honestly, well apart from the obvious. Look, everyone, my age has a Uni-fee overdraft, though not as big as mine. And *I* decided to do a *Masters* in the UK, nobody forced me to come here and do it. It seemed like a great idea at the time, and most of the time it is. I just hate 'Two-for-One-Wednesdays' that's all."

Lauren's mother remained concerned, "So how did you come to lose your job all of a sudden, what happened? I mean all over an olive. Sorry, half an olive?"

"Mum, you won't believe this. As usual, a typically chaotic day, non-stop with customers and screaming kids when a young couple came in. They sat down and ordered a large pepperoni pizza to share. So, fifteen minutes later the service bell pinged, and as I picked up the pizza from *the pass* to take it to their table, I spotted an olive, *the olive*, with my name on it. I plucked it up and ate it, carried on walking, and plonked the pizza down on their table. As soon as I did, I spotted a long saggy string of mozzarella stretching from my chin to their pizza. I nearly died. They both looked at me. I looked at them. I wiped my chin and ran off."

Lauren could see the transformation in her mother's mortified face at the other end of the Zoom call. The screen appeared as though it had frozen with her mother's mouth stuck wide open. Moments later her shoulders shook uncontrollably, as she made an unsuccessful attempt to contain fits of laughter with her head bowed and face in her hands.

She wiped tears from the corner of each eye, and said, "Well you always did love cheese, but when did you develop a taste for olives, I had no idea?"

"It's not funny Mum, but you're right I love cheese, although I seem to have gone off olives; can't understand why. So they decided to call the manager over and when I ended my shift, he finished me up. Nightmare."

"Oh Lauren, never mind love. Hey, before I forget, Gran asked about you, I told her you are fine, but she's not remembering much. I tell her the same things every time I speak with her. I told her you're home for a few weeks next year for Olivia's wedding."

"Mum, next time you see her, go in the morning and we can all share a Zoom. Just let me know. But I'll see her soon anyway, can't wait to see you all, even if it is only for a couple of weeks. I'm so sorry I can't be there for Christmas - December flights are three times the price and I need the hours and the tips. I'll be home for Christmas next year I promise. Besides, the wedding will be more exciting than Christmas. A few months will fly by, I can't wait, I've missed all of you so much."

~

Over the next few days, Lauren Eaves settled back into her hard-working routine, studying, and enjoying

Wales. She also found a new waitressing job the next day in the bustling and vibrant city of Cardiff. She studied at Cardiff University for an MSc in Geology and Business Management and needed to crack on with her dissertation, and then she would have to start thinking about finding *that* amazing job.

Cardiff seemed like the perfect location to continue her studies. As an English speaking steppingstone to explore Europe, it also provided a highly regarded faculty and the career pathway course she needed. Lauren loved her grandparents, who originated from the Welsh valleys, and she promised them she would learn more about where they came from and grew up. A handful of distant cousins had already made contact with her on social media.

She possessed a drive and determination to help fund the AUS$40k per annum university fee, and the associated lifestyle debt racked up over the past few years studying in Sydney, and now Cardiff. Although young, bright, enthusiastic, and confident, the AUS$200k total debt never strayed far from Lauren's mind.

Her parents, Harry, and Margaret were not super-wealthy people – far from it. They owned a small arable farm and a three-man gold mining operation back in Western Australia, one of the reasons Lauren chose to study geology. Many years ago, the business thrived. They did all right, but the mining aspect had declined in recent times, and breaking even every year became a luxury. In many mines similar to theirs, the return-on-investment business models began to show smaller and smaller returns of gold per tonne of raw unprocessed material. The running costs to work longer shifts with more manpower just to keep heads above water kept increasing. The future for the family business over the next few years looked bleak. Lauren had an inkling of their difficulties. She worried about how tough things were becoming for her parents and wished she could do more to help them.

Chapter 3

Speculative Issues

Spain - Mid-December 2021

Jason Price had made a significant fortune as a land and commercial property speculator. Over the years he had experienced many ups and downs. From humble beginnings with a construction company in Cardiff, going bust twice in the early days, before landing on his feet with the success of small infrastructure projects and industrial developments.

These days he preferred to focus on high-quality office blocks and luxury retail complexes. He either retained them and acted as landlord through one of his various companies or sold them as assets to specialist pension fund investors. The formula performed well in the UK, and with the help of trusted international property management advisers, he embarked on similar projects with a recent expansion into Spain, whilst setting up a home there in 2019.

The uncharted waters of the Spanish commercial market meant Price needed to start cautiously, but he soon experienced great success thanks to a more relaxed regulatory regime. Things culminated in late October 2021, as he moved into his new home – two months before his sixtieth birthday party – when a major opportunity emerged, and Price seized it.

One of his property management agents tipped him off, "Jason, you asked me to give you a heads up if something special came up. Well, guess what – here it is. Something happened this morning and you need to jump on it."

Price's ears pricked up, "What is it?"

The agent gave Price the brief, "A large piece of premium location land, once earmarked as a golf complex on the edge of Barcelona. The golf land deal fell through, all because the investors concluded that more than enough golf courses existed in the region and they got cold feet."

Price pressed harder, "How big is large?"

The agent explained, "Local planners have decided to carve up one-hundred-and-fifty acres and develop it into smaller retail, commercial and residential projects. This is good timing for you to make a bid and grab a piece, Jason."

"Perfect." Price identified a thirty-acre plot as a development target and made his move.

A slight problem existed; with money tied up in other projects, he didn't have the liquid cash or credit line to raise all the necessary funds to buy the land and build what he wanted. But he knew a man who did, someone who often expressed an interest in diversifying into bigger ventures - if they came along - his new minor shareholder, Declan Ryan.

Price and Dubliner Ryan originally met through mutual social acquaintances, during the summer of 2020. Then in October 2021, Price bought his new house, from Ryan, and as part of the house deal secured a modest stake in Price's business. The 'stake' knocked a big hole in the price of the €3M house and Ryan gained himself the exposure he had been looking for to enter the commercial property speculation business.

They occasionally played golf together and were friendly, though often competed for vocal bandwidth in café and bar group conversations. Price's window of opportunity for the thirty-acre project needed investment within weeks. A profit margin worth millions depended on it. Other potential investment candidates existed, but Price narrowed it down to the most obvious man - Ryan.

For most businesspeople, Ryan's name wouldn't have appeared near the top of their lists. Price understood the concerns of others having picked up snippets from friends about Ryan's international haulage business. Some suggested for decades he and his family hauled anything too hot for others to handle. One or two suspected Ryan was a drugs cartel baron but said nothing.

Price thought jealous people love to sensationalise and embellish with fake news. So he took most of it with a pinch of salt, remaining undaunted. Ryan seemed a wealthy legitimate businessman and family man. With years of experience, a successful entrepreneur like Price expected all businesspeople to sail close to the wind from time to time, including himself - though sometimes preferring to plough straight through the wind at ramming speed. He enjoyed the financial returns and thrived on the adrenalin associated with the occasional risky decisions of running a business. Whilst Ryan's attention flattered Price, he possessed a low opinion of some of the other people he dealt with, in particular anyone who didn't agree with his ideas. Although stealing the ideas of other people and claiming them as his happened almost every week.

The thirty-acre project would yield spectacular returns; Ryan acknowledged Price's expertise and the idea of becoming a property magnate offered great appeal to him. Both agreed on the potential of a partnership, and the urgency required by the timing led to the pair having a long conversation. It resulted in Ryan agreeing to consider funding five times more than Price's stake for the former golf course land, with more to follow for the construction work. This meant that Ryan would progress from being a minor shareholder in Price's Spanish business to a significant major shareholder.

"Jason, taking a small stake in some of your existing established business is one thing, a good thing. This casino thing is on another level. My pockets are deep, but even I will be digging deep on this one to see it all the way through. I need to speak to my financial advisors and family first, I won't mess you around, so give me a couple of days."

Ryan didn't need to speak with anyone, he kept millions in some accessible clean and laundered savings and investments. The agreement in principle fell into place forty-eight hours later, with clauses built-in exposing Jason Price to big penalties if things didn't go according to plan. Ryan's bankrolling of Price also came with a menacing personal interpretation of what 'penalty' meant.

Chapter 4

The Big Dig

Barcelona - 2021

The Irish ex-pat Declan Ryan studied a spreadsheet and made some year-on-year financial comparisons, *"Not bad, just sort the other shit out and I'll be happy."*

His international haulage business went through a satisfying growth spurt over the past seven years, with some modest profits.

"More luck rather than judgement, but who cares?"

The growth resulted from a perfect selection of Brexit-proof and pandemic-proof clientele. Ryan wrangled with one problem - cash. Not the money his legitimate business enterprise made, but the large bundles of €200 and €500 notes he amassed from smuggling people, drugs, and weapons around Europe, and into the UK.

CHAPTER 4

His dilemma began a couple of years earlier when international police forces famously hacked and exposed the dark web's *Enchrochat* encrypted mobile phone network. It led to the arrests of thousands of criminals, drug dealers, scumbags, and terrorists. All making news headlines around the world.

Ryan remembered the day it happened and the rumours that began spreading like wildfire. *"Who have they caught? Who's in the shit?"*

He thanked his lucky stars for his mature years, mid-fifties, and for remaining more of an old school traditionalist. His two burly, much younger cousins, Michael, and Aiden, both smart and streetwise, sometimes called him a Luddite. They only said it when he had not been drinking and when they distanced themselves by least five yards away from him at the time. When he could, he preferred to meet his clients and suppliers, or their go-betweens, face-to-face and look them in the eyes, rather than rely on modern technology.

Some of Ryan's criminal associates suggested buying an Enchrochat adapted phone for thousands of euros, to enable him to speak freely to anyone, anywhere, about anything illegal. *"This is the future Declan. What's the problem?"* So they said. Some of those ended up behind bars. Some of them ended up dead. He knew that for certain because he had personally killed two of them with his bare hands. The killings followed a tip-off that his victims would expose him and his family to the police – and just as infuriating – he discovered those *associates* had stolen from him.

The unfortunate pair were Susan and Ian Harrison, his accountants. An English married couple, on the surface living a normal semi-retired healthy lifestyle on the Costa Brava. Behind the scenes, they managed Ryan's huge money-spinning side-line of two restaurants, a handful of beauty salons, a dozen bars, various cafes, and a couple of seedy clubs. All establishments contained at least two, sometimes three or four slot machines, perfect for laundering cash. Positioned in the *right* bar, at the best central Barcelona locations open for long hours, some of his *slots* could earn up to €100k per machine, per annum.

The Harrisons made one single, careless, and fatal mistake. The pair called into an old bar, recently acquired by Ryan, just off Parc de Joan Miró. They needed to pick up ledgers, receipts, and go through the regular suppliers ordering process, to bring it into line with the other bars where they managed the finances for Ryan.

Some old memorabilia, in and around banquette style dining booths greeted customers upon entering the dingy, yet spacious bar. Along with a proud but dusty display of bullfighting *banderillas*, football scarves, club pennants and a multitude of pinned-up, tired-looking foreign currency notes adorning the walls. Close by, a ubiquitous gurgling Gaggia machine spat steam, before expelling a perfect regulation trickle of aromatic coffee for the barista. The aesthetic of the local's bar had not changed in decades, but it showed enormous potential for a new trendy venue.

The far end of the bar offered some loose tables and chairs, mixed amongst almost a dozen head high, booth style cubicles, created from bamboo and raffia sections. All similarly adorned with memorabilia. When the Harrisons came in together, they sat in a bamboo cubicle, preoccupied, and continuing with a heated conversation about Ryan's latest bar and their devious personal intentions for siphoning off a proportion of the bar's finances.

They thought they had chosen to sit in a quiet secluded spot, but the items pinned to the walls disguised their paper-thin structure. Cocooned in their cosy little zone, they failed to spot the person drinking a beer, alone at an adjacent table, obscured the other side of a raffia divider partition. They had sidled up close to their worst nightmare - Ryan's main lieutenant - his cousin Michael. They met him once, six months ago, but now, that life-changing day in the bar they didn't even see him, let alone recognise him. Just minding his own business, Michael wandered into the bar earlier, as instructed by his cousin and boss Declan, to check out a schedule of works for some much-needed refurbishments. He couldn't help but overhear the conversation taking place in English a metre away from him.

Two years earlier, a reluctant Ian Harrison agreed to his wife's suggestion to purchase and subscribe to the Enchrochat phone system. She told him they needed total discretion and security. That became a similar error for many other people also on the wrong side of the law around the world.

Ian Harrison hated the dubious work that he and Susan had slipped into over several years. He loved the money, and the lifestyle it afforded them, but a constant concern always hung over him. As the driving force behind their illicit scheme, the far more confident Susan did not share his concerns.

"Susan, why do we need to put some of *ours* in here? Haven't we got enough everywhere else? I worry that one day Ryan is going to find us out. You and your bloody Enchrochat phones. I'm telling you, we just survived one tough grilling from the Spanish tax department. How long before we hear a knock on the door from the police? One of these days – because those tax people gave us a warning. I keep wondering how much the police know about us?"

Michael Ryan's ears pricked up the moment he heard the part of a conversation that included a familiar word – Enchrochat, soon followed by another word *Ryan*. So he silenced his phone and sat quietly, listening to whoever they were, hidden from view on the other side of the partition.

Susan Harrison sympathised and pacified her husband. "Ian, I agree the phones were a mistake, but who knew eh? No one did. We are not going to get a knock on the door. They would have come by now. We are small fry and slipped through the net along with thousands of others. Don't worry, we are safe, in the clear and the phones are dead now – so relax. If the worst ever came to the worst, we go and tell the police all about Ryan's drug empire and they'll let us off the hook – simple as that. He's the big fish in the pond, not us."

Ian Harrison remained unconvinced, "I hope you're right."

Susan continued, "As for the *extra till* and the *extra slot* we can put in here, Ryan won't notice. He doesn't count them, or the money, does he? We do. He hasn't got a clue what we've been up to has he? We wash plenty of his cash, we make him a fortune every year, he's happy. Just let it go, Ian, calm down. Another few years and we can walk away from it."

Michael Ryan took no time at all to figure out who his obscured indiscreet neighbours were, and made a few crucial observations, *"Extra till? Extra slot? ...he's the big fish in the pond, not us...tell the police."*

Two days after their indiscreet conversation the Harrisons received an unexpected request to meet Declan Ryan. He claimed to have a large, unforeseen amount of new cash that he needed them to *take care of.* As usual, the Harrisons arrived in their Nissan Leaf at one of Ryan's warehouses, expecting to drive home with €300k in cash in the boot to launder. Instead, it was *they* who ended up in the boot - dead. Zip tied, duct-taped, and garrotted using a length of thick sisal twine and a 12mm ring spanner to apply the twisting leverage through the knot – carried out in person by Ryan, the traditionalist.

Minutes earlier, as anticipated he managed to extract the condemning information within seconds, assisted by a pair of rusty secateurs. He confirmed the pair had been skimming his profits and quite prepared to implicate him to avoid prosecution if they ever needed to when the police came calling, although only if the police followed up on the tax inspectors. Whilst they begged for their lives, the Harrisons also confessed to cleverly installing their own additional independent tills and extra slot machines in most of the establishments, diverting money to a clean private account in their name. When he heard it for himself, Ryan erupted with anger. The pair should have known better, but they got greedy and paid the ultimate price.

As Michael and Aiden drove off in the Nissan accompanied by their fingerless dead visitors, for a fleeting moment something crossed Ryan's mind. *"Who'll tell their twelve-year-old kid, in his boarding school on the outskirts of Bath, that both his parents have vanished? A pity."*

The cousins drove fifteen kilometres northwards, along the C-59 to a pre-prepared piece of deserted land, way off any tarmac road. Earlier in the day, they unloaded a mini excavator off the back of a trailer and Michael spent forty minutes digging a huge rectangular hole in the ground. Big enough to swallow a Nissan Leaf. To fill the hole back up, spreading and flattening the mound took them less than twenty minutes. A spare car left there earlier brought them back.

On the drive home, Michael appeared pleased with their abominable day's work, commenting, "Seamless, eh, big boy?"

Aiden looked up from finishing a text message, and agreed, "Yeah, seamless."

Michael sensed a mood in his brother and probed, "You sound a bit quiet mate. What's on your mind?"

"Declan. That's what's on my mind. He's losing the plot man. He's getting worse. What the hell was that all about today? Jesus."

"I know what you're saying Aiden, but they had it coming. You can't go around doing shit like that to Declan. Nobody can. Don't mess with him. That's the way it is with him - always has been, always will be."

Fifteen minutes later, Michael dropped his brother off outside his plush apartment in Plaça Tetuán. He wound his window down, looked at him and reminded him, "Just remember who pays our rent Aiden, money is like oxygen, and rarefied air isn't all it's cracked up to be. We do as he tells us."

~

The downside to the whole Enchrochat scenario caused Ryan to lose many of his money laundering conduits, and *that* part of his business became more difficult for him. Huge stacks of cash wrapped in cling film, accumulated faster than he expected. The stacks filled steel storage cabinets inside one of his high-security lockups. There were no other secure outlets for it and no experts standing around to advise him – because he had murdered them.

Then along came Jason Price, a friend-of-a-friend, whose wife knew Ryan's wife. Price had entered the market for his new luxury home and Ryan's house came up for sale. Ryan also wanted to diversify into land speculation and commercial property development on a much larger scale. He needed a mentor *come* business partner, and Jason Price ticked all the boxes as a legitimate international property developer, with no idea about Ryan's extracurricular activities. For Ryan, it felt like a marriage made in heaven and the road to developing his retail property portfolio to new levels and rejuvenating his stalled money laundering cycle – or so he hoped.

Chapter 5

The Party

Barcelona - January 2022

The vaccination saga reached a long-awaited conclusion months ago, with pandemic issues now a rarer news item compared to Russia and Ukraine issues. Nick Savvas looked like a satisfied man with a spring in his step, having fulfilled his lucrative three-month contractual obligations to a global mining corporation in the State of Minas Gerais, north-eastern Brazil.

The forty-nine-year-old mining consultant and semi-retired visiting Professor of Geophysics at the University of NSW in Sydney came from Brisbane but now lived in Spain. His professorship afforded him a reason for a trip to Australia once a year to combine lecturing with a family visit for seven or eight weeks.

Savvas excelled as an expert in his field - the identification and extraction of rare earth minerals.

Throughout the year he travelled and consulted for innovative precious metal mining companies around the world. These forward-thinking companies experimented with shifting some of their huge exploration resources to target defunct coalfields, an emerging section of the mineral mining market now yielding spectacular returns with everything *but* coal.

For the last five years, a beautiful home near Sitges, a few kilometres south of Barcelona, provided the relaxation and eclectic social life he adored with Mia, his Spanish wife. He and Mia enjoyed a fantastic lifestyle, with grown-up kids working in Australia and at University in Madrid, giving the couple freedom to go or do whatever they pleased. His occasional lecturing and periodic consulting work, combined with her digital marketing and web building business, contributed to an admirable bank balance.

After completing his latest and final two-week stint, Savvas arrived at Brasilia International Airport. A stack of emails and a few WhatsApps to respond to, but first, a telephone call to Mia to tell her he would soon be boarding. He wanted to catch up on things at home, explain how well the project finished up and organise a lift at the other end when he arrived in Barcelona.

Savvas started to think ahead to the next few days back home and asked, "Shall we have a quiet one this weekend Mia? What are we doing? I'm shattered. Jason's left me a bunch of messages; I must read them."

Mia reminded her absent-minded husband, "Have you forgotten? Saturday is Jason's sixtieth bash, everyone's going. Get plenty of sleep on the plane, you're gonna need it."

Savvas realised and said, "Damn, of course. How are they settling into their new place?"

"Nick, you should see the pictures, it looks crazy. Italian furniture, marble, and gadgets everywhere. So, Saturday evening, drinks to start near Las Ramblas and a motorboat to take everyone to his private jetty. He's also hired a celebrity chef for God's sake."

"Well, I hope the chef agreed on payment in advance, you know what he's like with money. I wouldn't trust him as far as I could chuck a €10 note."

Mia's mass of dark curls shook in irritation. "Yes, I know, you told me, a dozen times. Aren't you forgetting something? Like Jason's generosity - and that he donates thousands every year to a local children's hospital? Maybe you should give him a break now and again?"

"Fair comment. I can't fault him there."

Savvas first met the gregarious Jason Price two years earlier when their wives played tennis together, which led to a small digital marketing project for Mia. He liked Price, although Savvas mentioned to Mia, "Someone told me a story after we played golf with Jason. They said he did some kind of shady deal to buy his new villa from a dodgy ex-pat Irish guy. A *legit* loan, and a promise for the rest. He needs to watch himself."

Mia agreed, "Maybe a legit loan and a pound of flesh if you ask me. Look just relax, enjoy the flight and I'll see you tomorrow."

~

The Welsh entrepreneur, Jason Price, shared his time between a rural home in Pembrokeshire and Barcelona. Both locations enjoyed stunning coastlines and provided numerous fine dining options for the portly Price.

A tastefully planned and exquisitely executed mid-evening drinks gathering, at the Barcelona, Miramar Hotel, put Price's guests in a good mood for the sixtieth birthday party ahead of them. It set them up perfectly for the brief trip by motorboat to the jetty of his newly acquired sprawling villa, overlooking the ocean.

Tall and gangly, Nick Savvas's Mediterranean looks disguised his Aegean lineage as he held his wife's hand whilst they enjoyed warming remnants of the winter sunset during the ten-minute boat trip. He reminded her, "Don't forget, I'll give you a nod if I need rescuing when Jason's holding court later."

She laughed. "You mean if you're not holding court before he does? Don't worry, he'll be fine. He's on good form so far, and no expense spared is there?"

At that moment, neither one of the happy and contented couple had any idea that an innocent remark made in the next half an hour would have a dramatic impact on the rest of their lives.

CHAPTER 5

Along with a dozen other Gran Reserva cava fuelled enthusiastic guests, they arrived at the jetty and made their way up the torch-lit path to Price's new palatial home.

"See you at the top guys." He went on ahead of them and waited further up to greet everyone with a smile and hugs as other guests arrived in cars.

"Welcome, welcome. *Bienvenido a la fiesta,*" said Price, holding the hands of his excited three and five-year-old granddaughters, still going strong despite the hour.

They were on 'Barcelona time,' the moon glinted on the tips of what Mediterranean waves there were, and most people could smell the food as they made their way to the marble-pillared patio.

Price introduced his chef, announcing, "She once won the Spanish equivalent of MasterChef."

Whilst mingling with his guests, Price approached Nick and Mia Savvas. He caught a snippet of their conversation with another couple, smiling when overhearing his name mentioned in the same breath as marble pillars and ocean views. Price charged their glasses and conversations continued. He soon regaled a recent Tesla disappointment, explaining how he tried to jump the queue to buy one and they blocked him - *they* let *him* down. He soon relaxed and wanted to satisfy his curiosity as to where Savvas had hidden himself for the past few weeks.

Savvas reminded Price of his periodic consulting role in the mining industry. He thought to himself,

"You listened to this explanation from me a few times in the past Jason."

With an arm wrapped around her husband's waist, Mia read his mind, smiled, and gently dug her fingers into his hipbone as a *don't bite* signal.

Savvas got the message. But he possessed a strong passion for his scientific career and unusual experiences. He often worked in third world countries and always kept a death-defying story or two to tell up his sleeve. He couldn't resist switching into lecturer mode or offering nuggets of knowledge to impress and raise eyebrows - though not always with great success.

An opportunity presented itself, and he seized the moment to summarise his recent work in Brazil, visiting idyllic forgotten corners of the huge country and described its connection of competing in mining against China. He told them how the Chinese dominated the world supply of rare earth metals with their eighty-five percentage share of the market, holding global *tech* manufacturers and car builders to ransom.

"The metals are in high demand in fuel cells of electric cars, components in mobile phones, banknote anti-counterfeiting ink, lasers, MRI scanning equipment, wind-farms and many more applications. The list is endless."

Nods of attention and appreciation encouraged Savvas to continue.

"One substance exists called caesium. Used as a solid fuel propellant in space rockets, at least 140 times more efficient than current fuel, but rarer than rocking horse shit and super expensive." A few titters from his small audience pleased Savvas.

Although Jason Price smiled, his interest started to wane, because *he* wasn't the centre of attention during Savvas's scientific hobby horse presentation. On the verge of a *flekerl turn* to attempt an elegant shift to another group of friends, he stopped in his tracks. He caught Savvas mentioning, "...and disused coal mines are now gold dust."

Savvas's anecdote concerned the development of new innovative processes for extracting expensive rare earths and similar precious metals from coal waste materials and coal dust. The new coal field process came about due to the rest of the world's desperation to find ways to circumvent the Chinese. He also mentioned the extreme value of some of the scarcer materials, far greater per kilo than gold.

He added an anecdote, "Trust the Chinese to keep ahead of the game, hoover up all the easy pickings and make billions. Every week I hear stories of rare earth bonanzas happening around the world on defunct coal fields."

The germ of an idea formulated in Price's mind. As a wealthy, well-connected man with historical links to a large former coal mining area, his instincts told him to continue listening and harness Savvas's enthusiasm and expertise.

Chef declared the food ready and available. Staff deployed themselves in readiness for the select group of thirty or so friends, the third 'Jason's Sixtieth' party in a week for the Price family. The coal mining enlightenment ended up lost in the moment - but not forgotten.

The excellent food and the accompanying chat from the 'mic'd up' chef went down well with the guests. The entertainment transitioned into a solo acoustic guitarist strumming and singing a selection of classic 80s ballads.

Mia spotted someone and nudged Nick, "That guy, chatting with Jason, he's the one I told you about who used to own this place, Declan Ryan. I don't think you've met him, have you?"

"Not yet, sounds like an interesting character. Let's say hello and find out what he's all about shall we?"

Nick Savvas casually smiled and glanced in Price's direction who invited him and Mia to join their conversation.

"Nick, this is my good friend Declan, he sold us this place for a song - well almost. And decided he wanted a shareholding in some of my Spanish property business dealings into the bargain."

Ryan's hard, expressionless face tried in vain to produce an acquiescing smile. He didn't convey the impression of a man who sold anyone, let alone Jason Price, a huge property for peanuts. Ryan responded, "I gave you a hell of a deal Jason, but what are friends and business partners for? Working together in harmony."

Mia had previously explained to her husband that she recalled bumping into Ryan and Price not long ago, at a major local charity auction. She told him, "Nick, between the pair of them they must have splashed out €50,000 like confetti on some important artworks."

Savvas also remembered her remarking, *"Ryan has got a face only a mother could love."* Savvas could see what she meant from her description. A stocky, pugnacious bull of a man. He used to drive lorries around Europe, but now Ryan's soft hands had long since finished hooking up trailers to articulated lorries. He left it to dozens of men who worked for him.

For such a wealthy man, with an obvious full thick head of silver hair, Savvas couldn't understand Ryan's decision to crop it quite so short. He appeared to prefer an intimidating look, by displaying his array of scalp scars, along with a nose 'set' on more than one occasion, and a rugby hooker's cauliflower ear. All so incongruous with his Gucci loafers, silk shirt and the sparkling *Patek Philippe* strapped to his wrist. Savvas glanced again at the offending ear, and winced, thankful for having his ear medically syringed immediately, back in his Aussie rugby playing days.

Cava flutes clinked in mutual recognition. Watching them toast, Savvas' instincts suggested the faintest hint of awkwardness, or maybe a slight mistrust between Price and Ryan. No doubt still measuring each other up. He didn't know who trusted whom the least.

Price appeared keen to point out, "Yes, our first major development project - the casino complex - is shaping up, far better than expected. These are exciting times for us, and for me, sixty is the new fifty."

Savvas couldn't help but raise an eyebrow and nod in appreciation.

Price, remained full of enthusiasm, "Still time for you to buy-in Nick if you want to come and join the party? I warn you though, the casino we're building is Declan's baby, he reckons he's already commissioned a bronze statue of himself for the entrance hall."

Savvas laughed, declaring, "Gambling is like going to the dentist. Watching my money, or anyone else's money for that matter, vanish inside a casino is not for me guys. I think I'll stick to mining - where there's muck there's money. Best of luck, doesn't look like you're going to need it though."

Later, going home in the taxi, Savvas mentioned to Mia, "Jason and his new best buddy, are an interesting combination, aren't they? That Ryan guy must be worth a fortune. He made poor old Jason look a bit overshadowed for a change. He's got a lot riding on Ryan and his big wallet. Good luck to him."

She replied, "Jason's an arrogant risk-taker, but a successful and generous one. People, like him, learn how to find a pathway through life and business and always come out smelling of roses, don't they? Now and again, they appear to manage to navigate over or around the speed bumps when everyone else gets a broken suspension or worse. So glad you politely declined his investment offer. I won't be losing any sleep about it. The pair of them are bad news, mark my words."

Chapter 6

Early Adopters

February 2022

Early February, and a pleasant, calm fourteen degrees Costa Brava morning. Two kilometres from home, Nick Savvas felt the vibration in his back pocket for the second time in two minutes during his seven-kilometre jogging loop to Puerto de Garaff. He didn't have far to go and sensed the potential for a good time, maybe a personal best. No way would he have stopped to answer it, whoever it was and judging by the text ping and another mini vibrate they had left him a voicemail.

When he arrived home on the outskirts of his village he stopped, saved, and scrutinised his fitness app result, *"No PB. Close, but no cigar. Ah well, always tomorrow or the next day."*

Showered, and with a cold juice to hand in his kitchen, Savvas checked his phone. He could see missed calls from Jason Price. Plenty of texts in the past from him, the occasional email, but today, a first - a phone call, two within minutes - a real surprise.

Savvas' voicemail came from Price, *"How are you doing Nick? Jason here, I hope you recovered from the party? A hell of a night, eh? Listen mate I need to discuss something with you, a bit of business as it happens. How do you feel about an all-expenses-paid trip to a World Heritage Site? Call me when you have a chance thanks."*

Savvas poked a gentle finger at the iPhone's screen, silencing the speakerphone as it lay on his quartz worktop. He stared at the phone for a moment with a quizzical look.

Mia wandered across, "I caught the tail end of that message. From Jason? What's all that about?"

"No idea - but I'm going to find out. Fascinating stuff eh?"

Before calling Price back Savvas sat on the sofa, finished his juice and Googled *World Heritage Sites,* a familiar term to him. The Great Wall of China, Stonehenge, Machu Picchu, Venice, Taj Mahal, Grand Canyon, Westminster Abbey, Yosemite National Park, the remarkable list went on and on. More bucket list *to dos* and *to go tos* than he ever imagined. *"What's not to like and where's the catch? This is Jason 'scheming' Price we're dealing with here."*

Price answered before the second ring. "Hey, thanks for calling me back so soon. How is Mia? Say hello for me."

"Hi Jason, no problem, yes I'll say hello, she's popped out somewhere. So, what's up? What's this about a trip to a World Heritage Site? My top ten list is in front of me."

"Nick, I'm on the level, everything's genuine. But this is business and a bit complicated - you know how it is."

"I do know how it is Jason, and I'm wondering if *complicated* is a Welsh euphemism for *a catch*."

"When are you around? Maybe you can pop over for a chat at my place? And you won't need your list - I'll tell you all about it."

Later that day Savvas cycled solo the ten minutes to what he affectionately nicknamed *Price Towers,* although, with her usual smile and infectious laugh, Mia countered with *The Welsh Wing.* In fairness to Jason Price and his wife, either nametag would have done justice to their sumptuous prime location home.

Savvas passed through the high, oak security gate, and Price walked out to greet him on the patio with a warm handshake and a tap on the shoulder. The house looked bigger and more lavish in the sunshine which did more justice to the shrubs and manicured lawns.

"Come through, we'll grab a beer and I'll tell you all about it."

For all his happy-go-lucky attitude, people sometimes misunderstood Jason Price, and the shrewd, hard-nosed businessman side to him. Not always a detail man, he left that to others, but when he needed salient information to move along the scale to his next mini objective, he would demonstrate extreme focus. He saw things that other people didn't, or rather he saw things quicker than others. His wealth and track record in business demonstrated his success as an early adopter.

Savvas sipped his beer and Price placed his assortment of supporting information to one side.

Price gave Savvas a meaningful look in the eye. "Blaenavon."

A bemused Savvas replied in his Aussie twang, "Blaenavon? What's that? A thing or a place?"

"A place, a UNESCO World Heritage Site. In Wales - where I grew up."

Savvas brought his mental list with him, which proved useless because Blaenavon didn't resonate as one of his exotic World Heritage Site destinations conjured up earlier.

"Cast your mind back a couple of weeks to my sixtieth birthday party here. I know things became a bit foggy for many of us. You mentioned something that evening, and it struck a chord with me. I parked it for a few days, followed by some discreet research and it fascinated me. I'm hoping you can offer me your opinions, your gut instincts on something."

Now, with Savvas's full attention Price went on to provide a complete explanation concerning his speculative vision.

"OK Nick, sorry for the brief history lesson, but this is crucial to help you understand the important context, and why Blaenavon is a World Heritage Site. UNESCO doesn't dish those awards out like Michelin stars mate."

"We know how much you love those, Jason."

"So, *bear with.*" Price smiled and continued, "From the early 1800s, for about one-hundred-and-fifty or so years, eight square miles of the most valuable pieces of land on the planet sat at the top end of the Eastern Valley in South Wales. Situated at a small town called Blaenavon. There they pioneered the production of iron, followed by steel, all achieved in conjunction with the locally mined coal, ironstone, and limestone. If you check the history books, you'll find everything documented. You still with me?

Savvas nodded, with a, "Yep."

So, with the industrial revolution in full flow business boomed, until eventually, the steel production migrated to other parts of the world leaving the town to continue to thrive with its healthy coal production. That stopped forever in the late 1970s, by which time historians estimate the miners had extracted well over twenty million tons of coal. Now, here's the important bit Nick."

Savvas leaned in closer as Price carried on.

"Some estimates suggest another fifty or more million tons of coal waste and ironstone mining waste. Yes, over fifty million tons of coal spoil waste ended up either scattered or piled high into huge pyramid-shaped slag heaps. Some of it landscaped in the 1990s for aesthetic and safety reasons."

"Jason your sixtieth party is flooding back to me. I remember the conversation now, rare earth mineral extraction from disused coal mine waste around the world. I get the message."

"Well remembered, Nick. I'm thinking you didn't have as much to drink as me that night. So, I did a bit of amateurish research based on what you said. God knows how I remembered any of your conversation; my head felt like a box of frogs the following morning. I slept on the sofa that night - in the doghouse - but that's another story. The amateurish research I did soon turned into a significant chunk of in-depth research. Look, it appears this rare earth scavenging of old coal mine spoils thing is a relatively new phenomenon. The big boys like the Chinese and others have never heard of Wales. Well not yet. Can you see my point?"

Excited by what he heard, Savvas wanted to demonstrate how much he knew and interrupted Price, "Hang on Jason, let me correct you. This is not just a scavenging thing. People don't appreciate that the unmined substrate under the surface of the waste will hold as much if not more mineral product. So, if you described let's say, at least fifty million tons of waste on the surface, do the arithmetic, added to what's unmined under the ground, about maybe one-hundred to two-hundred million tons of potential in total. Can you see how it works? Here's the good news, if you strike it lucky, just one metric tonne, 1000kg, about one cubic metre of refined, processed rare earth metal is worth more than gold. If we have the extreme value material. So \$60 million or £40 million if you prefer old money. And that calculation is based on one part per million. Most rare earth mine samples are around ten or sometimes fifty parts per million. Let's not go there, it sounds too ridiculous for words doesn't it."

Price tried not to show his excitement, "OK, well even a billion tons would make no difference. If the soil doesn't contain any, or enough, premium rare earth metal particles, then mining would be a waste of time anyway. And that is where you come in Nick, if you're up for it and if you want to make an obscene amount of money? I'd like you to go and check things out, under the radar. No one must know about it, no one at all, that is critical. Because I have a plan."

A hooked Savvas looked across at him, smiling. "So what's the plan? How do we approach the project?"

By using a spare hand and fingers as an abacus, Price explained, "Firstly, I studied a handful of examples of former coalfields in China, Central and South America. You know all this stuff anyway, but the common denominator of the richest excavations ever discovered is the combination of high-grade coal, *tick*, limestone, *tick*, and ironstone used to make steel, *tick*. All are in Blaenavon, and no one yet has realised it, including the Chinese. Although maybe Blaenavon is too small for them, with too many honest local politicians."

Savvas agreed, "So far so good, and you have a point about the Chinese preferring to target third world countries, where they can *pay off* every man and his dog whenever they need to. They more or less *own* half of Africa these days."

"Nick, we don't want to jump ahead of ourselves here, but the interesting thing is the National Coal Board, now known as The Coal Authority, sold off all the land they owned surrounding Blaenavon years ago. A handful of sheep farmers own it now. And if we offer them well above going rate for what they see as useless boggy moorland, plus a few pints for good measure, I'm certain they will take it. They have to take it. And we explain to the council we'd like to open a new open-cast 'coal mine' providing environmentally conscious jobs for the local community. Then if we happen to find something else in the ground, *we find something else*, a lucky unexpected bonus for us." Despite his warning to Savvas not to get ahead of themselves, Price couldn't stop his voice from going up half an octave.

"But isn't that illegal Jason? I mean - that *is* illegal Jason."

"Oh, I don't think so, and you forget you're talking to an expert, Nick. Remember I do this for a living, week in week out. Besides, we'll cross that bridge when we come to it. In the meantime, are you up for a solo trip to Wales to check it out? I'll fund it. Can you do some on the ground investigation, or whatever it is you guys do? You're the expert."

Savvas smiled, "Yeah, I'm up for this Jason, but I have a better idea. We take one step back then two steps forward."

Price tried his best but couldn't avoid frowning, "What do you mean, one step back?"

"Jason leave things with me. To find the world's natural resources is never much more than a keystroke away these days. At my Sydney university, to avoid wild goose chases with my private consultancy clients, I use specialist mining and satellite imagery software for mineral mapping. A major defence and space exploration manufacturer sponsored the original development of the software for the college. We used to joke, 'It ain't rocket science finding mineral fields.' But to tell you the truth - it is. I log in and use it for my business on the side all the time. The Uni don't mind me using it."

Easy access to the state-of-the-art software came via Savvas's university affiliation along with his valid login passcodes.

Savvas added one final note of caution, "Jason, coal waste is a great place to hunt for rare earth minerals, but you should be aware of the implications and consequences. The environmental impact can be enormous, and a plant could be shut down in a heartbeat."

Price picked up on one word, "Could? Explain, *could,* to me."

"Ok, I'll try. For years, the Chinese have caused havoc, leaving huge pools of toxic mess behind them at their rare earth mines. Acid and harsh chemicals often used to separate the heavy rare earth metals are a nightmare. Remember the list of seventeen rare earth metals does not include gold or silver, but they are all minuscule heavy metals. The Americans discovered more sympathetic methods, some of them include using centrifuges, low ph-level fluids, and bacterial filtration. A big investment to get it right and environmentally acceptable in the UK. So there are other alternatives."

Price nodded, adding, "I understand, but first, we need to find out what the eight square miles around Blaenavon might offer us, don't we?"

"True, this is a serious long shot Jason, but stranger things have happened."

Savvas and Price came to a mutual agreement. Price had always lived his life with a sometimes 'quixotic half-full glass' and failure didn't exist. In his determined, over-optimistic mind, the Blaenavon project could not fail to succeed. And Price set this project aside from the Barcelona land and casino deal. One of Price's other UK-owned companies would handle the mining project and he would not involve Declan Ryan or even make him aware of it.

The men shook hands. Savvas said he would begin his research as soon as he got home, and they agreed to keep in regular contact over the next few days. Savvas retrieved his pushbike, strapped on his helmet, clipped into his pedals, and set off with a wave.

As he passed through Price's oak gates, he headed along the exclusive palm and orange tree-lined road and despite his earlier excitement, he started to wonder, *"What the hell am I getting myself into? And how am I going to explain this one to Mia?"*

Chapter 7

Curiosity

Lauren's dissertation entailed extensive global research. Despite studying for her MSc in Cardiff, her NSW University in Sydney, allowed alumni students to continue to access its various software packages and intranet portals. She found this facility hugely beneficial and used the portal regularly.

Whilst struggling to resolve a sedimentology module for her course, and with a deadline approaching, she found herself scouring her Australian college's database for information and related searches. She made slow and frustrating progress, and stumbled across a recent search-history correlation, carried out by one of her former flamboyant tutors, Nick Savvas. In between the nitty-gritty of the lectures, he often loved to digress and tell a story or two about his exploits somewhere in the world. It made some of the drearier topics far more palatable.

He did not lecture on a full-time basis. The University hired him for some specialist input during one of the terms. She liked him and absorbed his lectures with eagerness. Lauren recalled that he travelled extensively and lived in Barcelona, all adding to the vivid picture conjured up when hearing his anecdotal stories. All the more reason why she found discovering his cached search histories intriguing.

Despite frequent reminders, Nick Savvas never paid attention when he received regular warnings never to access private data, then leave behind on full view confidential information on public or shared computers – it was a bad habit of his. He ignored similar rules when logging in and using sensitive satellite-mining mineral-mapping software. A gift to a university, designed, created, and installed by an aerospace and defence company still required a degree of transparency in the event of an audit-trail request. A busy and absent-minded Savvas *didn't get the message* - he either forgot or couldn't bother himself to log out.

Bored, and tired, but more than anything Lauren needed a break from her coursework. Curiosity got the better of her and she started digging around and started to form a bit of a picture concerning what Savvas had selected to scrutinise. She could see his work targeted specific topographical information relating to the South Wales valleys and one GPS location in particular which highlighted a small town called Blaenavon.

Her mind paused for a moment, before realising, *"Wow. Blaenavon is less than thirty miles away from me here in Cardiff. What's that all about?"*

Thanks to his love of talking, Lauren knew all about Savvas' other well publicised, lucrative consulting business interests, and she began to do a little more digging.

Before long, a picture emerged presenting the curious Lauren with a large cache of information, which Savvas should have deleted, or encrypted but forgot to. The cache showed detailed satellite information, cross-referenced, and correlated using Blaenavon and historical finds from regions around the world of high-value rare earth metals. One of his search criteria involved coal fields, something she remembered from his lectures, and how they were emerging as the gold mines of the future, not containing gold, but far more valuable metals. But only if you possessed the capability to find and extract them. Nick Savvas had a reputation as an expert at finding and extracting them, and something he did for a living when not lecturing – one of the best.

In her third year as an undergraduate, Lauren attended four training sessions using the sophisticated software on her screen. She found the expensive resource fascinating, and back then, soon began plucking random uncharted regions in Africa and Asia as target experiments, to identify viable projects for mining. She understood how everything worked, like an elaborate video game, but by aligning satellites instead.

Her first reaction to Savvas' cached information relating to Blaenavon suggested it showed a false positive, maybe a simple case of a fake case study. Like when all the stars align, here is the perfect score, this is what it *would* look like. But after seeing it a second time she realised the truth; it was for real, a potential 'goldmine' that *could* be full of everything *but* gold. Results could be wrong, it had happened in the past, wasting hundreds of man-hours and other resources on the ground, but by the same token, it could be amazing.

Before exiting Savvas's information, she spotted a digital folder containing a file named *Test Sample Locations*. She opened the file created four days earlier, which presented her with a detailed map of the area and proposed soil test locations over a mile radius. All numbered and coded as - *Potential 'COAL MINING' Test Locations.*

"Gosh, this is so current - four days ago. He hasn't even been to Blaenavon yet. But he will be going there soon by the looks of things? And 'COAL MINING'? Really Nick? Pathetic. Coal mining vanished in Wales decades ago."

Lauren made some further exhaustive Google searches concerning the area, for evidence of any recent announcements of mining activity; nothing, no news.

She kept digging, no mines or mining companies operated in the area - nor had they for several years. Her coursework included a solid understanding of council planning processes, such as permissions, and applications to operate mines or groundworks. A search for those also proved a waste of time.

"A real mystery, Savvas is looking at something significant, but no one knows anything about it? Someone else must have an idea or be involved, funding or investing in it - but who? Surely, the landowners must know what he's doing? Or maybe not? What if he hasn't told them? Is that possible? Maybe. Shit."

She glanced at her watch, time to go home and change for work. Blaenavon and its lucrative rare earth mystery would have to keep for another day.

Chapter 8

Game On

Nick Savvas decided to take the initiative. At first, following his initial intrigue, and excitement he harboured serious reservations when he listened to Jason Price's over-enthusiastic explanation about Blaenavon's great potential. All tinged with some legal concerns, rebuffed by Price. But he underestimated Price's ingenuity and determination. Price had demonstrated remarkable substance to his amateur initial research. Savvas wondered, *"How could he have been so perceptive?"*

Price had a knack and a nose for making money. His radar picked up on Savvas's comments at the party, *"...and disused coal mines are now gold dust."*

Price followed it up with his usual dogmatic enthusiasm and he may have got lucky. Savvas would soon provide some initial, more professional validation to Price's groundwork. This time when he cycled over to see Price, he took with him a backpack, and armed himself with his laptop and copious notes.

They exchanged the usual formalities, Savvas preferring a cappuccino over a St Miguel whilst he hooked his laptop up via Bluetooth to Price's huge smart TV.

"As I said on the phone Jason, I think you might be on to something. I'm shocked at my findings. Let me give you some background on what I managed to establish so far - some geological indicators, and probable facts."

"What have you found? Is the ground likely to contain what we are hoping for? I told you how loaded it would be." Price had already started fidgeting and shuffling around on the Italian leather sofa, like a small child anticipating a birthday present.

Ignoring the intensity coming from the other end of the sofa, a determined Savvas continued to provide a professional backdrop to his findings. He had prepared some slides which explained the advanced technology, used regularly by him as part of his consulting business.

"This kit cost the best part of half a million Aussie dollars; the aerospace company use versions of it for all sorts of other applications. Many of them are confidential. I suspect they scrutinise parts of the earth's surface where western governments dare to tread."

A few slides popped up on the TV showing areas of South and Central America, with mainly far-flung places in Southeast Asia. Lots of colour-coded graphs, bar charts and pie charts linked into what looked like some kind of close-up heat map on the regions in question.

Savvas continued, "This is all connected with other historical data supplied into the mix. We make comparisons using our information and overlay it to where and what we know are exceptional rare earth mining locations. And we have some results."

Price's impatience manifested itself once again, "Nice. Impressive. So, what are the results? Let's hear it. Come on."

"Astounding Jason, bloody astounding. I anticipated something interesting, worthy of discussion, maybe a tick in a few boxes. But I hadn't bargained for this. I see information like this on other projects all the time, some parts of it are good some parts not so good, and they turn out as fruitful projects. But this is off the charts - good across the board. There is only one way to find out how good - go and do some soil sample tests and validate it."

Savvas explained to Price he often travels around the world with some portable kit, taking initial digital readings, before evaluating samples in a lab to produce more accurate and reliable data.

"So do you fancy a trip to Blaenavon over the next few weeks, Nick?"

"Depends how cold it is there at the end of winter? If the ground is frosty or frozen it will be a challenge. But it is just Wales in March, and not exactly the arctic tundra, is it? So, *we* should be fine. Wet and mucky, but fine."

The two men sat and talked for another hour. Price by far the more excited of the pair, though Savvas, even with all his years of experience, came a close second, he expected a positive outcome with the tests.

Savvas would have described himself as a confident man, but not a criminal or someone who wanted to flout the law or cheat people out of money. He again expressed his reservations to Price.

"Jason, are you serious about not telling the local landowners if we find the equivalent of a goldmine on their land? What about the local council? They won't be impressed either if our coal mining business suddenly goes stratospheric overnight. In South America, they would 'line us all up' in front of a bloody wall, I'm telling you."

Price smiled, "Relax Nick, I already carried out the research using local council land registry records. They aren't what you might call 'hardcore landowners' - they are a handful of skint sheep farmers. We'll be doing them a favour by offering them top dollar for the land. We make it worth their while, an offer they can't refuse. Besides, this is what I do for a living. I'm a land speculator. I buy land all the time and I develop it and make it profitable. They don't need to know *how profitable*, do they?"

Savvas' enthusiasm dampened, "Maybe we should build in an ex-gratia payment for them if and when the land produces what we are hoping for?"

Price peered across at Savvas, wondering, *"Maybe they have such a thing as a jab for STU-PID as well as COV-ID?"* Choosing to attempt a more diplomatic response he advised, "Nick, if you want to, then fine, but you can take it out of your money, not mine, and you might need an awful lot of it. If I were you, I would keep my mouth shut, because if they smell a rat, it will cost you and me more than we expected. Bloody lawyers and all sorts, they will tear us to shreds. Say nothing upfront and we'll be fine."

Part of Savvas remained conflicted, but he conceded and said what he thought Price wanted to hear, "You're right, we are in the mining business, or at least we might be if things go to plan."

Price could sense his blood pressure receding to its usual, but higher than is a healthy range. Although his permanent appearance of rioja induced, rouge faced embarrassment, which extended over his bald head, never seemed to fade. For a moment, his unscrupulous business mind conjured up visions of the legions of council officials, and 'professional' property management agents he had pressurised, sweetened, or simply bribed with impunity over the years to achieve his objectives.

The remainder of the men's conversation focused on a plan of action, dates, and timescales. The initial and most important steps were booking a flight to Cardiff, a hire car, and a hotel in Blaenavon for Nick Savvas's World Heritage 'sightseeing tour - with a difference'.

To aid the discussion, Savvas had come prepared with a printed copy of relevant sections of an online Ordnance Survey map of their target area. He pointed out he would need the best part of a week on the ground, alone, taking samples from fifteen to twenty distinct locations highlighted on the map.

On a roll, Savvas had parked any previous concerns, and his attitude shifted more towards geologist mode, as he stated, "We need to book something more substantial than a basic hire car, I need a decent four-wheel drive with plenty of luggage space for the testing kit. Now, let me show you where I intend to take some samples, way off the beaten track and away from prying eyes, with a bit of luck."

In the event of someone asking what he was doing, Savvas had a perfect cover story. He would explain he worked as an external consultant for *Natural Resources Wales* and the *National Rivers Authority*, and that every five years sample tests take place to check for soil pollution harmful to local wildlife and rivers. He would even rehearse saying, '*So far everything appeared better than expected.*' If asked. No one would have any concerns and would let him carry on with his work.

Price found listening to Savvas' intent fascinating, and exciting. A satisfying reassurance for Price to observe his friend's increasing commitment to the project, sensing a determination in his 'new partner', with his full-on professional approach. He recognised at that moment it was 'game on'.

"Oh, and one other thing Jason. I will need some space to set up a mini-laboratory. A hotel in town won't cut it, but there are a couple of suitable Airbnb's just outside town. They say there is good Wi-Fi, which is important, as I need to send and receive some digital samples to an old friend. She will assume the work is just another one of my regular requests and won't be suspicious."

Price nodded in agreement, "Nick, I told you I'm funding this end of your work. I'll transfer you three grand today to cover your costs. So, you can make all the bookings yourself. If things don't work out as we hope after your trip, I will also reimburse you for your wasted time. At your daily rate. Let's hope I don't need to do that eh. Besides, we are going to need to raise a huge pile of money for mining equipment."

The cycle back home for fitness fanatic Savvas differed from the last time he left Price's place on his bike. This time, before he got on, he looked at his smartwatch which displayed his heart rate as up over 115 bpm, without having turned a pedal. His head spun with ideas, the challenge, the adventure, and he dismissed all his previous thoughts of not trusting Price as far as he could throw a €10 note. He couldn't remember the last time he felt such excitement and rush of adrenalin.

As Savvas walked through the door and saw Mia sitting in the kitchen at the breakfast bar typing furiously. He offered her a broad smile and shrugged his shoulders. She understood what it meant, and peered over her glasses, "So when are you going to Wales? What are you intending to do?"

Grabbing a coffee Savvas pulled up another stool and joined Mia, "I need to clear the decks of some outstanding projects and give myself a full week. So, I'm aiming for the week after next. You're welcome to join me if you want? A chance for you to visit Wales, Blaenavon has got a fully operational mining museum with a miner's cage to take visitors underground."

"It does sound interesting, but can you see me in a miner's helmet with these curls, or even worse standing on the side of a mountain with you digging samples out of the ground, in the rain, surrounded by sheep?"

Savvas laughed, "You do have a point. Wellies will be the order of the day, most days. You'll just have to come back with me in the summer. If everything goes to plan, but I have a good feeling about this one. Jason did some extensive homework before I got involved and validated it, and he might be right. But there will only be one way to find out with any certainty, I must go there and get dirty. He's already transferred me three grand, he's not messing around."

Mia knew what his plans were, and warned him against it, "Nothing's going to change your mind, so I may as well say keep quiet."

She recognised her efforts as a lost cause. In the end, she supported his decision. They had both reconciled themselves to the serious deceitful nature of the Blaenavon project if it progressed with any success - but perhaps it would not be an illegal project.

The upside to everything was they could be worth a fortune, and the money aspect transcended every other argument. But there were still occasional nagging doubts for them both - could there be any legal risks unaccounted for?

Savvas joked with Mia and told her, "I'm going to Google UK land fraud when I have some spare time."

That evening Savvas booked his return flights from Barcelona to Cardiff, organised a Ford Ranger 4x4 pick-up truck, and plumped for a cosy self-sufficient Airbnb cottage in Llanover, a rural location just outside of Blaenavon. The Airbnb nestled close to a tiny old pub, surrounded by fire-break forestry trails. A perfect retreat for privacy, jogging and achieving what he needed to do.

He relaxed in his lounge and picked up from his coffee table a hefty silver coloured metal ornament the size and shape of a Rubik's cube, mounted on a round, similar metal base. The Chinese presented him with the expensive piece of art on completion of the high profile mining project he had masterminded for them a year or so earlier. It represented one of the numerous periodic table elements he helped them to discover.

He passed the tactile, solid rare earth block, from hand to hand, cool to the touch. Gazed at it once more and wondered, *"Maybe some more like this are in the pipeline soon."*

Chapter 9

The Bumpy Ride

Westonia, Western Australia

Snuggled into a train seat, Lauren wondered what she would find at home when she got there. Almost twenty-seven hours door to door, not including the extra three hours train ride the other end to transfer from Perth airport to Merridin, near her parent's home. They lived almost 300km east of Perth in Western Australia, where she grew up, near the tiny town of Westonia, within a farming region called the Wheatbelt.

After completing her studies in Sydney, Lauren spent six months at home working on the farm and mining business, often driving combine harvesters and huge dumper trucks with aplomb. Then eighteen months ago she left to go to the UK to study. This trip home came sooner than she would have preferred. She needed to return to Cardiff, to finish her dissertation and attend her MSc. graduation - if things went to plan - as they should. Lauren enjoyed the UK, the culture, and the people, although she preferred the Western Australian climate. Working in the UK long term appealed to her, and she saw her career starting there. Whatever that would be - her ideas remained fluid.

The local train ride and familiar sights triggered more thoughts of home, she thought to herself, *"I came all his way for Olivia's bloody wedding and all I want to do is see Mum, Dad, Gran and my friends and relax without all of the wedding fuss."*

Four years older, Lauren's sister Olivia and her partner, both teachers, were tying the knot after living together for several years. The sisters always got on OK, but they never considered themselves as close, and certainly wouldn't confide their deepest secrets to each other, they didn't rub along like that. Olivia never really got the knack of driving a truck - plenty of other things always seemed to take precedence, which grated a little bit on Lauren.

Lauren scolded herself for her churlish thoughts, reminding herself that Olivia deserved a nice wedding and all her family there for her big day. Her other concern centred on the cost, Lauren hoped her parents could afford to contribute towards the wedding without borrowing, she knew things were tough for them.

An iPhone snooze alarm came to the rescue, transporting a tired Lauren back from serving pizzas and Peronis on *Two for One Wednesdays*, to glancing through the train's dusty window at a familiar landscape. Pan flat shrublands, broken up from time to time up by the occasional arid looking mulga tree, as Highway 94 drifted alongside the train track for endless stretches disappearing into the horizon. Hundreds of thousands of square kilometres of the same thing, with the occasional cluster of a dozen buildings designated as a town. Not the outback but it did become hot and dusty on the roads in the summertime. A glance at her watch showed five minutes to her stop.

As Lauren stepped off the train, Margaret Eaves ran along the tiny makeshift platform and held her daughter in an emotional embrace for what seemed like an eternity. Zoom could never substitute for the real thing, and an untouchable 15,000km made it 15,000 times more challenging. Moments later she positioned Lauren at arm's length, gazing and smiling with relief, sensing she looked healthy and not too skinny.

Keen to set off for the twenty minutes to home, Margaret squeezed Lauren's bags into the boot of a battered, old Toyota hatchback. A car Lauren had not seen her mother driving in the past. The two women chatted and laughed as they sped along the dusty roads, leaving a tell-tale red cloud behind them in their wake on the bumpy ride.

"What happened to the nice GMC pick-up truck Mum?"

"Oh, the lease expired on that nine months ago, so it went back. This car is fine, Dad got the air-con recharged a month ago, it needed doing, and two new tyres on the front, it drives fine. Dad just called me, he said he is going to need another couple of hours. One of the water pumps seals on the plant is misbehaving, he won't take long."

The Eaves family lived in a modern, tastefully decorated, smallholding with smart furnishings and a kitchen that went in three years earlier. The large low-level building possessed a raised walkway bordering it on every side, complemented by a stylish, overhanging, grey tiled sloping roof, and punctuated by slim white vertical pillars and a smart white picket fence. It provided essential year-round shady verandas and some usable relaxation space, all with outstanding views for as far as the eye could see. Pods of solar panels tucked away in discreet locations around and about on the lawn areas generated free power.

Thanks to innovations in conserving and producing water from dams and desalination plants, fertile agricultural land surrounded them, although the Eaves's were not extravagant with their precious water commodity usage and didn't own a pool. They had a lovely home, typical of many in the area. There were neighbours, but all about a ten-minute drive away or a brisk and sweaty one hour walk.

When she arrived home, Lauren looked out on her feet and her father's water pump seal problem gave her time for a couple of hours sleep. Two hours later, with the local school lessons finished for the day, and the water pump fixed, a late afternoon family reunion commenced. First Olivia arrived, she and Lauren looked so much alike, definitely sisters. Both were fair, tall, and willowy. Although that day, Olivia had tucked her blonde hair neatly up into a bun with her school swipe card still dangling around her neck. She rushed inside to subtle squeals of excitement. To cap things off Lauren's father, Harry, came and swept her off her feet with a broad grin. There were so many things to catch up on, Margaret had not been so happy in months.

After an exuberant early tea on the decking, Lauren and Olivia gravitated to the kitchen, clearing away, and washing up. They continued to talk, mostly about the wedding, less than a week away, and Lauren's life in Cardiff.

Olivia gasped in astonishment and laughing, shouted out to the veranda, "Mum, Dad - Lauren's just told me the olive and the mozzarella story. Oh my God, I wish I had a picture of that, I'd pay good money to see it."

Lauren saw the funny side, "I'll bet the manager of Luigi's has got it on the security camera footage, he would probably sell it to you, Olivia. Shall I call him for you? I'm not sure he's still speaking to me though." At which point Olivia ended up in tears of laughter, whilst at the same time realising how pleased she was to have her younger sister back home. She had changed - perhaps she had grown up more.

Lauren could already feel herself recalibrating to life back in Westonia and sensed a little buzz of excitement at the prospect of dressing up and meeting friends and family not seen in years. Folks were coming in from all over the region for the wedding - and she did love a party.

Still in the kitchen, with music playing in the lounge and everyone in high spirits, Lauren decided to ask Olivia how their gran, Harry's mother, was doing at her nursing home.

"She's OK in herself, but she forgets lots of things, names, faces, events. Well, she is nearly ninety, so fair play to her. And then out of the blue, she comes out with something unexpected and random about Dad's birthday or our holiday to Phuket last year, so 'she's all there', it just comes and goes."

Wiping a saucepan, Lauren, decided to ask about something closer to home. "And how are Mum and Dad doing with the business? I'm sure Mum doesn't tell me everything that happens around here. I know things are tough - but how tough? She thinks I'll be worrying instead of studying; I mean I'm not a kid."

"They are just about keeping their heads above water. They had to lay a couple of part time-guys off last month, and Dad's pulling the extra shifts himself. I spoke to him about it, and he says he's fine. He's fifty-seven but still thinks he's twenty-seven, he is his own worst enemy. I help out at weekends and after school when I can."

Lauren smiled inwardly and ensured her raised eyebrow remained an invisible one.

Olivia continued, "And when a piece of machinery breaks down Dad needs to fix it himself instead of getting someone in like he used to, plus the cost of parts, and sometimes we are talking big bucks. Mum has got a part-time job doing accounts for one of the wholesaler farm food suppliers. I'm sure she'll tell you. Look, they are OK. Mum said they had some savings, and this place is mortgage-free because when times were good years ago, they paid it off. A blessing now."

As she listened to her sister, Lauren started to worry about her parents. Now she could see for herself the daily difficulties they had to deal with and the challenges ahead. The wedding came at a good time and would be good for everyone's morale.

Cardiff's *gig economy*, and her unrelenting bakery night shifts, meant Lauren's body clock had a thick skin. She could sleep at the drop of a hat and manage jet lag like just another day at the office for her. So, for the next two days, with breakfasts long before dawn, Lauren spent time helping Harry work through his well-organised list of priorities around the business. It also proved a wonderful opportunity to spend some more time with him.

Harry had inherited the farm from three previous Eaves generations. He had adamant views that the family originally came to Australia as prospectors and farmers from England and not on a one-way transportation ticket. Insisting, tongue in cheek, Botany Bay was 10,000 km away, knowing full well Perth once ran a penal colony named Swan River and some of his ancestors did originate from there.

As they explored sections of the five thousand acres of land checking and repairing fences Lauren noticed some changes to the boundary and asked Harry what his plans were for them.

He explained, "Look, you know things were a bit tight over the last couple of years and we needed some capital. The farm and the business kinda pay for themselves, most of the time, but I sold a few hundred acres, so that will help see us through. We still own the river and mine. Our neighbours made us a good offer, so we took it."

Lauren not only thought the world of her father, but she also had enormous respect for him as a hard-working, shrewd businessman. But some things were out of his control; COVID was one of them, many farms and mines had taken a big hit due to the pandemic affecting the health of workers and trading within the industry in general. They were luckier than most.

"Dad, I guess you had to do whatever it took, you know what you're doing."

Harry Eaves left school at sixteen and went straight to work for his late father in the mining part of the business. As just a tall, skinny, young kid with jet black hair and glasses. Harry drove huge earth-moving excavators and dumper trucks, depositing hundreds of tons of soil into a gold refining plant beside the river on their land.

Over forty years on, other than for a bit of salt and pepper, contact lenses and a cracked old pair of aviators, he still looked almost the same. Lauren convinced herself that his faded navy boiler suit must have been older than her.

What knowledge Harry had not learned the hard way about mining, he could write on the back of one of his cigarette packs. He was also a highly intelligent man and tried to keep up to speed with current ideas and new processes, forever trying to find efficiencies and economies of scale throughout the business. He became well aware of the global demand for rare earth metals many years ago and made some initial investigations, back then, on his own land. At that time, the land he owned appeared unsuitable for finding anything other than red dusty soil and seemingly less and less gold.

Deep thinking and well-respected Harry had good connections in the Perth area mining industry, and he listened intently when Lauren began to tell her story. She explained what she had discovered concerning Nick Savvas and Blaenavon. She emphasised his well-publicised speciality in converting coal mining waste to rare earth fortunes, and how that aligned, to some extent, to her work in progress dissertation.

"When I arrive back in Cardiff, I'm going to borrow my friend's car, take a trip up to Blaenavon and treat it as a geology field trip. It will boost my rare earth knowledge and enhance my dissertation. It will also give me a chance to take a discreet sniff around to find out what my old lecturer is up to, other than on the Uni system. I can't find anything anywhere about his activity in Blaenavon. It all appears a big secret. Maybe not for long though eh, Dad?" Smiling as she said it.

Driving home, Harry glanced across the bench seat of the truck at his daughter. They were both in need of a good shower, and he recognised the steely look of determination on her face as she spoke. He had seen it many times as she grew up; learning to swim, studying, the horse-riding unexpected dis-mounts and instant re-mounts. Lauren was like a resourceful dog with a bone, and he realised there would be more to come from what she had told him. She would get to the bottom of it one way or another - even if it was a wild goose chase.

Lauren didn't spot Harry looking across at her, she was too busy gazing through the windscreen of the truck as mulga trees and telegraph posts flashed by. She sensed a determination to help resolve her parent's financial crisis and had a plan formulating in her mind. Part of her plan depended on Olivia's wedding, and something her father mentioned in conversation earlier.

Chapter 10

Mind Blowing

An excited Nick Savvas refreshed his memory on the early morning flight from Barcelona to Cardiff, his tablet offered him an array of historical downloads to remind himself of facts concerning Blaenavon. In recent years, his work encompassed coal mines all over the world, but a two-hundred-year-old Welsh mining area registered as a first. Also, his first visit to Wales and looked as though he would need some waterproof clothing to deal with the well documented late February wet Welsh valleys at that time of year.

With an array of cases and accoutrements, he caused HMRC officials to raise a cursory eyebrow as he retrieved his kit from the baggage carousel before he collected and loaded the rented Ford Ranger pick-up.

Less than an hour after clearing customs, he started to recognise the tell tail, brown historical monument road signs for the intriguing destination that would be his base for the rest of the week. Rather than head directly to his Airbnb, his eagerness compelled him to modify his plan. Instead, he took a circuitous route to gain an initial impression of the town and surrounding landscape. Leaving the outskirts of Abergavenny, Savvas passed hardcore cyclists grinding the steep two miles to the ridge of the Blorenge mountain, adjacent to the Keepers Pond.

To his surprise, he realised lambing season must have started weeks ago. The local obstinate sheep were out in force as he dodged an unperturbed ewe and her lamb, whilst passing over the ridge at the top of the steep mountain road. A perfect roadside viewpoint presented itself, so he pulled over, taking in the scene as the clouds gave way to emerging sections of a blue winter sky. In an instant, the new light transformed the damp monotone landscape that sprawled into the valley ahead of him. It then led his eye westwards, across to the opposite side of the valley, up to the opposing Coity mountain, a mile or so away, the river and valley meandered north to south. Sunlight refracted off wet heather-clad hills and mounds making them sparkle, lighting up the surrounding terrain with the town of Blaenavon 'cwtched' in silence at the hub of it all, beckoning him closer.

His peaceful artistic vista shattered in an instant. A pair of motocross bikes roared by in front of his parked truck, ascending several of the old man-made mounds, carving up and spitting backwards chunks of clay and dark grey soil. The dark grey coal waste soil, lay almost everywhere he looked - a perfect reminder as to the reason why he was there and not lounging in the Barcelona winter sun with his wife.

He had work to do and thought to himself, *"So this is where all the magic once happened, and where it should be happening again soon, with a bit of luck."*

Savvas unfolded a pair of maps, each one had handwritten markings in red ink corresponding to more precise GPS locations on his tablet. The locations provided his 'exploration roadmap' and he saw that some were within two hundred metres of his parked truck. They would keep for another day. He felt compelled to move closer to the Coity mountain, riddled with historical mines, and the famous Big Pit mine. Big Pit's huge winding wheels were prominent in the distance, still able to spin, operating as a functional mining museum as part of the town's heritage status. The pit cage took curious visitors from all over the world way underground to the pitch-black depths of an authentic old coal mine.

His pre-prepared maps showed where he intended to take samples, but they also showed where numerous old, smaller pits, once stood. He needed to understand where they were, what debris they had spewed out in the last century and where the miners scattered it, with as much accuracy as possible. Hi-tech software and Google Earth were both helpful tools, but nothing quite compared to getting hiking boots on and seeing and touching things first-hand.

Parking up again on the opposite side of the valley at the base of the Coity mountain, a long and steep walk rewarded him with a breathless view looking back to where he had come from an hour earlier. Big Pit dominated the scene just a few hundred metres below him and it soon became apparent what one-hundred-and-fifty-years of unhindered mining had done to the land. Old photographs on his phone helped pinpoint where huge pyramid-shaped slag heaps once prevailed, dominating the area. Now significantly flattened, a section had been made into a thriving nature reserve, a genuine oasis. Less obtrusive open cast areas further afield were not easy on the eye but blended into the industrialised landscape with relative ease.

Nothing, not even the film crews capitalising on the areas rugged appearance for film sets over the years, could hide the lurking secret - that at one time a huge industrial mess existed. All well documented in the local museum. Now, thanks, to the valiant efforts of local government, some gorse, and a rare moss that grows almost nowhere else other than on the slag heaps, he could see a unique beauty to the landscape.

Savvas savoured what he witnessed, thinking, *"Nature doesn't leave things like that, people do. You can't 'paper over' almost a hundred million tons of coal and iron spoils."*

His map showed several disused pits: to his left Kay's Slope, Milfraen and Dodds, to his right Coity and Garn drift. As a poignant reminder, research also told him, over the years hundreds of men and small children lost their lives in those places with either pitfalls or explosions.

Savvas's stomach reminded him he had grabbed a coffee and toast seven hours ago at Barcelona airport. He could see a pub called the Whistle Inn, two minutes' walk from his vehicle and it fitted the bill to perfection. He walked into the old pub and thought he had stepped back in time. He stood out like a sore thumb, opening his mouth, and ordering a beer and a sandwich with his Aussie accent and winter tan, the neon *tourist* arrow pointing to his head lit up. Nothing subtle about it, he soon realised this pub had a real local feel to it, albeit a friendly one. Mining lamps and railway paraphernalia hanging from the walls made it obvious he had found the right place to embrace a feel for the authentic local culture.

One middle-aged man sat in the corner caught his eye, or at least his sheepdog caught his eye. The fine-looking dog lapped itself to a frenzy with a bowl of water on the flagstone floor, near a raging log fire.

Savvas had made eye contact and felt obliged to issue a polite and discreet, "G'day, beautiful dog. Still a pup?" He raised a courteous pint of lager a fraction off the table.

"Aye, a year old, and she's earned that drink of water this morning. Bea, she's a *Welsh sheepdog*, my working dog, but she's still learning the ropes."

Savvas shuddered. The pub regular had presented him with a sudden reminder that the Whistle pub nestled amongst the land owned by the local farmers, but he had not come in expecting to bump into one and start a conversation. He simply came in for a quiet beer and a sandwich. If things went according to plan, it would be Price's job to make approaches to the landowners in the coming weeks, not his.

The genial man offered some information, "Brewed just down the road."

Savvas looked across again and responded with a quizzical look, "Sorry?"

"Your lager. The brewery is on the edge of town. Mind you they stopped making lager last year and made lorry loads of alcohol gel instead." The farmer chuckled to himself.

"I had no idea. Well, one thing's for sure, it tastes a damn sight better than hand rub. A good pint, and better than that Aussie rubbish."

A self-deprecating Savvas amused the farmer and the eavesdropping landlord who both managed a chuckle.

"Back out to work for you and Bea this afternoon then I imagine? I could think of worse places to work, like underground in that coal mine I'm going to visit in a minute."

"Yes, back to my sheep and lambs for an hour before the kids come in from school. Lambing season has still got a few more weeks left, it keeps Bea busy, and teaches her a more careful approach. How about you - you a tourist then, or working around here?"

Savvas did not expect such direct questioning and it jolted him. He arrived in town not long ago, and immediately found himself under the spotlight, experiencing an uncomfortable, unwanted warmth.

He realised he needed to stick to his pre-prepared flaky alibi, "A bit of both. I'm doing some part-time work for the Environment Agency. They need to take a few soil samples every few years to make sure everything is clean and tidy. You know what *Welsh Government* is like, making mountains out of molehills, but who cares as they are paying me. You might see me around and about over the next few days up to my neck in muck. I won't interfere too much with your land, most of my work will be on common land between the farms. And on a couple of bridle paths on the edge of the farming land."

There were plenty of paths, tracks, and unfenced, undefined areas criss-crossing the land, more than enough locations over a wide area, to provide the sampling required. The grinning farmer nodded his head in approval, muttered something tongue in cheek about taxpayer's money, and appeared to fall for the subterfuge.

Savvas finished his pint and sandwich, stood up to go, and stroked an appreciative Bea, "Nice to meet you, I'm Nick by the way."

"I'm Dai. Those are my fields over the road. Enjoy the pit and the ironworks. You're a tall one, so keep your head down when they take you down."

As Savvas rummaged for his keys walking across the car park, it occurred to him that Dai came across as a decent, friendly, family man. He drove away in silence, anxiously digging a thumbnail into the steering wheel. To make matters worse he had officially started digging more than one hole for himself.

~

A loud clang reverberated, as the hi-vis clad liftsman slammed shut the steel-framed door of the lift cage. Two bleeps of a safety button and the small group of tourists descended to the bottom of Big Pit in less than thirty seconds. The group consisted of a family of four from South Carolina with their two small kids and Savvas. They had all attended the safety briefing and wore hard hats and a belt with a battery pack feeding the light on their helmets. It smelled dank and cold as they exited the lift and began the fascinating tour.

Savvas felt mildly embarrassed. For many years he had travelled the world as a coal mining expert making himself a small fortune from the business, even writing books and white papers on the subject. Yet, this was the first time he had ever visited a proper old-fashioned coal mine. All his work over the years involved gigantic open quarry type mines, but never anything like Big Pit. He felt just as intrigued and excited as the Carolinian's were.

By the end of the tour, Savvas realised he had learned more in half an hour than in months on end lecturing and researching his subject. An hour later he had finished wandering around the above-ground museum. Although he had arrived only hours earlier, he could sense a strange connection to the historic town and the hardships and oppression the Blaenavon people endured back in the early mining days. The same as coal mining towns all over the UK had endured. A stark picture emerged, far beyond the books and wiki pages, of a typical tough Welsh valley town, whose glory days had vanished decades ago. The free of charge visit to the pit did something else; it also reinforced his knowledge of the hundreds of millions of tons of coal and waste that came to the surface. He tingled with excitement at the prospect ahead of him, before continuing his tour, across the famous town with a visit to the historic ironworks, where a local industrialist invented steelmaking in the mid-1800s.

Late afternoon and time to find his Airbnb, but on the way, he planned a drive through town. Leaving the pit, he saw long rows of Victorian terraced houses, some of them simply designated as *A Row*, *B Row* and *C Row*. *"Bloody Imaginative,"* he thought.

He then appreciated how hard COVID and its effect on the local economy had hit the town, as he passed by several boarded-up shopfronts and *To Let* signs in the main street. He stopped for a few provisions and left the small town behind him to find his secluded cottage, tucked away in a rural area a couple of miles outside town. So far everything appeared just as he hoped - maybe even better than he hoped.

~

The following morning, more rain, *"Mia was right, she knew what she was doing by staying home in Spain."*

Nothing would hold Savvas back, rain or snow, his mission had started. Invigorated by a good night's sleep, and a decent breakfast, he didn't need the goosebumps to remind him of his eagerness to execute his plan. As always, his meticulous planning didn't let him down. He had brought with him a full set of gear; a Gore-Tex jacket, matching trousers, boots, gators, and a spare pair of wellies if needed. He would be warm and dry no matter what Blaenavon attempted to throw at him.

The breakfast bar enabled one final check of his map and a cross-reference with his GPS locator. His schedule involved spending the best part of a day in each of five locations. From each two-hundred-metre radius location, he planned to retrieve up to ten soil samples using a hand-operated mandrill device to extract one soil sample.

The device consisted of a 500mm long by 30mm diameter 'worm' tube, which he tapped with a soft mallet, to begin with. He then twisted it manually into the ground always trying to avoid rocks. He added extension pieces making a penetration below the surface of up to two or even three metres wherever possible. When extracted the inside of the hollow mandrill tube contained a soil sample, which Savvas would eject into a polyethene sheath, seal off, label, code and register on his laptop. He would be making long soil sausages all week, and it would involve hours of arduous work.

Each evening back at his temporary lab in the cottage he would take further samples from each sausage for analysis. He finished off by sending them electronically to a specialist lab in Switzerland for the ultimate 'forensic' validation. The precise origin of the sample remained undisclosed, and they processed hundreds every day. They didn't care where the samples originated.

The Swiss lab provided a prestigious and fool-proof facility, but it took time, twenty-four to forty-eight hours depending on how busy they were. Whilst he awaited the official results, Savvas had brought with him a secret weapon, a Bruker S1 TITAN Handheld XRF Spectrometer. A state-of-the-art, lightweight, battery-operated analyser. It would provide him with accurate readings, almost as reliable as the Swiss lab, in less than a minute. It looked like a traffic policeman's speed gun, but it cost twenty times as much and didn't generate any penalty points.

Savvas decided he would target one of the prime locations for his first day of sampling. In hindsight, he was glad to have broken the ice with 'Dai' the farmer and explained himself. At least then if he ran across anyone else, he would reference his conversation with Dai in the pub, pretending as though everyone knew who he was, and why he was in town, no big deal. He also felt more comfortable, as the prime locations were almost out of sight from *The Whistle*, he could relax and carry on with the work.

As it turned out, overshadowing the first location, he found a foliage-covered ten-metre-high by eighty-metre diameter circular mound, the remnants of what was once an ugly gigantic conical coal slag heap, named Coity tip, which in its day rivalled almost any self-respecting Egyptian pyramid. Nearby were other small mounds and a handful of gorse bushes, all offering almost total seclusion. The pick-up truck enabled Savvas to drive in close to the sample zone and with a few shuttle runs hauling the equipment by hand and he began. After a few rock impeding false starts, an hour later the first sausage emerged.

Struggling to contain his excitement, Savvas mused, *"Well Jason this is the moment of truth."*

The earlier rain had ceased and the bed and tailgate on the back of the pick-up made for a good impromptu workbench. Using a Stanley knife, he made incisions in the two-metre-long sausage, splitting it open lengthwise in four places, allowing the moist dark contents to squeeze out onto a dust sheet.

The previous evening, Savvas had programmed the handheld spectrometer with four of his chosen rare earth expectations. Setting 1 was Rubidium, which he knew traded on the Nasdaq (National Association of Securities Dealers Automated Quotations) at approximately $16,000 per kg. Setting 2 looked for Scandium trading at $20,000 per kg, then 3, Iridium at $60,000, and 4, Caesium at $62,000. His research also told him that as a comparison gold traded that day at approximately $42,000 per kg, but there would be no gold found here.

His hand trembled in anticipation as he pointed the device close up at the first of the spread-out lumps of muck and squeezed the trigger button, registering a successful attempt. The forty-five seconds it took to analyse the sample seemed like an eternity.

A bleep and a digital red reading appeared. Setting 1 stated 119ppm (parts per million).

He frowned as he looked at the results, "That can't be right – can it?"

He sighed and made a double-check. He wondered if he was seeing things or were his hands shaking? Same setting, same sample, same remarkable reading.

His vocal cords struggled to utter more than a whisper, "Holy Mother of God." That was the most overt his Aussie-Greek Orthodox upbringing had manifested itself since he was a kid.

He paused, took a few deep breaths, checked the equipment one more time, changed the settings through 2, 3 and 4 and carried out the procedure again and again. Taking as much time and care as possible he spent the next thirty-five minutes examining and testing the same two-metre sausage sample. He had used the Titan spectrometer hundreds of times all over the world. He always found it reliable - flawless, and he knew how to use it as well as anyone. In the past, the Swiss lab consistently corroborated his handheld tests. The multiple checks he made all registered between 117ppm-122ppm across all of the four rare earth particles he searched for.

Sitting in silence, cocooned in the driver seat for two minutes, surrounded by bleak grey clouds dominating even greyer mountains, Savvas savoured the temporary refuge as adrenalin coursed through him. There he took stock, assimilating what he had witnessed and what he knew were genuine, irrefutable facts.

He gave up smoking over twenty years earlier and figured in the small minority of one of those people who never missed it, not once, not even when he was out with his mates having a few too many beers - nothing. But at that moment he yearned to fill his fitness fanatic lungs with smoke and nicotine.

There was no doubt, he had hit the jackpot. This was the holy grail of rare earth discoveries, a geological freak. It could be worth tens of millions of dollars, perhaps billions.

Price had sent him regular WhatsApp's throughout the day. Where are you? What's happening? Any news? Savvas fended him off with one message, *"I'm in a poor signal area. Will go through all results later -looks promising."* There was a great temptation to ring him and yell. But he composed himself, he would take another two samples from this location and tear up the plan by going sooner than scheduled to another location, less than a mile away, and repeat the same process.

Before he set off to the second location, he called Mia, he wanted to tell her the amazing news. She had not read any of his messages, and his call went straight to voicemail. He chose not to leave her a message and would call her again later.

At Location 2 Savvas stood on top of what was once a thirty-metre-high tramway viaduct.

Originally, the track came through a one-mile-long narrow mountain tunnel, then across the viaduct over a small part of the valley towards the town's historic ironworks. The viaduct no longer existed, neither did that small part of the valley, because, in just thirty years, during the late 1800s, almost a million tons of iron and coal waste materials filled the huge void. Since then, nature had reclaimed the land, replacing the huge space with thousands of square metres of flat fields with trees used by grazing horses. During a one-hundred-and-fifty-year period, a scene of industrial devastation took place. No one had any idea, nor did they care, how much material would come from under the ground and end up scattered on the surface. Now it offered Savvas even greater riches.

By 16.00 Savvas had decided to call it a day. Location 2, a mile from Location 1, had provided almost the same startling results.

Price answered his phone in an instant, "Nick, how is my hometown? What's happening? I tried to reach you all day. What have we got?"

Savvas, a man never lost for words, paused for a moment trying to think how to respond, "Jason, Blaenavon is amazing. They should twin it with Barcelona. Maybe they will do after you hear the amazing news that I have for you."

"I'm all ears, go on."

"Listen, I have worked with the best of the best, in China, Brazil and Australia on high-value speculative excavation projects, just like this one. Many of those proved fruitful, but by comparison, these results from Wales are off the charts. I wanted to call you earlier, but I needed to double-check a couple of locations. Remember, this is day one of five, but so far, the results are astonishing. And I mean *astonishing*!"

Savvas concluded by reeling off several price comparisons to gold. Explaining a kilo of gold fluctuates significantly daily, depending on anything from flu outbreaks to sabre-rattling by North Korea. He then told Price the rare earth metal values, per kilogram for Rubidium Scandium Iridium and Caesium, stating the values of the latter two were typically forty percent more than gold. He added that technically they were not 'rare earths'. They were on similar rows on the periodic table of the most valuable of the metals but scientifically classed as noble metals or precious metals. It was sometimes easier to generalise and call them rare earths.

"Jason, in case you're wondering which, if any, of those I found in high concentrations within the Blaenavon samples, the answer is …all four of them. And we don't even need to go digging for it. Most of the stuff is just sitting here on the surface waiting for processing."

"What? You're joking? I'm writing this down. Are you certain? I mean how sure are you?"

"Jason, I wrote books on this stuff, and I once did a live Global *TED Talk* (Technology, Entertainment, Design) in San Francisco. This is for real - mind-blowingly real. Look, as soon as I arrive back at the cottage, I'll send today's samples digitally to the guys in Switzerland. The results are always the same as my handheld results, *always*. But they have the scientific licence and the geological accreditation to make it official, so the next step with those guys is necessary. We do the same thing again tomorrow and the next day. You need to start getting your shit together Jason and make it happen. This is big, massive. Oh, and by the way, I met one of your new potential clients yesterday – David Davies."

Chapter 11

Uncle Jack & The Intrepid Trio

Since arriving back home in Westonia, Lauren's first week had been a busy one. She had reacquainted herself with the dark art of unrolling coils of wire fencing, and her arms, shoulders and back ached every day from wielding a fifteen kg, bell-shaped, fence post rammer. In between the manual hard work, she had found time to do some more feminine things including buying a new dress for the wedding, enjoying a spa day with Olivia and Margaret, and surviving a messy hen party in the neighbouring town. Embarrassing, tagged-in photos were still emerging on her Instagram page, and somehow or other a TikTok video involving a blindfold and a red balloon filled with lager, went viral.

Lauren realised how much she missed home; she missed her friends and most of all she missed her family. At the time, leaving high school and heading off to college in Sydney meant the world to her, almost to the exclusion of everything and everyone else. Nothing could stop the determined, independent young woman who exuded confidence and more than her share of sassiness. That week back in Westonia allowed her to stop and smell the roses and appreciate where she came from and what she had.

Olivia could sense the change in her normally feisty, younger sister, maybe Lauren had matured more in four years than anyone realised, including herself. Of course, the wedding dominated many of their conversations during the week, but they still found time to reminisce about the fun events they had growing up.

A chilled-out afternoon in Merridin gave them a chance to grab a coffee in one of their old haunts as teenagers, *Fab&Jay's* a cosy arts and crafts shop that served amazing homemade cakes, surrounded by local art and cool music.

"Oh, God Olivia I miss this place. I want to own something like this somewhere, but it would never be the same as this would it? I love coffee and I love cake, I'm in paradise."

"I'm with you on that one, but I don't want to own one, I'd eat all the profits."

The sisters laughed and joked, "Lauren, can you remember that time when we were little, and Mum and Dad took us to the big new department store in Perth? You were such a nightmare back in those days - uncontrollable. The lift doors opened, you rushed in through a crowd of people, the doors closed, and you vanished on your own. Mum was frantic and tried to run the wrong way up an escalator, with a security guard chasing her. He thought she was a shoplifter legging it. Two minutes later the doors opened and out you popped as if nothing had happened. So funny."

Lauren giggled and smiled, "I'd forgotten about that one. Mind you #mozzerella-gate recently would take some beating, wouldn't it?"

Olivia laughed aloud causing a few heads to turn and look, she didn't care, no one did, "Oh my God, don't get me started. That was the best story ever. I'm going to pay good money for that CCTV and if you ever get married. You'll see that cheese and the olive again I promise you."

They could have talked for hours but they needed to run a couple more errands.

As they drove around, Lauren spotted a few old school friends and waved from the truck as they passed by and then Oliva asked her once again, "So where are you going to find a job when you graduate? What's the plan?"

"I wish I had an answer Liv. I like the UK, and Europe, there may be something coming up in Wales. I'm still figuring it out - I should have a clearer idea in a few weeks. But right now, I'm enjoying spending time at home and seeing everyone."

A few more horns tooted in recognition of the Eaves sisters before they picked up some groceries and made it home.

CHAPTER 11

~

The wedding at the local golf club far exceeded Lauren's expectations, Olivia was not religious and wanted a less formal wedding, but it still looked special.

"I don't know what it is about weddings, but they make everyone so excited, and so happy. Such a great time to catch up with and to see people again," Lauren thought to herself. She had no idea how much she missed the family dynamic, and how much Olivia really meant to her.

Once the speeches were over, and some initial festivity excitement had taken place, Lauren found time to catch up properly with friends and relatives not seen in ages.

She vaguely recognised a woman who was chatting with Margaret, but could only see her back and couldn't place her, *"I can't be sure from here who that is chatting with Mum? How many aunties have I got?"*

Then Harry came and joined them with a huge, ginger bearded, bear of a man who looked like he could have made a good living as an extra on *Game of Thrones* - Uncle Jack. Of course, the woman talking with her mother was Jack's wife, Sara, she looked so different with a hat on. Uncle Jack Tennison, not really family, but a childhood friend of Harry's. Lauren always had a soft spot for him, and she knew he and her dad went back, more like brothers than friends.

"Uncle Jack, it must be years since I last saw you in the flesh? So lovely to see you again," Lauren said smiling, struggling to wrap her arms anywhere remotely close to around his barrel-shaped body for a hug.

Jack smiled back at her and spoke with his authoritative, baritone voice, "And as you can see there's more flesh on me now than back then as well, eh? But I suppose three hundred km makes it hard to pop over for a quick beer and a sandwich, doesn't it? Hey, speaking of long distances, Harry says you're learning Welsh and taming dragons or something Lauren, is that right?"

"He's not far wrong Uncle Jack, but I had a bit of wake-up call this week working on the land again, for sure I did. My arms are on autopilot, they are killing me. So how are you all doing anyway? You're both looking so well." Lauren glanced over towards her mother and *Aunt* Sara with a smile.

"All good thanks. The last couple of years, whilst you were away, were a bit of a blip with the pandemic and everything, but Sara and I are in one piece thank God. And production is getting back to normal for us, touch wood. Although I know your dad's playing catch up, he'll be fine, wait and see."

Harry wandered off offering to fetch them both another drink, leaving Lauren and Jack to it. They chatted for ages about family, Olivia, sport, life in Wales and her college course.

"I need to visit there one day. They tell me some of my relatives are over there somewhere - Welsh and Irish they reckon. Can't you see the connection?" Stroking and tugging at his stupendous bushy beard.

Lauren smiled and explained more about her MSc. and the dissertation, "I'm well ahead with it, polishing and editing now more than anything. Another month at the most and it will be ready for submission. The course work is fascinating, and I found myself gravitating towards rare earth mineral mining. Isn't that your speciality Uncle Jack? Didn't you switch from mining other stuff to focus on rare earth minerals several years ago?"

"You're right. You could say we kinda transitioned into it. We didn't want to put all our eggs in one basket. But then it was obvious that the land was well suited, it was fruitful, and we could sustain it, so we switched over entirely. Not all land is viable, your dad had a look at his ages ago, and at the time it wasn't a good shout. I keep telling him to reconsider it, processes are different and more efficient these days, thanks to the Chinese. Bloody clever they are."

"I hope you're right about Dad's land. I'll try to pep him up. But there is something else I wanted to ask your opinion about. Can you spare me ten minutes before the music kicks in?"

Lauren and Jack took themselves off to a quieter corner and she explained everything she knew about Nick Savvas, Blaenavon, her university software and how astonishing Savvas's preliminary geo software mapping results appeared – if they were true. She also told him she was studying less than an hour down the road from Blaenavon and intended to check it out when she went back to Cardiff. If nothing else, it would be a handy course fieldwork analysis.

"If I'm honest Uncle Jack, this is a long shot, but if there is huge potential in the soil in Blaenavon, and only a handful of people know about it, then maybe everything will be fair game. There could be a mineral treasure trove sat waiting for someone to excavate, and it might be an opportunity for someone who understands what they are doing to make some money? What's your advice? How should I approach it? You're the expert. The landowners won't know what to do with it, they would need people who know about rare earth mining to assist them and work with them Maybe us - if they haven't already sorted out a deal with Nick Savvas, which is possible – but not certain because he hasn't been to Blaenavon yet. I don't know what he's up to yet, a mystery – and he is describing it on his information as testing for coal mining testing – it stinks to me."

Jack and Lauren found themselves ensconced in a deep technical and commercial conversation when Harry arrived minutes later juggling three ice-cold schooners. Jack looked at Harry and said, "We all need a proper chat mate, Lauren might be onto something and not something we should ignore."

Jack and his wife were staying at the Eaves's for a couple more days. Lauren and Harry agreed to speak in more depth with Jack the following day so that everyone could relax and focus on the biggest priority for the rest of the day - Olivia's wedding.

CHAPTER 11

~

Olivia had moved out of the family home three years earlier and Margaret and Harry had no sensations of losing a daughter, her new husband was like an existing member of the family. Harry was a happy man, and all of his other worries were far from his mind.

It was late afternoon the following day, by the time Harry arrived back in Westonia after dropping the honeymooners off at Merridin train station. The Tennisons, their two teenage sons, and Lauren were still in great spirits and swapping pictures, despite a few hangovers and dance inflicted blisters.

Margaret loved to bake and emerged with pride from the kitchen carrying an almond cake, mugs of tea and a jug of lemonade, "Last time I checked no one had a nut allergy so get stuck in. And I'm guessing nobody needs a beer yet, do they?"

Lauren, Harry, and Jack sat on the patio helping themselves to a second slice of the delicious almond cake.

With a fork in hand, Jack targeted the tip of his new slice, and looked up, "This morning I had a little more time to think about what you said yesterday Lauren. I also did some research of my own into this Savvas fella. He is one of the main men in the rare earth mining business at the moment, from what I can see of it. He knows his stuff."

"Yes, he is. If you ever meet him, he won't mind telling you about it either, he loves to talk. He enjoys the attention and considers himself as a pioneer on the subject."

Jack continued, "Which is all the reason why we should give this thing some serious attention and consideration. It doesn't take a genius to recognise the significance of the data you uncovered, and I know you're sure it is the real thing. So why is he keeping so quiet and calling it coal mining? Something is happening or will be happening, and you are in a good position to look into it, Lauren. Blaenavon is on your doorstep, and *we* can carry out a bit of a recce of our own, can't *we*? Well, *you* can when you go back to Cardiff, with some remote teamwork and assistance from *your Uncle Jack* and your dad."

Harry remained silent, listening to every word, and smiling to himself. He was aware of where the conversation was going, Jack had chosen his moment earlier and mentioned it to him.

Jack was a true entrepreneur and continued to explain his thoughts on the matter, "It could be an investment opportunity for us all with your local help and involvement to get us started, Lauren. The landowners would make the ultimate decisions on who they needed to work with or go into business with. You know, over the years your dad and I did all right for ourselves with our businesses, and it didn't come about by accident. Don't get me wrong, we both went through our tough times, but with hard work and smart thinking, we made it through them. This project might be one of those moments that comes around once in a blue moon. Some people know how to grasp it, and some don't. Some people can't even spot an opportunity staring them in the face - I'm not one of those people, neither is your dad, and we've come up with a plan."

Harry picked up the conversation, dovetailing with Jack, and for the next twenty-five minutes Lauren listened, often contributing with some smart ideas, and the red flags they should avoid. Between them, they had the land and assets to raise capital, and they were confident other trusted entrepreneurial investors would also come forward to fund a 'pilot' mining project. Everything was dependent on finding something of consequence worthy of mining.

Jack explained to Lauren, "I can brief you, and share with you, as much of my knowledge as possible in a short space of time. How to carry out soil testing, produce the necessary readings and interpret them."

Similar tests to those that Nick Savvas was completing, almost 15,000km away at that exact moment. Lauren possessed a pre-planned road map, thanks to the carelessness of Savvas, highlighting where he considered the prime test locations were.

Lauren commented, "I've already copied the data he had stored on the Uni system to my laptop. All I needed to do, is turn up and find the same results." Little did she know then, the astonishing results waiting for her when she went there.

Jack explained, "I've got all the equipment you need and it's portable."

By coincidence, he owned an earlier version of the spectrometer Savvas had used. Functional, and adequate for what she needed.

He added, "Lauren before you go back to Cardiff, we can spend a couple of hours going through stuff and what you need to look out for. Ideally, it would be better if you were hands-on, on the ground. But hey, enough business talk, for now, you're here for your family, not for me."

"Dad, Jack, as you said, this could be the chance of a lifetime for us all, and yes, I have come to see Mum, you, Olivia and the family. There is a solution though. My ticket is flexible - I didn't ask for it, but it was in the deal. I should be able to extend it by a couple of days if there are some seats available on a later flight back. I'm sure there will be. Give me a minute."

Lauren opened up her Qantas app, and a minute later declared there was plenty of space on a handful of future flights, at no extra cost. Jack agreed, offering to take her to the train for Perth airport when they finished his mini spectrometer training course if she still wanted to go and see him for a few days.

Jack cautioned, "Just one thing though Lauren when you arrange your flight, book another luggage spot for the extra kit."

Lauren smiled, "Great news. I'm all set. I'll tell work I missed my flight. I hate Wednesday's anyway, so even better."

~

CHAPTER 11

The following week, Lauren said her emotional goodbyes to Harry and Margaret as they saw her off to go and see Jack Tennison, a couple of hours away on the train.

The last time she sat on a similar train she had just come off the back end of a long haul flight. This time, although sad to leave, she realised it was not just the start of a journey back to Cardiff, but perhaps the beginning of a much bigger journey. Her naïve enthusiasm needed tempering to stay focused and in the present. Harry and Jack's expertise would channel Lauren's efforts in the right direction. Both experienced miners and businessmen – and they provided her with inspiration, confidence plus even greater determination.

The train had a good wi-fi signal and out of curiosity, Lauren did another internet search using the same words - *Nick Savvas Blaenavon.* She didn't expect to see any hits since her previous search, about two weeks ago.

This time she sat up ramrod straight in her seat, uttering, "Wow, are you kidding me?"

She found a surprising result. An online travel review, of a cottage on the outskirts of Blaenavon, posted days earlier, from a man describing himself as - *Nick Savvas, Spain.*

It occurred to Lauren, that Savvas's careless online attitude had manifested itself once again. After giving it further consideration, she realised, *"Of course, why wouldn't he?"* No one had the foggiest what he was doing in Blaenavon other than himself, or so he thought.

She was not lacking motivation or enthusiasm, but this little tell-tale slip-up by her loquacious former tutor gave her even more impetus. Not only had he carried out the extensive research and planning concerning Blaenavon, which was valid - he was acting on it, and not wasting much time.

She looked out the window of the train for a moment to concentrate and to think, *"He's not doing this on his own, is he? Who else is involved? Who's behind it and funding it? What are they planning to do? They think they are smart about it, but they don't know Nick Savvas as well as I do."*

The online review was for a small, isolated, and self-contained cottage. Suggesting he had stayed there for about a week and left a few days ago. *Five stars- Idyllic - A beautiful, peaceful place to stay and relax after a long day. Surrounded by forestry and great views, in the middle of nowhere with all the comforts of home, and the quaint Goose and Cuckoo, a cosy little pub tucked away just down the road. Ample parking. Good, much-needed Wi-Fi. Historic Blaenavon is a ten-minute drive through the lanes. Planning to come back again soon.*

Lauren, mused, *"Planning to come back again soon? What's that supposed to mean? I think I know."*

Before she left Westonia to meet her Uncle Jack, Lauren had set up a WhatsApp chat group entitled *The Intrepid Trio.* Jack and Harry received the first of many messages to the group from Lauren. The message included a link to the online review, which was a great reassurance for them all, causing a flurry of responses within their group.

Jack, *"Bloody hell. Sightseeing? My arse."*

Harry, *"What a clot. He couldn't resist, could he? Like you said he loves to chat. Whatever he's doing can't be without the say-so of the local council. After that, he's going to need a mining license and permission from the landowners. I bet none of them realises anything yet. It must be too early. Great news."*

Jack, *"I will make a discreet check on applications for a mining license in the area. Nothing that will tip Savvas off, just something vague and obtuse. Like I'm a writer or a tourist asking a question from a historical angle."*

Harry, *"Go easy Jack. Try to look online without speaking to anyone."*

Lauren, *"And I'll take a proper sniff around when I go there next week."*

They all agreed they were on the right track, and Savvas and his associates had no idea – not yet.

~

Lauren learned almost as much about geology, and in particular mineralogy, during her forty-eight hours with Jack and his small team as she had in a year of studying. This precious time was the glue that pulled much of her theoretical work together and proved invaluable. Her business studies knowledge improved by understanding the difference between a mark-up percentage and a margin percentage, until then she thought they were both the same thing.

The highlight of her rare earth mining business crash course came when she learned how to extract samples from the ground and measure the particle contents. She used a set of portable tubes which screwed seamlessly together and fitted in a dedicated shoulder carry bag. Exactly as Nick Savvas did a couple of weeks earlier.

"You can find yourself a heavy mallet in Cardiff, Lauren. No point paying Qantas to fly one over for you."

Using his battered looking but fully functional spectrometer, Jack explained, "This is what we are looking for Lauren, this is the good stuff. More than 7ppm or 8ppm and we are in business in Wales. This is what you will be taking with you in a hard case. Keep it well charged. It could do with a new battery, but it should be fine."

Lauren got the hang of it in seconds, saying "The lab in Cardiff Uni is well equipped. They have a research department there, and I had some training there not long ago, so I'll be able to carry out some more precise tests to validate the initial results. It should be easy."

Jack helped her to pack away the kit, and said, "That was the easy part. The hard part is the commercial stuff and coming up with a business case. The crucial element will be to differentiate our proposition from the competition - Nick Savvas and his mates whoever they are. I need to do some background work on how we should approach things. But I reckon you're good to go."

CHAPTER 11

As the miles passed by the train's window, Lauren's mind began to think about the long flight back to the UK, when her mother called, "Hi Mum."

"Darling, thank God. It's your dad. We are at Merridin Hospital. He's had an accident."

Chapter 12

The Inquisition

Barcelona, a city famous for its adventurous approach to design and architecture. Gaudí, the Catalan 'Godfather of Impact' led the way, with his Sagrada Família and many other notable buildings.

The urban planners and administrators at Ajuntament de Barcelona, the city council, receive a plethora of ideas and proposals to address every day, with high expectations from the public. The mayor herself personally rubber-stamps many of the more prestigious ideas.

Fifty-six-year-old Xavi Zamora, a wily, urban landscape senior planner and citizen council committee member, thought his Friday morning would be a straightforward one. That was until he had a call to attend a meeting at Casa de la Ciutat, the city hall – the mayor's office – with his boss. The call meant a short walk from their offices, across the

Plaça Sant Jaume to the unscheduled meeting. Rare, but it was not the first time to receive such a sudden call to a meeting.

As Xavi strode across the concourse, he asked his boss the same question, three times in as many minutes, "What's this about?" Then, "What's going on?" Followed by, "What does she want?"

"No idea. It wasn't her anyway; she's away on holiday. We're meeting her new deputy; I saw him once from a distance, but I never met him."

~

Visible through the railings and orange trees that securely enclosed Jason Price's opulent Spanish property, was his sizable backside, displaying an unpleasant valley, as he crawled on his hands and knees. He was trying to retrieve his iPhone from underneath a prickly Spanish Broom, gorse like bush. The phone landed there moments earlier, following a call he received from a property management company intermediary. Price looked furious, frustrated and bleeding from scratches to both hands and the crown of his head, the blood indistinguishable from his shiny red pate.

Earlier, Price's caller passed him some disconcerting news, "Jason, this is off the record. You have not heard this information from me, my friend. There will be an announcement in an hour. From Monday the council are going to suspend all work on the casino project until further notice, pending a corruption investigation. They have suspended Xavi and two others."

"What? ...*What*? Are you serious? He's your cousin, you promised me he would be careful. Safe, experienced and impenetrable, were your exact words."

"My English is perfect. I know what I said. I meant what I said. He is, he *was* - safe. The casino project did not blow him. Something else did. He got greedy on other stuff and so they came looking for him. The casino is a by-product. It will be complicated and drawn out. Many people, like you, are involved in *unprofessional* jobs across the city. But the government and the police need to prove it first, it won't be easy. He was greedy, but he also tried to take great care, it will be someone else's word against his. How did you pay him?"

"Bitcoin, the equivalent of €10k, as he asked, he's not a novice, is he? There is nothing to prove it was me, no emails, no text messages, no phone calls. You set it up, I met him once and paid him. Planning consent went in my favour. Simple as that - easy.

"Then stay calm, play it cool. You will be fine, so will I. These things blow over, this is Spain after all."

Price's usual cultivated Welsh accent reverted to the rapid valley twang he grew up with, "Fine for you to say stay calm and play it cool. It may be dodgy, but you're missing the point. If this project gets suspended, then I have a huge problem with my investors. Massive. We've all got millions tied up in the land, and in the work in progress, with enormous overheads. There are a pair of thirty-metre-high cranes arriving on-site next week. This is the worst news of my life. There will be huge chunks of money leaking from the project like a sieve. My money."

Price hooked his phone out from the prickly bush with a three-iron - relieved to find the phone still worked and made one of the most uncomfortable calls he had ever made. Bad news travels fast, even in Spain, and he needed to ensure he was the one bearing it, and not someone else.

~

Whilst Jason Price was about to deal with the fallout from the Catalan corruption scandal, Nick Savvas was reaching the end of the greatest week of his illustrious career.

Every day he spent in Blaenavon, he had expected to encounter some dubious readings, anomalies compared to the amazing first day. There were none, every day proved as good as the day before, a consistent across the board set of excellent results. Even staff at the lab, in neutral and unemotional Switzerland, passed enthusiastic comments. They asked him where he did the tests, "China, western China," he proclaimed.

On the final evening of his trip, Savvas had diligently sent off his last set of results, expecting that they would match the handheld readings when they came back. He had jogged, showered, changed, called

Mia, and answered most of his emails - apart from one - from an old acquaintance.

Savvas's inflated ego had made mental preparations for his next book *The Mineral Pioneer* all through the week. In his head, chapter upon chapter unfolded. His feet were not touching the ground and he harboured ludicrous, romantic notions of appearing on the radar of the Nobel prize committee. He could match anyone in a confidence competition, though he lacked the necessary killer instinct and determination possessed by successful entrepreneurs.

The email which arrived two hours earlier came from Dee Munchetty, an American woman, almost twenty years his junior, whom he had met whilst working in China, pre-pandemic. Most of her time involved contracting with National Geographic as an edgy environmentalist and geological documentary filmmaker, often dodging active volcanoes, analysing potential earthquake patterns and glacial shifts. She split her time between a home in Boston and a company apartment in London.

Weeks before the phrase *social-distancing* entered global vocabularies, funds were in place and National Geographic were all set to produce a one-hour *Rare Earth and Our Future* programme. A spin-off article would follow in the Nat Geo magazine about a mine Savvas had pioneered in China. Savvas was the intended focus, demonstrating the ever-increasing global hunger for rare earth metals. They planned to highlight the constant stream of new technological and scientific applications for it. The key message though would have focused on the finite availability until it all disappears, or scientists find new alternatives in the next hundred years. Every year the value of the precious commodity rises as sources shrink.

COVID and the vilified Chinese government had blocked the documentary, and the news had devastated him. A minor celebrity-academic profile would have done wonders for his book sales, particularly in the US, and increased his non-existent social media following. He had scrubbed up his Twitter and Instagram accounts in readiness - he was all geared-up. Then the world changed and everything and everybody came to a standstill.

Emails from Munchetty popped up once in a while to keep him on the hook and updated. As a journalist, her real agenda for keeping in touch meant she would find out if he had any news. She often pressed him hard, to use his contacts, to try to find a conduit back into China, with the permission of the Chinese government, now that COVID no longer threatened. Savvas had no news, nor any route back into China and of course, he would have contacted Munchetty the moment he did.

What he did have though involved a new idea. A much bigger, far better idea than the Chinese project, combining a historical and human-interest significance to it. After a few days in Wales, he found himself itching to divulge what he was doing to Munchetty and start the ball rolling again. Somehow, he managed to restrain himself, the timing of telling her, and the risk of a leak, could ruin everything.

For the next hour, Savvas fought his egotistical demons. He became paranoid with visions of busloads of Chinese tourists eyeing up the potential within the coalfield landscape. But worse than that, something Munchetty mentioned in the email troubled him.

"... Nick, I wanted you to hear it from me, personally. The Discovery Channel has approached me. They too have taken an interest in the rare earth phenomenon. One of the Nat Geo producers switched allegiances and joined Discovery Channel a few months back. She is planning a similar documentary. You must be aware, there is a huge mine in Russia, with a great back story. You, China, and Nat Geo would be a far better TV show, that combination would be my preference. But time is running out and my bank manager tells me I didn't make many programmes last year..."

~

The *Thinking Cup* is a large trendy coffee shop on the edge of downtown Boston, Massachusetts, over the road from Boston Common and serves great coffee. The *Cup* is always packed, either with tourists, locals or well to do students and is situated a brief train stop or two away from MITT and Harvard. Early afternoon Boston time, Dee Munchetty's iPhone danced around on the table beside her MacBook.

She inserted her earpods and answered the call with an enthusiastic tone, "Hey Nick, what a lovely surprise. How are you and Mia keeping, both fit and well, I hope? And how is Spain?"

"Hi Dee, we're both fit and well thanks, and Spain is better than ever, you must come and see us. You sound as though you are out and about? Are you home in Boston, at your London office, or are you travelling? And is this a good time?"

"Yes, now is good. Just grabbing an espresso and a bagel in my favourite Boston coffee shop - and getting some work done at the same time. I came in three hours ago and have not moved a muscle since, I need to stand up in a minute before I seize up. Come to think of it, when I emailed you earlier, I was right here, in this seat."

"I love Boston, you're so lucky. I picked up your email an hour ago, hence the reason for my call. I didn't want to write back - I wanted to speak to you about something. Something important that couldn't wait."

"Go on." Munchetty had her Moleskine and pen poised in anticipation.

"OK, you might need to hold off on that Russia thing you mentioned. Right now, I am working on something spectacular, mind-blowing - I promise you. You must trust me on this. But only two of us are involved in it so far, me and a business partner. That's how sensitive it is. We are carrying out some tests and the results are outrageous, but there is more to it than that. There would be a terrific historical story to marry up to the scientific aspect of it."

"So where is this taking place? Where are you? I mean, are you there now?"

"In the UK and yes, I'm here now."

"What? You mean the *story* is based in the UK?"

"Yes, I know, not exactly the gargantuan Chinese rare earth black hole mining operation you might expect. It won't be. It doesn't need anything like that. The geology is different, and has off the scale concentrations of minerals."

"Where in the UK Nick?"

There was a pregnant pause, whilst Savvas considered his words.

"I can't tell you that, well, not yet. But I will as soon as I can. This whole thing is complicated and sensitive. But it will all be resolved soon."

"Nick, I need more than that, for my own satisfaction and peace of mind. I could be booking flights to St Petersburg and hotels in Veliky Novgorod as early as next week if things go to plan. Our fixer in Russia is all fired up. Which is why I put my cards on the table in the email, out of fairness to you." She lied.

Munchetty realised, as soon as his name popped up on her phone, responding to her email, that she had Savvas on a piece of string. She kept giving it a gentle tug with every sentence.

Savvas was just an occasional drinker, but the completion of the work on the ground in Blaenavon, the euphoria of it all and the expectancy led him to the Goose and Cuckoo. He was enjoying a quiet, solo, celebration, and a fraction more alcohol than he intended. Not much more, but enough to loosen his tongue as he continued the conversation.

"Help me out here Nick, you know I'm with you on this one."

"Dee, you need to promise me, you will tell no one. It must stay between you and me."

"You have my word, Nick. When did I ever let you down?"

"OK, OK, I'm in Wales, at a former coal mining area. Millions of tons, maybe thirty million, of coal waste and iron waste ended up scattered all around during the last couple of centuries. Dozens of men and boys died back then mining it, in pitfalls and explosions. Like I said there is a big human-interest story here for you."

"Where is this place?"

"Blaenavon, the town is called Blaenavon. UNESCO even made it a World Heritage Site twenty years ago."

Savvas, could not help himself and spilt the beans. The whole can. Though he refused to divulge the names of his business partners, other than stating they were wealthy ex-pats living in Spain. Munchetty got what she needed. There was no trip to Russia, no fixer, and no genuine plans. The only factual comment she made earlier referred to her colleague moving jobs and she had not even started her job yet. But now Munchetty had her teeth into something special, she would not let it go.

"Listen, Nick, I'm coming to London soon to finalise another project. If we are both in the UK at the same time, I think we should meet and catch up on this one. I think it could be going places, it sounds exciting."

"OK, Dee, I'm going back to Spain in a few days. But I expect to return to Wales, in a week or so, nothing fixed yet. Let's keep in touch."

Realising that alcohol had loosened his tongue more than he had intended, he insisted, "Dee, this is serious, and big, so I need you to sign a non-disclosure agreement, I'll create one later and email it across to you. OK?"

"Sure, no problem, I'll sign it. Send it over."

Her agreement reassured him. If she did ever sign it, she realised her US legal team would laugh at it and tear it to shreds, although she had no expectations of such a set of circumstances ever emerging. Munchetty would involve Savvas, if anything developed, he would be perfect. But she liked to keep her options open, and she held the trump cards.

As soon as the phone went dead, Munchetty opened her social media and took a closer look at some recent acquaintances on Facebook posts. She used Facebook on rare occasions, considering it a necessary evil, but an essential tool for any respectable investigative journalist. Mia Savvas, whom Munchetty had met several times was a friend of hers on Facebook. Within a few moments, a picture emerged, Nick Savvas celebrating at a sixtieth birthday, with his land speculator friend Jason Price, accompanied by Declan Ryan – both ex-pats. Munchetty had put two and two together and correctly concluded who was backing Savvas. She dug deeper on social media and business media for more helpful background information in case she ever needed it.

~

"Declan, we've hit a bit of a snag with the construction work. There is no easy way of saying this, but they are suspending building work from next Monday. It could be for weeks, perhaps even months. Nothing is official yet, but you need to know. There will be an announcement in an hour."

After a moment of hush, Ryan reacted, "Suspended? *Suspended?* What the hell do you mean? Have they found an unexploded bomb or an earthquake fault-line or something? What the fuck is going on Jason? Tell me, what do you know?"

"Nothing like that Declan. There is, or there was, a guy in the Barcelona city planning department, he's high up. Influential. He makes things happen. His name is Xavi Zamora. I do some work with his cousin, a local property agent. He contacted me a few minutes ago to tell me about the problem. Xavi sanctioned the planning consent for the casino and retail job. He ensured, with his colleagues, that the vote passed it through. The thing is, the guy voted lots of things through recently, and is now caught up in a backhander scandal."

"Shit. I'm all ears, Jason - and I don't think I want to hear it."

"To cut a long story short, I *sorted him out* with some Bitcoin months ago, way before you were on board. Now it may have come back to bite me. There is no evidence and no connection to me, or you for that matter. But now someone has dropped him right in it. With his bank accounts loaded, he and his new girlfriend went on a giant spending spree. Bloody idiot."

"So, when me and my family handed over millions of our *hard-earned* to you Jason, you forgot to mention it to me then? It must have slipped your sixty-year-old fucking mind or something. Maybe you thought I would back off if I were aware of some stinking fucking backhander deal that could eventually jeopardise the project and my fucking money and my business. You, fucking prick." Ryan's voice started loud and by the end, Price sensed vitriolic steam and saliva spraying through his earpiece.

Throughout his life, Price's thick skin and devil may care attitude towards most people who got in his way proved an effective facet of his personality, though not the most endearing. As time progressed, growing up and through adolescence, the people, and friends he circulated with were just as hardnosed. They were kindred spirits, never far from trouble, no compunction or moral compass. He and his career in the land and property business were a marriage made in heaven. The ultimate dog eats dog world, with Price never far from the top of the food chain.

All of a sudden, for the first time in decades, Price sensed an unusual and uncomfortable feeling

- vulnerability. Deep down, he had figured out that Ryan was far more cutthroat than most of his acquaintances. He had ignored it because it suited him, he needed Ryan on board. Now, the normally *bulletproof* Jason Price could feel the heat - he was a worried man.

Shaken by Ryan's understandable reaction, a sheepish Price responded, "Declan, I'm sorry. I had no idea it would come to this. In all honesty, I had forgotten about paying that greedy bastard. He was *at it* for years, a master. You know what *they* are like *they* are all doing it, no big deal. Now he goes and gets greedy and gets himself caught - fucking clown. It should blow over soon, but we have no way of knowing how it will pan out, not for at least a few days."

"It better fucking blow over Jason. It had better. Otherwise, you won't be having a sixty-first. This mess is all at your door, and all your problem to fix. Get me my fucking money back, are you listening to me? Get me my money back - otherwise, you will have a fucking big problem. The casino will be the least of your fucking worries. I promise you. I'll fucking kill you."

Chapter 13

The Fall Out and the Make-Up

Friday - always a busier day than normal at most regional airports. People heading home after work trips or flying off somewhere for a weekend break, and as a rule, with everyone in a good mood.

Savvas was no exception. He had returned the pick-up rental and his check-in went as smooth as silk. He breezed through custom control and found himself a seat with a newspaper fifty minutes before boarding when his phone rang.

It was Price, calling again, *"He is relentless, he doesn't let go."* Savvas found Price exasperating.

Price and had also called late the previous evening to listen and glorify in more good news from Savvas as he wrapped up his week. The Friday airport call was ten minutes after Price had heard the news about Xavi

Zamora and less than one minute after he finished speaking with an angry Declan Ryan. He needed some solace and a lifeline.

"Jason, you can't get enough of a good thing, can you? What's up, mate?"

The tone of Price's voice was barely a whisper, gone was the ebullient Welsh lilt that Savvas was sick of the sound of.

With none of the usual pleasantries, "Nick, what time are you landing? I will be there and pick you up, as I need to speak with you. Something urgent has come up."

"Mate, Mia is already fixed up to fetch me. We are going out as soon as I arrive back home. What's happened, Jason? You sound like crap?"

"You need to put her off for an hour. I wouldn't ask if it wasn't important, you know I wouldn't. Look, there is no problem with Blaenavon, nothing like that. But something else, and I need to get a few ducks in a row with you."

"OK, I understand, see you in a couple of hours, I'll send you my flight details."

Mia replied to Savvas's text message and said she would wait at home. She had heard no other news about Jason and wondered if anything was wrong and waited.

~

Price at least managed a genuine smile, when he shook hands with Savvas as he emerged from the arrivals gate at Barcelona airport.

As they drove off together, Price glanced sideways and managed a joke, "Did you bring me a stick of rock, or should I say rare earth rock from my hometown?"

"I had to dump the dirt before I left. Customs get funny about stuff like that. There will be a bit of residue on the equipment if you're that desperate Jason? Besides, the best gift is in the digital results, they are what matter the most."

Savvas, realised Price was desperate for something, but what? He chatted about the successful weeks' work and decided to wait for Price to explain himself when they arrived at Price's home minutes later.

The two men sat in the kitchen, as Price poured them each a brandy, "Sorry to haul you off your schedule like this Nick. But I, *we*, have a huge problem with Declan. A huge problem, which needs a resolution – tomorrow."

"Problem? What kind of problem? And what does it have to do with me?"

Price took another gulp, he looked like he needed it, "Let me put all my cards on the table."

Price started to explain to Savvas the entire story, from start to finish about the original golf course land coming available, which Price obtained at short notice for the casino project. How the specific piece of land he wanted happened to fall into his lap, with some local assistance. He described the land procurement deal, the tip-offs, the associated bribery of Xavi Zamora and corruption at a high level. All, in an easy matter of fact fashion, like it was nothing more than a mere everyday transactional occurrence.

At first, the news shocked Savvas. It prompted him to remind himself that the work he planned to embark on in Wales was irregular at best, and at worst breaking the law, although he never once considered contemplating the word, *fraud*.

"And now I'm under severe pressure from Declan *fucking* Ryan. Look, Nick, all sorts of dodgy people have made veiled threats towards me over the years. This guy worries me, he scares me - I'm not stupid. I took his feisty reputation with a pinch of salt at first. Since then, I listened to other stories coming out of the woodwork. I need him off my back. I need time - a lot of time, before we resolve the casino problem. We need to tell Declan about the rare earth project. I need to cut him in. So, we must go and see him and tell him what you and I discovered and what it will be worth once we get it over the line. I want you to come with me – tomorrow - with your geologist's hat on."

Savvas could feel the pressure, oozing itself from Price's shoulders onto his, "I thought you were business partners? Isn't he going to ask why you didn't tell him before?"

"He does have a stake in some of my business ventures, the Spanish ones, including a massive stake in the casino project. He's aware I have others, in the UK, but that was always my business, and they were never on the table. I didn't want him involved in Blaenavon, I hoped we wouldn't need him involved.

But things just changed. You and I were always going to have to raise funds, we discussed it loosely before you went to Wales."

Savvas had to agree, "I know we did, but now this is *game on* everything is a reality."

"The dynamic will just need to change a little bit. Since you told me about the news from Wales, I spent some time earmarking a few trusted potential investors over the past couple of days - tentative approaches. The Blaenavon project is ours fifty-fifty, that was our starting agreement if it were to get off the ground. From now on in we have to dilute our shareholding equally. Tomorrow I will tell my accountant to register a new 'mining company' to handle it. But if Declan doesn't believe what you say and understand the significance - you might be on your own. To tell you the truth, he's a vicious bastard - he rattled me."

Savvas realised that the thick-skinned Price sounded scared - fearful. Savvas, had an immediate wake-up call, that he was now playing with the big boys, but he had far too much at stake to walk away, "OK, Jason. OK, let's go and see him tomorrow. You need to speak to him first, this evening, then let me know things are calmer. I'm not going in there with you tomorrow stone-cold. No chance."

~

The next morning, Savvas's lift arrived, and he had barely clipped in his seatbelt before asking the burning question, "What did Declan say to you last night?"

Price pulled away and responded, "He was much calmer than earlier in the day, more rational, prepared to listen and help to find a way through things. I said there is a rescue plan up my sleeve if he wanted to hear about it. I made sure it would sound interesting to him. Of course, it did, and here we are."

Holding back a pair of muscular, boxer dogs, on short leashes, Ryan invited the two men inside his property. As they approached the door, Savvas gave an admiring glance back towards a gleaming blue Maserati MC20, as Andrea Bocelli's voice and *Con te partirò*, disconcertingly filtered through to them. "Come on in guys come and sit down. I hope you enjoy operatic music - I love it and so do the dogs, it soothes them - keeps them quiet and calm. I used to have a decent voice but not as good as his. I'm making tea if tea's OK for you?"

Price and Savvas looked at one another, neither had any inclination to suggest an alternative.

They moved into the kitchen area, and there were Italian chairs and stools everywhere, which reminded Savvas of a Vitra showroom he once visited in Milan. The three men sat around a gleaming ten-seater steel and polished oak table.

Savvas had not taken his eyes off the pair of beautiful but intimidating-looking creatures since they arrived. In return they sat staring at Savvas, silently sizing him up, "A handsome pair of dogs Declan, and well trained. They haven't barked or growled once, have they?"

Stroking each dog behind the ears, Ryan revelled in his favourite pet subject, "These two bad boys are Alfie and Bow. Just about fully grown now. Their dad was a *Reserve Best in Show* at Crufts. Cost me an arm and a leg, but I adore them. They are so loyal, and it is incredible how intuitive they are. I've owned other dogs over the years, mostly, big aggressive, dogs - noisy and hard to handle. With these guys, I decided to get them professionally trained from day one. You know, with the grandchildren coming along and everything. So I hired a top-notch obedience trainer, cost me thousands, but they don't make a sound unless they feel threatened or if they think I'm getting threatened."

Price nudged himself forward on his seat, and asked, "Can I stroke them?"

"Not if you want to keep your hand, Jason. Family and close friends only."

Price got the message loud and clear that he didn't make it into the latter of those two categories. After exchanging some defusing pleasantries, Ryan opened up, "So what have you got for me, guys?"

Savvas deferred and allowed Price to lead, "Declan, the casino will come back to us. Just a matter of time, this is Spain and things move on."

Ryan interrupted, "What makes you so sure?"

Price was undeterred, "The unions are involved, and lawyers will intervene. The council have no idea where the problem originated. Perhaps it was the people selling the land? Or maybe any of the three or four outfits, like ours, who were buying the carved up pieces of land?"

Another interruption, "As simple as that? You reckon?"

"Declan, I'm telling you, they have not got a clue about my favourable planning consent, other than for a smoking gun - and his name is Xavi Zamora. Besides, Xavi's cousin, my contact, has heard a rumour they will finish him early with a black mark against his name - early retirement. A slap on the wrist. I will be fine, I'm not concerned. The project will resume. The problem we both have is we have money tied up in it until it does resume."

"What a fucking understatement!" Despite Price's reassurances, Ryan still struggled to keep a lid on his temper, and the effect of the raw nerve that Price just trod on.

Both dogs bristled at their owner's minor outburst, silently flexing, and demonstrating their shredded withers and shoulders.

Price ploughed on, "In the meantime Declan we have an opportunity, which will eclipse the casino project. I touched on it last night, which was not the best time to go into detail, so we are here now to explain. Please remember, Nick only arrived back in Spain from the UK last night, this is genuine and fresh news."

Price, looked to Savvas to continue, having primed him with the approach to use whilst in the car earlier, and to, *"Keep it pithy and positive."*

Savvas took a few moments and reminded Ryan of his impeccable credentials as a renowned Professor of Geology. He explained his speciality was working within the global rare earth mining sector, with outstanding results. Ryan looked impressed and a gentle nod of acknowledgement signified he would continue to listen.

Price chipped in with, "Now it gets amazing."

An agitated Ryan glanced in Price's direction with a *who asked you for your opinion* expression on his hard face. Price got the message, *zipped it*, and sat back in his chair.

Savvas carried on and capped it off by referring to the university software mapping, followed up with details concerning the soil and his substantiated tests. He placed on the table printed graphs and reams of datasheets, comparing statistics from other mines around the world, to the more favourable ones from Blaenavon. Everything thing he said had corroboration and backup, including a small amount of soil residue in a small polythene bag and his spectrometer, which he demonstrated and reproduced the excellent PPM results for Ryan.

Ryan commented, "OK, so I'm impressed with stats and with the chemistry experiment, now where's this heading, Nick?"

Savvas added, "The other crucial factor here is the volume, there are millions of tons laying there, untouched, loaded with high-value rare earth particles. With the right equipment, we could process an acre every few days or so. We only need a final processed and refined output of a ton to make $40 million. That will be simple, and less than a year's work."

Ryan smiled for the first time in twenty minutes, "So, why are you telling me this. What's the plan, Jason? And what could possibly go wrong?"

Price looked more confident now, "I can't control the casino project controversy, we have to wait for it to play out. But this Wales thing is a project where I *will* make a load of money within a year and repay your casino investment. I'm sorry, but you would need some patience of course. There is another option."

Ryan had listened to every word, and asked, "Which is what?"

"Nick and I need investment for Wales. We can recruit investors at short notice; it will be easy. I have connections and so does Nick, there will be a queue around the block. But if you want to join us as one of the main investors, we can keep it between ourselves. We are inviting you in."

"So, what do I receive in return for my investment - apart from a huge return?" Ryan meant what he said.

Price explained, "We need to buy the *worthless* coal spoil land, that provides the best road access, from a couple of farmers, about four-hundred to five-hundred acres at least, offering them three times what they paid for it from the National Coal Board years ago, which was not much at the time, or whatever it takes to obtain it. They don't know the true value of the land, so we can get it for next to nothing, whilst they think they have got a good deal. But they must sell it to us though - they have to."

Ryan asked, "How do we ensure they will go for it. What else is in it for them apart from decent money? The money won't last them forever."

Price suggested he had a fool-proof plan. "We offer to buy the land with a legally binding covenant. To make us obligated to hand the land back to them in three years - for nothing, but we must own it outright upfront. I suppose you could say we are borrowing, or leasing, the land from them, and from the start, we take out a legal *option to purchase* applied to the rest of the land to stop anyone else from owning it. That way we don't need to spend as much money upfront on the whole project."

Savvas hadn't heard this commercial detail, it impressed him, "Brilliant idea."

Price, continued, "Then we need to obtain a mining license from the Coal Authority in Nottingham. That will be a formality with the correct technical application. Wheels are in motion to instigate that. The final piece in the jigsaw will be to guarantee the blessing of the local council, to avoid any problems from that end. They can even block us, but I have an undeniable, eco-friendly, job creation plan ready to go. By the way Declan, we will need some tipper trucks and logistics, you can have a premium-priced contract for a nice piece of transportation work."

Savvas began to understand why Price made such a success as a businessman, he anticipated and planned for everything, and made it look too easy. There was never a shred of doubt conveyed from the persuasive and sometimes charming Price. A convincing man on a mission.

Savvas commented, "Oh, and there is a disused drift mine on the side of the mountain, adjacent to the farmers land. Built years ago and looking a bit scruffy, but it would be the main site and perfect base for our operation. There are some outbuildings we would need to utilise."

"What's a drift mine, explain that one to me?" asked Ryan, sounding confused.

Savvas sketched on the back of a piece of paper, "Like this, a couple of tunnels side by side, like shotgun barrels, bored almost horizontal into the mountain, a six-degree slope is a more precise term. We can try to mine that, but *they* cleaned it out of coal, so it won't produce enough of the soil that we want and accessing those tunnels will be a nightmare. We need the farmland to come with the mine as a package. The farmland has the spoil-heaps on the surface. The spoil-heaps are a bit greener now though than they once were, hence, the sheep. The bottom line is, the mine and the farmland are integral, we need them both."

Price added, "That drift mine might be trickier to obtain. Looks like the owner is based in the Cayman Islands and could be hard to find. But they sure as hell don't want to own a *worthless* piece of mountainside anymore, they will sell. Whoever they are."

Ryan's eyes lit up, "The Cayman Islands you say? This gets better by the minute." He had an idea.

"Just one more thing," Price added, "We are expected to pay someone a commission for everything we extract and on the profits we make."

Ryan, winced, "What? Who? Why?"

Price, smirked, "The law of the land, The Crown – H.M. The Queen. – God save the Queen."

Everyone laughed, including Ryan, before he added, "I don't think she needs to know much about the first few tons of rare earth though, does she?"

A serious question - and everyone agreed.

Price had a separate, but equally serious question, "Declan, I know this has come on the back of the Xavi thing and not great timing. Once again, I'm sorry for the temporary cock-up, but I hope you can see I will resolve it - one way or another. So what are your thoughts about Wales? Are you coming in or staying out? As you know, we don't need you *in*, but it would be great if you came on board, and if you did you would enjoy the lion's share with the rest of us?"

Ryan declared, "In principle, I am in, but we need to discuss the money. You need to figure a bloody good compensation package percentage for the 'Xavi thing' as you call it Jason. By the way, I want to buy the drift mine from whoever the owner is in the Cayman Islands - some plans spring to mind for that. Before anything happens, I need more evidence about your results Nick. Two of my lads are outstanding at digging holes. I need to send one of them over next week for a day or two to take some samples for myself. I will organise independent tests and when the results come back, and if they are good results - we are in business. Nick, you can explain to my lad where he needs to test and what he needs to do, basic stuff mind, he's thick as shit."

Ryan had plans for the mine the moment he heard about it. He had bundles of unlaundered cash to spend. There was a possible recipient for it, with a ready-made bank account and a shell company in the Cayman Islands.

"OK, the way I see things, Jason, if you're right the casino project will sort itself out, and my investment is sound - even if you have to sell the house that I sold you a couple of months ago. If I don't invest in the Wales project, you can pay me out of your profit from Wales. If I do invest in Wales, I make even more money. We call that a win-win-win situation in Ireland. Either way Jason, you *will* be getting me my money back. Now I need to make some phone calls lads. You know your way out. Oh, and don't worry about the dogs they won't bother you – the *big dog* is the only one that bites in this house."

Chapter 14

Re-Grouping

"What happened?" Lauren could barely mouth the words through the tears as she hugged her mother, the moment she entered the hospital.

Margaret explained, "He's Ok, he will be fine. He got dizzy and had a nasty fall. Dad came in from work, a normal day, nothing unusual, so he says. He never says his day was an awful one. He had a shower and then he started getting a pounding headache. Next thing, he collapsed on the floor and banged his head. There was blood everywhere."

Lauren put her hand to her mouth as she inhaled sharply, "Oh, my God Mum."

"He was conscious. Somehow, I carted him over to the truck and drove him straight here. That was the quickest way rather than waiting for an ambulance. I called Olivia earlier, she is distraught. She was coming home tomorrow anyway, as planned. The nurses are still doing tests, nothing conclusive yet, but heart attack and stroke are both ruled out so far. The doctor thinks it could be dehydration and heat exhaustion. He's staying here until all the tests are back, and we know what's happened."

"Can I see him, Mum?"

"Of course you can. It's a few hours since we came in, so he's settled and sitting up now, and chatting. Look - don't alarm yourself love, but he's got a drip and wires, coming from him with computer screens bleeping all-around monitoring things. Standard procedure. Oh, and there is a whopping great bandage around his head. He'll be so pleased to see you."

Harry Eaves's face was normally a weather-beaten, tanned shade of rouge. Lauren walked towards him and saw a grey smiling face, in stark contrast with the white bandages, greeting her. The image almost stopped her in her tracks. A kiss on the cheek with a gentle, cautious hug, was all she wanted to risk without dislodging any of the wires or the drip.

"What have you done to yourself Dad? I warned you not to hammer those fence poles in with your bare hands and I hope that isn't premium strength lager going straight in?"

Harry smiled again, "I wish. So good to see you darling, so good." Harry instinctively gripped Lauren's hand even tighter as he said it. "Not sure if this is good timing or bad timing. Another day and you'd be halfway to Cardiff. I messed that up for you big time by the looks of things, all my own stupid fault."

"Dad, everything is fine. Qantas came up trumps for me again, I called them earlier, they were amazing. I can fly back whenever I want. So just relax. I'm staying over for a while longer. I can work on my college stuff from here and finish off that fencing for you. My arms are ripped now, feel them." Lauren faked a little bicep flex, which amused Harry even further.

"He's overdone it. The temperature has hit the 40s all week and he's not getting any younger, none of us are. This is a wake-up call Harry, I'm serious, you need to slow things down." Margaret meant it and was fighting back tears of frustration to accompany the tears of relief that her husband was going to make a good recovery.

Lauren made a list of priority jobs from Harry and promised she would make a start on them first thing in the morning. She refused to allow her father any unnecessary worry about anything, which he would have done had she not taken the initiative and put his mind at rest.

Before Margaret and Lauren left to go home Harry asked Lauren how she had got on with Jack, and if there was any more news concerning Wales.

"It was a serious education for a couple of days Dad. Jack was great, I learned everything I needed to know. No more news, nothing that can't wait a few weeks longer. Besides, we've got to get you back on your feet first."

~

The following morning, before going back to see her father, Lauren made the arrangements for her extended stay in Australia. Qantas reaffirmed her open ticket special medical dispensation due to her family circumstances. Her work in Cardiff appeared less than impressed and wouldn't promise her a job when she arrived back. The course tutor wanted to know if there was anything he could do to help and reassured her that the modules already submitted were in good shape and to focus on her dissertation. She had plenty of time up her sleeve to finish and submit it.

The pressure was off for a while. Harry came out of hospital after two days of observation with a clean bill of health, nine stitches in his forehead and two swollen, bruised bags under his eyes. He had strict instructions not to leave the house for another two days and only then to supervise and keep Lauren company. Olivia was back from her honeymoon and running around like a Tasmanian devil. Friends dropped by and helped out when and wherever there was a need for some extra hands.

A week after Harry's accident, things cautiously started getting back to normal, including the completion of some of the more necessary heavy-duty groundworks. They found nothing pressing that would involve Harry rolling his sleeves up for and sweating buckets all day. He needed to spend more time at the gold mine, but the property demanded repairs, heavy rainstorms would often wash out roads and he tried to find the balance between the two revenue streams. They didn't keep many cattle and focused on growing wheat.

Lunchtime arrived so Lauren and Harry parked up in a shady spot. One of the few places in the area offering respite from the baking sun, where an incongruous outcrop of reddish sandstone rocks must have sprouted millions of years ago.

Harry seemed back up to full steam, though under strict instructions to stick to tractor driving - fetching and carrying duties. All from the inside of an air-conditioned cab for most of the day. The cool box packed by Margaret provided a well-earned lunch. With careful attention paid to plenty of cool drinks ensuring Harry's fluid levels stayed much higher than where they were previously.

Harry mopped his brow, and took a long swig of water, "It never happened to me before - flaking out like that. I watched plenty of other fellas get the shakes and hit the deck over the years. I must have lost track of the time, skipped a meal, and didn't drink enough water. It crept up on me, nothing sudden. Then bang can't remember a thing. Glad your mum was there."

"So am I."

"Small margins out here sometimes Lauren. Some people have difficulties and emergencies a hundred kilometres from anyone, with no mobile signal and no sat-phone. Now that *is* when it gets tricky. I was lucky."

"Let's not go there, Dad. At least you only have about twenty square kilometres to worry about, thank goodness."

With lunch done and packed away, they had one more light job planned for themselves for the remainder of the day, which involved cleaning the dust off a small solar panel installation near the house. A regular but important chore.

"Dad, before we go back to clean the solar panels, I wanted to show you what I'll be using next week when I go back to the UK. The kit that Uncle Jack gave me and trained me up to use. I wanted to check I remembered everything he told me and give it another go, around here. Have you ever seen how this works?"

"He told me about it and how you were better at using it than he was by the time you had finished."

"Jump in the truck Dad, I saw a spot earlier we can try it on, away from these rocks. At least you'll know what I'm doing in Blaenavon when I get there. That won't be practice - it will be for real."

"Yeah, as I mentioned to you before Lauren, we checked out rare earth potential on this land when you were a toddler. People realised the potential for it even back then. The gold was going well here at the time, and making us a decent living, so we weren't that bothered when they drew a blank with rare earth stuff."

Lauren had no preconceived ideas or expectations of decent readings, she was just curious and enthusiastic to demonstrate her new skills to her father.

They pulled over to an exposed area of land, one never farmed or planted - just cooked for millions of years. Ridley Scott could have filmed The Martian there and saved themselves a fraction of the cost of a studio in LA.

Lauren set up and tapped the first length of auger type tubing into the ground, twisted it, and added another length of tube. It bored into the ground without much effort, considering the arid compact nature of the soil.

"That looks well over a metre, Dad. It should come out as easy as it went in. With luck, Blaenavon soil will be as receptive."

Harry assisted to retract the length of tubing. With an old blanket laid on the dirt near to the back of the truck, Lauren used a plunger to press out the sample.

As the soil emerged onto the blanket Lauren quipped, "Have you ever seen those TV food shows where they stick one of those skewer tools into a big block of hard cheese, twist it and out pops the cheddar or the parmesan? Same principle, different taste."

Harry chuckled, "Don't make me laugh, you'll give me another headache."

Lauren opened up a battered, old, hard aluminium *photographer's* case, "So that was the first thing we do. Then I use this device called a spectrometer to measure for any interesting particles. Like this."

She spread the dirt from the middle section of the sample. Took aim from close up, pulled the trigger and waited for the spectrometer to produce an audible satisfying ping.

Harry wondered if something was wrong with the equipment, Lauren seemed frozen, deep in thought,

"Don't tell me Jack didn't give you any batteries when you came away?"

"It worked fine Dad, it pinged. Just a bit confused if I'm honest. Let's try another piece."

Taking great care, Lauren spread out a decent coffee mug's worth of dirt from the lowest extreme end of the tube, which came from one-hundred-and-ten centimetres below the surface.

"So when they did the tests twenty years ago Dad, what did they do? Can you remember? Were you there watching?"

"Yes, I gave the guy a hand. I drove him around to a few places; we had a couple of shovels and a bucket. We filled half a dozen plastic bags. He labelled them up and off he went. They didn't have anything handheld and electronic back then. Jack swore by the guy, he helped him find stuff on his land. It cost me a couple of hundred dollars, I remember that for sure. He posted me a report, I think I kept it somewhere if you want to see it?"

Lauren gave her father a serious look, "Dad, don't get too excited, but these readings are decent. Well better than that, they are as good as the ones I saw on Jack's land last week."

Harry gave Lauren a bemused look, "Are you kidding your old man? This is a wind-up, right?"

"No Dad, I'm serious. How are your energy levels? We might need to skip the solar panels and hit a few other locations. We also need to ring Uncle Jack, but after we tell Mum."

Lauren and Harry targeted two more locations, with the same levels of success, before calling it a day. Harry still couldn't get his head around it.

Lauren sounded bullish, "Dad, I'm sure the guy who did those tests for you back then did a thorough job. If you look at his lab report, he may even have found some small traces of rare earth on or near the surface. But not enough to raise an eyebrow in the 1990s. Since then, REE (Rare Earth Element) prices have skyrocketed. What you have in your soil is a viable mining proposition – if there is a widespread deposit of it - which looks almost certain."

Despite all his years of mining experience and encyclopaedic knowledge, Harry smiled and showed a hint of excitement, "What the hell do we do next? Where do we start?"

"We go home and have tea with Mum. Don't know about you but I'm ravenous? But let's send someone a message first, shall we?"

The Intrepid Trio WhatsApp group's message pinged in Jack's pocket, *"Jack, hope you're up for a quick Zoom call later - in about an hour? We have some exciting news from our end."*

~

They arrived home late afternoon, to find Margaret on a ladder completing one of the less pleasant annual jobs – clearing out the roof gutters of the single-story house. Harry hated spiders, everyone hated spiders - Margaret was fearless, gloved up, and nearly done.

"No creepy crawlies all day," she declared as they got out of the truck.

All three decided they had earned a cold bottle of beer before doing anything else. They were all covered head to toe in dirt and dust. Harry did the honours as they sat in the shade on the porch, where Lauren and Margaret had settled into the swing frame double seater. He then told Margaret about their news, in great detail as Lauren filled in the gaps.

Margaret's initial reaction was to laugh, before stating, "Well I think they call that a bit of a turn up for the books, don't they? But before we rush off and spend the children's inheritance, how certain are you, Lauren? I mean, I'm sure Jack taught you well, and we all realise you know your stuff darling, but what happens next? If this were the doctor's surgery, I suppose we'd ask for a second opinion, wouldn't we?"

"Mum, I don't blame you. Dad and I were both as shocked as you are. But technology has changed and is far more reliable, mineral values have gone through the roof, hundreds of percentage increases with some of them. The world is a different place. We all need to clean up by the looks of us. I stink for sure. Then we can catch up with Uncle Jack and ask his opinion in a while, he said he would take a Zoom call with us when we are ready. He must think I'm mad. He doesn't know what we want to chat to him about yet, he thinks *Project Blaenavon*, would be my guess. He'll be wrong."

Margaret was still smiling and sensed an element of substance to the big news story, "OK, I'll put the oven on. Let's all take a shower and give Jack a call before dinner, shall we?"

The Zoom call opened up to reveal a screen filled with Jack's weathered face, his wavy ginger hair and omnipotent curly beard. In both hair and beard, an arm wrestle was taking place between *ginger and grey*. Ginger appeared in the ascendancy, at that moment.

Jack, intrigued by the earlier messages spoke first, "Lovely to see you all. How is everyone doing over there? You're looking better than you were the other day Harry - if that is you? You look like a psychedelic panda mate."

Everyone roared with laughter, including Harry. Jack, didn't give anyone a chance to respond, "So what's all the fuss about guys? I must say, your messages earlier on teased me a bit."

Harry explained, in detail, the findings he and Lauren had made earlier, and how radically different they were to those findings in the report carried out twenty years ago. "Jack, either your machine is on the blink, or we are on to something here. Which one is it?"

Harry's comments took Jack by surprise, "Bloody hell. Wow. Well, first things first, let me put your minds at rest. The spectrometer I loaned to Lauren, might look a bit scruffy, but it's top-notch. From time to time, I take samples with that myself and check them with the lab - they are always spot on. So, no worries on that score. The other important thing is that Lauren, you know how to use it. You used it with me dozens of times over here the other day, didn't you? In fairness, Harry, she showed me extra functions on the thing I never realised existed before she left. Kids, and technology, eh?"

"I'll give you a high five next time I see you, Uncle Jack," said Lauren.

The Zoom call continued, and discussions centred around a plan of action for Harry's land. Lauren needed to carry out more tests the next day and then she would send them to one of several labs in the region. Harry had an account with a couple of them and they would have results back within days.

Harry sounded concerned, "Jack, if the results are good what about the plant and equipment needed to refine it all. Won't that be millions?"

Jack intervened, "Hold your horses mate. It won't cost you anything to refine it. All you do is dig it, nothing else. You fill 30-tonne tipper trucks with unprocessed soil that goes to the train station. They dump it in rail wagons for the railroad, having checked the raw material and ship it to China for refining. This is common practice in the industry. The Chinese are buying your raw material. On average, the Chinese will pay you way more than half the value of the rare earth plus your trucking costs. Sounds like a lot of *commission* to hand them, - but not really. No headaches. No outlay from us."

Margaret spoke up, "Lauren I think your original jobs for tomorrow are cancelled. Your new schedule is taking samples, with the panda, to send them to the lab. In the meantime, the champagne will stay *on ice* for a few more days."

Chapter 15

Acceleration

Once he had left Ryan, avoided the boxer dogs, and sat in his car with Savvas, Price experienced a brief euphoric sensation. Somehow the anticipated Ryan hurricane breezed through with all the gusto of a gentle zephyr.

Savvas spoke to a relieved Price before they set off, "Well, that went OK, didn't it?"

"Understatement of the year. Thanks, Nick, you did well, but I wouldn't have expected anything less."

Savvas, thought for a moment, *"I think that was a compliment? But I'm not sure?"*

Price continued, "We're not out of the woods yet, though. Now we need to pull it all together and make it happen - but this is where I come in, it won't be a problem. This is getting exciting."

The threats, the worries had subsided. Price was a different man to the concerned one who trudged into meet Ryan less than an hour earlier. He was on to his next objective like nothing happened in there. Savvas couldn't believe how he managed to take it all in his stride, *"How the hell does he do it?"*

~

"Jason, I found him. Bloody nightmare, I spent all morning, but his name is Feisal Hussein. He's Jordanian, living in France - Paris by the looks of it. When ISIS overran Jordan and trashed it several years ago, many wealthy Jordanians legged it. I'd say, he legged it with the rest of them and took a King's ransom with him for good measure."

Price's legal adviser never let him down. A delighted Price congratulated him, "Brilliant, fantastic. What else have you got on him? How do I contact him?"

"Well, I think there is a way. He's got a handful of shell companies in the Cayman Islands to his name. Some are dormant, including one that owns the old drift mine in Blaenavon, which at one time, or still is, a part of a much larger mining operation. God knows why he hasn't sold it off. The Blaenavon mine is doing nothing and worth peanuts to a man like him. My guess is it appears as a tiny line entry on a balance sheet that no one can bother to delete. The top of the pyramid is Petra Holdings, I'll email you the details. There's even a phone number for their Paris office. Nothing special, their reported turnover is about $15M with steady profits, some mining, but mostly chemicals and plastics – and I suspect, plenty of other *off the record* stuff."

Price had some high priority objectives to tick off. He wasn't sure why, but Ryan wanted to buy the mine in Blaenavon for himself. If he wanted to, he could have it. Nothing else mattered more for Price than keeping Ryan happy and off his back.

Price did some background research himself and came up with not much more than he managed to learn over the phone earlier. He decided to make the call to Petra Holdings, expecting to hear a recorded message, if he was lucky.

The voice of a confident young woman, came across crisp and clear, "Bonne après-midi, Petra Holdings."

It took Price by surprise, and he completely overlooked the fact that anyone answering would reply in French, just because they were in a French office block in Paris.

He composed himself, and hoped for the best, "Ah… bonjour madame, please do you speak English, merci?"

"Yes, of course, sir. How may I direct your call? And what's the reason for your call today?"

"Oh, wonderful thank you. My name is Jason Price, calling from the *UK*. I would like to speak with *Monsieur* Hussein, if possible, please. It concerns a business acquisition proposal that I have for him. Thank you."

"Which Monsieur Hussein Sir?"

"Oh, Feisal Hussein, please."

Price found himself listening to the dulcet tones of Celine Dion for a dozen or so seconds before another

English-speaking voice answered – that of a mature sounding American woman.

"Good afternoon Mr Price. I'm afraid Mr Hussein is unavailable today. I do hope I can assist you, I'm Amy Frey. I manage corporate affairs at Petra Holdings. I understand from my colleague that you wish to discuss an acquisition proposal?"

Price hated getting the run-around, a narcissistic misogynist trait manifested itself, and couldn't resist thinking to himself, *"Yes Amy, and HR and the post room too, I'll bet."* He wrongly assumed the owner of an international chemical company, albeit a small one, would drop everything and speak with him, even if he were there.

With a subterfuge prepared and practised in his head, Price explained to Frey that he originated from Blaenavon and was approaching two other landowners. He clarified the legal ownership of the drift mine stated Petra Holdings, and that he recalled passing the mine on one of his recent hikes. A blatant lie. His only exercise, other than climbing into a hot tub involved the occasional round of golf. Even then his regular playing partners tagged him with the nickname of *Mr Magic Pencil.* His scorecard numbers never tallied with the number of strokes taken to get out of bunkers.

He reminded her that Blaenavon's location and World Heritage Site status meant it attracted tourists, hikers, paragliders, and mountain bikers. The only thing lacking was an activity centre, and he needed a hub for his well-advanced proposals. The drift mine towards the base of the mountain would be a great contender if it were available, at a sensible valuation compared to other locations under consideration. He implied there were other options up his sleeve. Of course, no other locations were under consideration. There was only one thing Price wanted – the mine – or at least Ryan wanted the mine.

"Amy, I'm sure you and Mr Hussein have numerous thriving revenue streams to contend with every day. I'm guessing the dormant old mine in Blaenavon is not a regular topical conversation starter?"

"Mr Price, *Jason*, although I have never visited Blaenavon – but maybe one day – so your observations are reasonable. The particular asset you mention served us well in the past. We receive enquiries like yours from time to time, though I'm afraid our general response is to politely decline any interest. That said, I will discuss this *small* matter with Mr Hussein, and we will be in touch with you. Please email me your contact details. A pleasure speaking with you, Jason."

Amy Frey ended the call, replaced the receiver on its cradle and looked at her curious boss who had listened to every word from the desktop speakerphone. "An interesting one Feisal, to say the least. What do you think?"

Feisal Hussein, smirked, "I think I will *pay him* to take that headache off my hands tomorrow if he wants it. But maybe we can make some money instead. Let's check out Jason Price first before we email him with a valuation. Who is he? Is he a genuine mountain bike mecca man or someone else?"

Over the next 24 hours, one of Price's activities included the application for a mining license. It soon became apparent from the documentation, an application to mine coal in the UK is a carefully scrutinised process. The wording of the documentation made it clear that both *ownership* and *expertise* within the mining industry was almost a necessity. Cowboy 'happy-go-lucky' coal miners had a short shelf life. Expertise to tick the box would emerge in the form of Nick Savvas, as for ownership of a coal mine – the drift mine remained in progress, although not yet secured. The application needed to wait until the reaching of an agreement over the old drift mine, so not the certainty, and immediate tick in the other box, Price had hoped for.

His other research and planning centred around the real crux of the matter - the Blaenavon landowning farmers. Without them, nothing would happen, and some unhappy faces would be looking in Price's direction. Price drew a deep breath and looked at schedules for the next flights to Cardiff. He needed to go to Wales as soon as possible. His second home in Pembrokeshire would be his base until he resolved the next hurdle. He needed to meet some farmers in Blaenavon and make them offers they could not refuse - with or without the procurement of the old drift mine from Feisal Hussein.

As it transpired, Price didn't have to wait long to find out if he would be with or without the drift mine. Within days Amy Frey and her boss decided to off-load it. She was in the process of emailing Price with a take it or leave valuation. A bold decision, but Hussein was correct when he sensed Price needed it far more than he did, and he had a bad taste up his sleeve for Price to savour when he, or at least Declan Ryan, took rightful ownership of the mine.

The lengthy email arrived in Price's inbox. Along with a valuation, it showed a detailed explanation concerning the technical and geological structure of the mine. A hefty series of pdfs also included surveyor's reports, evidence of regular adherence to Coal Authority standards, their inspections, and safety certificates. Also included was an inventory of the declining coal volumes extracted, month on month, the scale of the outbuildings and old plant and machinery with a handful of photographs.

In reality, the mine was a soggy mess, even a thousand well-directed tins of WD40 would never manage to unseize the dilapidated machinery. It didn't matter, all Nick Savvas needed was a hole into the side of a mountain and some outbuildings to create a new hub.

All Declan Ryan wanted was an opportunity to spend some of his unlaundered cash and legitimately own an asset. One that would appreciate through the roof, skyrocket in value once they announced to the local community and mining world the amazing mining discovery stumbled upon by modern-day coal miners in Blaenavon. A perfect money washing opportunity.

Much depended on Price re-negotiating the initial valuation for a sale and Hussein agreeing to take some or all of the money in Euro notes from Ryan, which was how he told Price he wanted to do his business - if possible. What the vendor did next with the Euro notes was of no concern to Ryan. Hussein could stick it under his bed or bank it in his Cayman Islands account, Ryan didn't care which.

Price shared Amy Frey's email with Ryan, who did not appreciate the bullish valuation, "Shit, €960k for a pile of rubble? God almighty, a piss-take or what?"

Price realised his phone call would not go down well, "Declan, listen €960k is just an opening stance. Besides, what's €50k on either side of that - peanuts. You did say you wanted it all to yourself?"

"I do want it. But I've got standards - and limits. Cheeky bastard whoever he is."

Price changed the subject slightly, "How is your cousin doing taking the samples, any news? Has he finished yet?"

Ryan sounded optimistic and happier, "He's gonna do what Nick told him to do. No, he only got there today and should finish by tomorrow. He's much brighter than he looks, so fingers crossed he will send the right stuff to the lab when he gets it all done and dusted. We sourced a lab. They seemed to know their stuff and said the results should take two or three days. I had a long conversation with the lab people, so I already know what bad, good, and bloody brilliant are meant to look like on the results when they come through. This better be *bloody brilliant* Jason."

"Nick is world-class. He hasn't stopped doing cartwheels for days now. It will be on the money. Trust me."

The instant the words came out of Price's mouth, he wanted the earth to open up and swallow him, he knew right away he would regret using those words *trust me*. True to form Ryan responded, "Yeah, I already did that once, and you fucked it up. Good results in Wales and I'll be happy. By the way, does this guy Hussein know it will be me he's gonna deal with and not you?"

"Not yet, but I'll let him know when we get to that stage, following your lab results."

"OK, send me the contact details for this Amy Frey, and I can take it from here. When the time comes - if the time comes."

Three days after speaking with Price, the time did come, just after breakfast. Ryan's inbox pinged with a message from the lab, "Bloody hell. Well, well. I need to go and buy myself a shitty old drift mine."

Chapter 16

The Rolling Stone

When Ryan told Price and Savvas he needed to make some phone calls, that's exactly what he did. Ryan was also a man under intense pressure. He and his lucrative logistics operation were an integral link to a much bigger and far more powerful chain, an Algerian organised crime drug smuggling cartel.

Ryan's business, a key conduit for smuggling had begun to look like the weakest link. There was a noticeable cautiousness in his activities since the incident with his accountant business partners, he pressed the pause button whilst he thought things through. Often, he declined smuggling requests from his regular clientele, cherry-picking the easiest consignments via the safest routes to the UK.

He gleaned all the information required from his English accountant *partners* before killing them. They told him they both underwent interviews with a Spanish tax department who threatened them with hefty fines or worse if it transpired, they had a connection to illegal activities. The money laundering at the various establishments appeared like excessive income, and caused a red flag. Investigators *invited them in for a discussion* and grilled them, but not under arrest and promised leniency if they divulged more details about the revenue streams. Both were lightweights and worried. At one time they panicked and started discreetly selling assets and made tentative plans to get out of Spain before any more attention from the police came their way. When nothing happened, they shelved their plans, stayed put, and continued raking in money for Ryan and themselves. Ryan realised they would cave in and drop him in it one day, so he acted swiftly off the back of his skimming suspicions. His suspicions proved correct ones, and so he 'cleaned house'.

Meanwhile, the Cartel were unhappy and wanted to understand the reason why Ryan's activities had become cold and cautious. With a thriving business to run, Ryan was causing them and himself big problems. His saving grace was a long and trusted relationship with one of the Algerian family, Karim Nasri, whom he had met when both of them were young men.

~

Before moving to Dublin, as a teenager in the late 70s, Declan Ryan grew up in the border counties in the north of the Republic of Ireland. His father and uncle, both staunch Republicans, owned a haulage business and were long-standing senior members of a notoriously brutal Irish paramilitary group.

Following a period of tit for tat kneecappings and killings during the autumn of 1982, the uncle vanished, and no one ever saw him again. The Ryan family were targets of the security forces and rival factions. The family were not simply hauliers and occasional terrorists, they were gangsters and local tough guys who ruled the roost, involved in everything from robbing banks, extortion and prostitution to drug smuggling and gun-running. Politics and religious divides were often an excuse to murder competitors muscling in on their turf and revenue streams.

Declan Ryan's family reputation preceded him at school in Dundalk and he chose to live up to it. Occasionally dishing out threats and beatings in the schoolyard, until all contenders rightly stayed well out of the way of the school *alpha-kid*. In those days, the rugby field was as good a place as any to assert your authority in the front row of a scrum and kick off a punch up. It was part and parcel of the game, broken noses and split lips were far more common than sending's off in the 70s and 80s, and Ryan loved a scrap.

By the time he reached nineteen years of age, Ryan had managed to get himself banned from most pubs within a thirty-mile radius of where he lived. One particular Friday night, late into the evening during his ban, just inside the entrance of a packed local pub he decided to attack a solitary doorman who had refused him entry. Ryan headbutted the unfortunate doorman sending him reeling back into the pub. He rained heavy punches on the man, and repeatedly kicked him in the head as he lay in a pool of blood on the floor until Ryan's two friends managed to drag him off, into a car and away.

Within less than twenty seconds the bouncer had received a broken jaw, a broken nose, a fractured eye socket and lost sight in one eye. Someone used the payphone and called the local Garda who arrived within minutes. Out of well over fifty drinkers in the pub, no one saw anything, not even either of the two bartenders - one was *changing a barrel* in the cellar and the other *had his back turned at the till.* As the vicious assault took place half a dozen young women sitting at a nearby table found themselves sprayed with droplets of blood and pieces of nasal cartilage. The bar staff advised them all to leave and go home before the garda arrived. *"Make tracks, it could get complicated sticking around."* They understood and they *did* go home.

By the time he was twenty, Ryan was more or less a one-man crime wave. Combined with his growing involvement in his father's republican activities, Ryan junior may as well have worn a target on his back, and he knew it. Threats ranged from serious people to amateur chancers, all popping up on his radar. One such threat, involved a gangly, helmet wearing, young pillion passenger who attempted to shoot him. He had waited for Ryan to come out of a betting office, and somehow, he managed to miss three times from the width of the road before misfiring and tearing off. It wasn't a warning, plenty of people wanted Declan Ryan maimed or dead. A queue had formed - with weapons to do it not hard to come by.

One day, not long after the shooting incident, Ryan walked into the yard where his father was changing a tyre on a truck with a huge torque wrench, "Dad, I did some thinking, I'm going away for a bit. I'm going to do some travelling. See a bit more of the world you know. About time don't you think?"

Never had a father shown so much relief and delight on his face in the space of a minute, wiping the brake dust from his fingers as he spoke, "Bloody hell. You're a dark horse so you are Declan, but I think you should do what you need to do son. Where are you planning on going to? America? There are dozens of Ryan's over there on the east coast who would welcome you and your County Louth accent with open arms son. Have you spoken to your mother about this yet?"

"No Dad, you're the only person I've spoken to about it so far. This has played on my mind for a while now,...and with everything else going on. Do you know what I mean? America can wait, I'm going to Europe for a bit. Not sure where yet, play it as it comes, or until the money runs out."

Ryan followed through on what he said, although he knew exactly where he intended going to in Europe. The following morning, he said his goodbyes to his family, took a one hour train ride to Dublin and boarded an afternoon flight to Marseille. It was the first time he had ever flown or left Ireland. He had already decided to join the *Légion étrangère* - the French Foreign Legion. He turned up at the *Aubagne* recruiting office with some spare clean underwear, t-shirts, his passport, a birth certificate and five hundred francs. He had read that their recruitment offices were open all day, every day of the year, including Christmas Day. He walked in and signed up for the mandatory five years - if he could survive the induction training.

The gruelling basic training lasted four months, it commenced at a base in Castelnaudary, in the south of France, nicknamed *The Farm*. During this gruelling time, Ryan met another young recruit, a French-Algerian named Karim Nasri, who spoke a little English. Together they helped each other to improve their language skills.

Ryan thrived on the infamous and harsh training regime, in particular the mental challenge of coping with the premeditated psychological stress they subjected him to. Described by the trainers as *personality, logic, and motivation evaluation*. Right from day one, intense psychological pressure arrived straight after the initial interviews,

"Why did you join?"

"What is your problem Irishman?"

"Who are you running away from?"

"Tell us everything you're hiding from us otherwise you will not pass out with your kepi blanc."

Some men were running away from something. Most people had a *problem* or a *past* which was why they were there. Every man had the opportunity given to them of assuming a fictitious name, a practice that continues to this day. As long as Interpol did not want to interview any candidates, then everything was OK. Ryan kept his name and harboured a strong determination to make it through, pass out, and earn his kepi blanc. He did.

The tradition of the kepi blanc is synonymous with the legion. The white cap, held in such high regard, that the officer in charge symbolically places every *passed out* soldier's monthly pay inside it. Next, the soldier puts the cap on his head with - his pay still inside it.

In early November 1983, Ryan and Nasri had barely finished shaking off the excitement of the *passing out* celebrations when they found themselves on an aircraft along with dozens of other soldiers belonging to the 31st Brigade. Their posting: Beirut, where all hell had broken loose a month earlier.

At the end of the first world war, Lebanon came under a French Mandate, and France considered itself as the trustee of the country, making the region almost into a French Colony, despite independence many years later. If flare-ups occurred in Lebanon, France would lead the way to sort it out, along with the Americans.

Flare-up was an understatement. Backed by Syria and Iran, on the 23rd of October 1983, two Hezbollah suicide bombers had just detonated truckloads of explosives at the French and U.S. barracks killing over three hundred soldiers.

Beirut became home to Ryan and Nasri on and off for the next few years. A divided city, the Muslim west and Christian east with armed militia roaming around on pick-up trucks converted into mobile mortar units or speedy heavy machine guns. They would shoot and bomb lumps out of anything standing in their way - buildings, cars, men, women, and children, from Lebanon or from overseas. Foreigners were a preference, and on occasions high profile kidnappings took place.

During this dreadful time, the authorities found it impossible to find a balance between peacekeeping and asserting control. Ryan regularly witnessed death, sometimes on a large scale and became immune to it. Section seven of the Legionnaire's code of honour included *acting without passion and without hate, respecting defeated enemies.* Ryan hated everyone other than his comrades. He enjoyed killing his enemies, often glorifying in it, and on two occasions he killed them with his bare hands.

Once, after bursting into a room with Nasri and another platoon mate, they surprised two assailants, whose AK-47s leaned uselessly against the wall beside them and shot the two men several times. Moments after they shot one of the bearded men in the chest and stomach - disarmed, disorientated and bleeding heavily – he somehow found the strength to attempt to rise from his knees. He made a slow, futile lunge at Ryan, who calmly drew his seven inch *Camillus* knife from the scabbard in his belt, plunging the blade into the man's throat rather than fire and waste another risky round in the small, crowded room.

The second killing happened during a close quarter encounter in a bombed-out block of flats whilst closing in on a sniper. Evading capture, the sniper fled and ran down an internal darkened stairwell, skipping four steps at a time. Just a teenager, no more than eighteen, a handful of years younger than Ryan. The *kid* wore sandals, faded wranglers, a black Rolling Stones t-shirt emblazoned with the famous *red lips and protruding tongue logo* and a *keffiyeh* scarf draped loosely around his neck.

He rounded the corner of a flight of steps and collided with the well-prepared, armed to the teeth Ryan, who had heard him descending the noisy staircase two floors earlier. Ryan was a great advocate of a rifleman's unwritten rule, to stuff every spare pocket or orifice in your kit bag with extra ammunition - you never know. Ryan weighed a ton, and the kid ran into an Irish brick wall.

The sniper's loaded weapon bounced to the floor, firing a deafening round into the wall which echoed off the poorly tiled confined concrete structure, stirring up a dust cloud. The sniper, startled, stunned and defenceless by the unexpected confrontation, proved no match for the determined Ryan's superior training and sharpened instincts. He instantly smashed the butt of his FAMAS F1 assault rifle into the teenager's face - dropping him to the floor. Instead of choosing to shoot him, he seized the opportunity to pounce on him, locking two meaty hands around a fourteen-and-a-half-inch neck. The stunned kid's legs and arms flailed around in desperation, slapping the floor like an overwhelmed *octagon* fighter, begging for submission, and *tapping out*. A relentless Ryan, far more powerful, and heavier, straddled him in the corner of the stinking, dusty concrete doorway. Exertion and adrenalin both demanded more oxygen for the underdog's lungs, there was no air available. Over a minute later all movement ceased, feet and hands flopped out motionless to the sides. Ryan had strangled the life out of the young man.

Nasri arrived and witnessed the aftermath of the scene, "I heard the single shot. I thought maybe he nailed you?"

Ryan smirked, "It was a close one. He ran into trouble - me. The little fucker stuck his tongue out at me - I never did like that."

Both men, satisfied with the outcome, didn't display an ounce of remorse. They had lost friends at the base, and a teammate from their unit, some tortured then killed. Neither of them cared anymore who died, from the other side, or how, so long as it was someone else other than them on the receiving end.

Nasri picked up the sniper's M21 rifle, cleared the chamber, removed the magazine, and smashed the telescopic sights against the wall. He stamped on the barrel over the concrete steps to bend it, rendering the rifle useless, before tossing it on top of the dead body. They left the decommissioned weapon and the sniper amongst the urine stench, rubble and graffitied walls then radioed the building as *clear* - another daily encounter brutally and safely dealt with.

By the end of *Caporal* (Corporal) Ryan's grim five-year *European adventure,* a service extension, and the possibility of making *Caporal-chef* (Senior Corporal) was a brief consideration, but he decided to go home. Enough was enough. His father was not getting any younger, Ryan missed Ireland and had not seen his family since he left Dundalk. During that period, his parents had moved to the outskirts of Dublin, near the coast. Ryan went home and reacquainted himself with the haulage business. Karim Nasri went back to his family's importing and exporting business in southern France. Both men remained great friends and eventually became business associates – trading partners. Nasri controlled the main supply chain and Ryan was one of a handful of trusted wholesalers and distributors.

~

The two old friends met whilst Ryan awaited the soil sample results from the lab.

Ryan had not seen Nasri for almost a year, although he had learned of the unexpected departure of Ryan's accountants. Nasri had other business to attend to in southern Spain and met his old comrade for lunch in a restaurant north of Barcelona, in Port de Badalona. Away from the hectic tourist areas of the main city, but busy enough to blend in unnoticed as a pair of grey-haired locals having a chat. Nasri possessed a North African complexion, with a thin grey moustache. Made of slender build he looked like a marathon runner. He always came out on top as the fittest in the unit, winning the aerobic physical tests when they were younger men, but he could match few of the other men for strength. His aerobic fitness surprised many because Nasri smoked over forty liquorice scented *mahawat* cigarettes a day. He rarely went anywhere without a cloud of smoke following him around, other than when they were either training or on the parade ground.

Ryan always cut it fine, and Nasri was already inside waiting, sipping water - he did not drink alcohol. He stood up and embraced his old friend, who ignored the familiar scent of tobacco which always accompanied the Algerian.

"You still don't look bad for a *fifty-something* Irishman. Good to see you, my friend."

"And you Karim. You look slimmer every time I meet you. I need to cut back on my Guinness intake, so I can stand next to you without feeling guilty."

The men chatted and reminisced as they always did. Both ordered some fresh fish before they got down to business.

"Things are quiet at your end Declan. What's up my friend? You're like a big old Irish mouse.

We need you full throttle man, not bits and pieces. What's going on?"

"I've got a few other projects keeping me busy - I'll tell you about them in a minute. I also moved house a few months ago which was a bloody nightmare, never again, at least not in Spain. Then we said goodbye to some old friends who caused us a few ripples and it caused me a time-consuming recruitment issue. So decided I needed to slow down and take stock of things - just for a while, nothing permanent."

"You're getting cautious in your old age Declan. Either you have too much money or your wife isn't spending it as fast as she used to?"

"Well, I'm a grandfather now and I can assure you my Mrs can spend as good as any woman I've ever met. I'm not exactly suffering from a *cash flow* problem at the moment, I have a *cash mountain* problem. I mean I'm fucking swimming in the stuff. I had it all worked out then things went pear-shaped on an investment project. To make matters worse the Spanish *feds* might be sniffing around, keeping a close eye on some of my businesses, since the tax people had a little friendly chat with my former English business associates."

Nasri looked up, a hint of seriousness showed on his face, "I'm glad you got that sorted out straight away. You had us worried for a while."

Ryan spotted the concerned *tell*, "All sorted they told me everything, *everything*. We have no problems. Nothing to worry about, just a bit of vague speculation to deal with. As far as any concerns from the tax people and their suspicions, or the police if they ever had any suspicions, most of the money came from the dozens of slot machines in the bars. They have nothing to go on. The was no connection with me because the Harrisons managed it and ran it every day. I'm the established, reputable businessman remember."

Nasri appeared reassured, "Good. So now I need a favour from you. Something to get us back on track. The downside is your cash mountain will get a little bigger. But it means a lot to me. Kind of a *family business* thing from my end. Nothing extraordinary, the same process as always. I have a few wooden crates coming in from North Africa, let's say a van load. Might need a fork-lift truck? We are going to need them in Zeebrugge, mixed into a big container consignment and shipped to Immingham, in the UK. A seamless, dependable shipment process is what we need. So, therefore, I need you Declan."

Fine details and questions continued until the men were about to stand up, embrace again and go their separate ways.

Before they did, as always Ryan insisted Nasri told him what was coming in the boxes. He had a good idea that it wouldn't be bananas. The unshockable Ryan's jaw tightened when Nasri told him, and also informed him he had the recipient lined up. The consignment contained all the components and sub-assemblies required to assemble a sophisticated industrial 3D printer made by one of the market leaders in Taiwan. Pre-programmed with the data for producing the end product, and with enough justification for it to pass as some new technology for a college laboratory. The worrying aspect involved the raw materials also coming in the crates. Dozens of boxes, shrink-wrapped onto pallets, each box containing blank pieces of high-strength nylon-based polymer known as Polyamide 6.6 and Polymer 2 and a selection of innocuous un-machined metal pieces – small-diameter precision steel tubes and packs of hardware store style, tiny springs.

Ryan was about to import into the UK all the technology and raw material required to manufacture perfect replica, premium quality, Glock 17, semi-automatic, 9mm pistols. Made from composite materials. Tens of thousands of them.

"Jesus, Karim, are they for drug dealers or someone else, are you trying to start a fucking war?"

"Like I told you Declan - supply and demand. This is just a new line of the family business. Salespeople in our line of work in the UK need to defend their businesses. A lucrative business for all of us." A thinly disguised lie from Nasri appeared to have satisfied Ryan.

Most normal peaceful people find it hard to comprehend why doctors, architects, teachers, and many other ordinary British people would ever leave their families, and comfortable lifestyles in the UK, to go to Syria and join a death cult. It might be easier to understand why a ruthless Algerian drugs smuggler would choose to involve himself with, and sponsor, a North African Islamist terror group - Wilayah al-Jazair - one of many groups associated with ISIL.

Chapter 17

Native Title

It took a day or two for the euphoria to settle down at the Eaves' farm and for Harry's rainbow bruised eyes no longer beguile Lauren with the look of *Kaa*. The champagne remained on ice to celebrate the rare earth find on their land.

Lauren had spent another day completing the collection of samples and sending them off to Jack's lab for verification.

Harry, always a man of action remained on light duties. He took the opportunity to use his time wisely. An initial phone call to an old acquaintance at DMIRS (The Department of Mines, Industry Regulation and Safety) prompted a train ride with Lauren to their regional offices in Bunbury, near Perth. The Eaves land lab results were back, and they were as good as expected. The next step involved obtaining a new licence from the regional office to mine a different much larger section of his land for the minerals. He already owned a gold miners license but that was not acceptable for his new plans to extract rare earth minerals on a bigger scale.

Lauren had postponed her flight, with no plans to return back to Wales for at least another week, until she felt confident her father had fully recovered. The doctor wanted to take a final look at Harry before giving him the official all-clear. As they sat on the train heading west, Lauren asked, "So why all the fuss about a new mining license Dad? Is it that complicated?"

Harry answered, "Things are different these days, the rules and regulations are far more stringent than they were thirty years ago. There is a load of stuff to go through and forms to sign, so in the end, I decided I wanted to meet this guy and get all the answers. Emails and phone calls don't have the same effect as a proper chat. It might save me weeks and time is against us. I need to start mining and making money."

After his long train ride, followed by his DMIRS meeting, Harry had the face of a man suggesting he had lost a shilling and found a penny. Despite great optimism for the future, the short term did not look as rosy for the Eaves family's new mining venture as Harry had hoped. Despite having all the forms completed, then signed, provisional legal and environmental issues complied with, yet more and bigger hurdles thwarted them.

Harry looked unimpressed, "233 days? So, you mean nine months of doing nothing? Is there anything else that can speed things up?"

The DMIRS officer continued and sympathetically reiterated, "Harry, *Native Title* in Western Australia for an exploration licence goes through the *Expedited Procedure* – which means obeying the law. This is a standard-issue process that makes life easier for both parties. That takes about 233 business days or nine months, and there is little one can do other than wait for the process to conclude. Trust me mate, this *is* fast-tracking. But it is the correct procedure and will avoid a *section 29 notification* with objections and tribunals taking even longer. Those are the rules and just the way it is these days, Harry. At least you're on day one and the clock is ticking in your favour. From what you just told me about your test results it will be worth waiting for, with reasonable money sitting there for you to scoop up on your land, good on you."

Harry, replied in a more conciliatory tone, "Yeah, you're right mate - sorry just eager to crack on. We will wait and get things sorted out, in readiness for the *b* of the *bang* in nine months. We don't have much choice, so there it is."

The train journey home seemed to take an eternity. Harry would normally have plenty to chat about, yet even he seemed preoccupied with the never-ending string of mulga trees passing by the train window. He restricted his conversation to *bloody bureaucracy,* and it is *my land – I own it.*

Lauren didn't help matters by suggesting, "But Dad, the land once belonged to *them*, until *we* came along a few hundred years ago. We must be respectful and patient. Then we can start planning and making preparations. Besides, 233 days will fly by. As the man said, the clock is ticking."

Harry didn't avert his gaze from the endless miles of farmland on view, "I know Lauren, but waiting doesn't make our situation any easier, or much fun sitting around scraping a living, does it? Planning is fine and is free. Making preparations is another matter, which means diverting labour and resources and will cost money. Preparation can wait."

Lauren could sense the anguish in her father's voice, she understood the immense struggle he and Margaret were going through. If anything, her extended few weeks home for the wedding had brought her closer to Olivia and her parents and made her more determined than ever to help them pull together as a family.

She decided to change the subject, "Oliva's pregnant with twins dad."

"What!"

"Only kidding." She stifled a laugh.

Harry managed a smile, despite his elbow slipping off the train's internal window frame, causing him to almost bump his healing head wound on the glass. "You're not too old for a clip across the ear, there might be a first time for anything." He laughed as he realised Lauren had tried to distract him from their disappointing meeting.

"Olivia's been good as gold since the wedding Dad, we're tighter than ever. Oh, and we're taking Mum off for another spa day before I go back, a bit of a treat. They gave us a deal before the wedding. Can't have enough of a good thing, can you?"

"Ah, nice, she'll love that. When are you going back to Wales? Qantas must be pulling their hair out with you."

"The end of next week, I think. At least I won't need to worry about work, they 'let me go'. My dissertation is pretty much, done and dusted, and I managed to add some new ideas and information thanks to the Blaenavon thing and working with Uncle Jack. But I need to get back and catch up with my tutors and a few lectures. After that, I have to find a proper job with decent money."

~

Harry's doctor gave him his green light, but he didn't exactly ease himself back into things. He hit the ground running trying to catch up for the lost time, with Margaret and Lauren keeping an eye on him, ensuring he hydrated himself to the max every day.

During the quieter moments in the evenings, and in between some last-minute socialising with her old school friends, Lauren kept searching for any new information relating to Blaenavon and Nick Savvas. It pleased her every time she drew a blank, it meant she still had a slim chance to get in on the action and speak with the farmers before anyone else did. She assumed they had no knowledge of anything yet.

One evening she decided to do some more digging around. She ploughed through some of the original information she had discovered during her *accidental* bit of nosiness on the University of NSW in Sydney intranet a few weeks earlier. She widened her search and hunted for anything with Nick Savvas's 'fingerprints' on it. Looking in a few new places, she found nothing startling, other than a few folders tagged as 'National Geographical, for Dee', and a couple of folders designated as China and Blaenavon. The Blaenavon folder was new, less than a week old, and replicated the salient pieces of information Lauren had previously found.

"National Geographical? Dee? Who's Dee? And what the hell is that all about?"

It didn't take Lauren long to find out more and give herself some clues. A Google search with some relevant keywords including – 'National Geographical Dee mining' - produced some hits.

"Jackpot! Dee Munchetty." An image appeared of an attractive woman with shoulder-length black straggly hair and dazzling teeth. Her smiling face, framed by the hood of a bright blue, quilted Rab jacket.

"An American documentary filmmaker and environmentalist. Wow, she's even got her own Wikipedia page. Born in Boston, 42 years old. Studied at Stanford University. Divorced. Nominated for an Emmy and won an IDA Documentary 'the Oscars of the documentary genre'- and it appears she's connected with Nick Savvas and Blaenavon. This is crazy. What is Savvas up to? And how is she involved?"

Lauren spent the best part of twenty minutes reading all about Dee Munchetty, although she found no images of her with Savvas, and no articles linking the two of them. After scouring all of the articles concerning her activities and impressive filmmaking exploits, Lauren decided to try a different tack. She hunted through Nick Savvas's back story and social media.

"'China for Dee', another folder said. Let's see what you did Nick and with whom."

Savvas had a multitude of professional social media accounts and business associations with numerous snippets of unhelpful information amongst them. Then a link caught Lauren's eye, for a TED talk given during a conference in San Francisco just before the pandemic. Twenty-five minutes of the film described as *'Nick Savvas, the Rare Earth guru. He explains his recent cutting edge mining concepts in China, extracting tonnes of riches from the soil to feed the starving technology industry which is screaming for more and more of the commodity to run our electric cars and gadgets'.*

Lauren considered, *"Twenty-five minutes of Savvas's smarm should be entertaining, but more than enough for anyone. I'll skip through the presentation slides."*

As he closed his presentation, Savvas popped a *Nat Geo* logo up on the screen and gave a small but exuberant comment, "I can't say too much, but this particular project, with all of its peculiarities, and environmental aspirations, will be the subject of an upcoming National Geographical documentary. Watch this space in a year or so time – thank you and have a good evening."

Lauren was so pleased with herself for her dogged detective work, *"And then the pandemic arrived, he got stuck in Spain and hasn't gone back to China since. I know he went to Brazil, and now Wales. Someone pulled the rug on him in China. Now he wants to do a different documentary and become a minor celebrity, using Blaenavon, I guarantee it. He can't resist it."*

The Intrepid Trio WhatsApp group pinged with Lauren's update for Harry and Jack, highlighting the new information she had found concerning the *Blaenavon Project*. The update included a quick explanation about Dee Munchetty and Savvas's documentary aspirations, with a link to the TED talk and a little comment to skip to the final two minutes.

Lauren added, *"Another week or so and I'll be in Blaenavon joining the party."*

With Blaenavon on Lauren's *student* doorstep in Wales, going to the former mining town and carrying out a few tests would not cost much. She wondered if she and her family were expecting too much, and from a few warmish pieces of evidence. *"Is Blaenavon a genuine commercial rare earth mining opportunity? Why can't I find more solid evidence of it? Am I biting off more than I can chew? Am I over-ambitious? Then, I'm going to march in, and try to steal the show – literally, steal the show, bold as brass from Nick Savvas."* Doubts tried and failed to get a stronger foothold inside her gritty and determined head, *"Sod it. I'm going for it. What have I got to lose?"*

Whilst Lauren continued to think through her plans, Jack had spent some time searching and found no mining applications. But his efforts had been just a fraction too early in his search. Because a few days later, Jason Price started putting the wheels in motion for his coal mining licence – not any other minerals and was taking care of it. But Price realised the timing of the application was crucial, so as not to alert the landowners before he could buy the land. Price's plan was coming together nicely, all his ducks were in a row, and he had started the process of knocking them off the complicated sequence.

Meanwhile, Ryan had agreed more or less to come on board and would stay off Price's back for the time being. Ryan's lab samples, taken by his cousin were in, and they had substantiated Price's lucrative promises, so Ryan sensed the beginnings of a huge investment payback.

Feisal Hussein had been informed by Price that Ryan was the man intending to make the purchase. He knew that Ryan would be in contact to continue the initial process, finalise negotiations and purchase the drift mine, which would not take him long.

All that remained for Price was to seek out and meet the local sheep farmers and secure the agreement of the local council. Although the council agreement mattered, his main priority was to get the farmers on board. He specialised in sorting out land deals and gaining council agreements, one way or another, although Welsh councils had reputations for being squeaky clean. He needed a professional approach, but never doubted for one moment, that in a matter of weeks he would have full control of everything needed to make a fortune – he was already in Blaenavon, making inroads. But an unanticipated series of events would soon start to overtake him.

Chapter 18

Cash is King

The Blaenavon sample results were back from the lab. Exceeding Declan Ryan's expectations by a mile, they were almost off the scale and led to a second test by the 'stunned' lab as a double-check. He appreciated the commercial investment significance of what the results represented and had practically interrogated the unfortunate lab technician over the phone, even before the completion of the soil testing. When Ryan wanted answers, he became impatient, relentlessly bulldozing and bullying his way through people and processes.

He breathed a deep positive sigh, as he punched one meaty fist into the open palm of his other hand. He now had confirmation of all the facts that he needed to convince him to invest. They were remarkable but useless without ownership of the nearby mine, its disused buildings, the land which accompanied it, and the most crucial element – the farmer's land.

In this instance, the cart needed to come before the horse. Purchasing the mine needed to happen before the procurement of the farmers land - to get the mining license, to appease the council and for leverage with the farmers to persuade them to do the deal with a credible mining organisation. But the farmers were Price's responsibility.

Some tricky hurdles still required careful navigation, including the local council, which could make things awkward if they were not on board, but Ryan consoled himself that the local jobs boost would resolve any of their concerns. Nick Savvas gave him great confidence, and when Savvas said they needed to buy the mine, Ryan would do just that - buy the mine – for more reasons than one. The slight problem was Jason Price, he did not instil as much confidence in Ryan, and had not covered himself in glory with the stalled casino project - still haemorrhaging money for the time being.

"This is your opportunity to redeem yourself, Jason. You need to make damn sure you do," Ryan thought to himself.

~

Ryan had plenty of extremely wealthy friends and associates. Over the years, he witnessed some of them spending many millions buying a private plane or a luxury yacht, like the equivalent of buying a second-hand Ford for normal people. The same rules applied when he decided to buy a shabby piece of property in Wales for less than a million. If the will to sell and the desire to buy existed, a deal would happen in no time.

An exchange of emails took place between Declan Ryan and Amy Frey. She understood the relationship between Ryan and her original contact Jason Price, and that Ryan was the main interested party in buying the mine. She also did her research and credit checks on Declan Ryan and his rapidly growing logistics business. Everything appeared legitimate and satisfactory. All her diligence culminated in the arrangement of a private conference call between Ryan and Feisal Hussein.

From the warm friendly tone, they sounded like they had known each other for years, "Declan, what a pleasure it is to speak with you, at last. My apologies for some of the initial complications and delays in arranging our discussion – I was travelling extensively – a necessary evil. Although I understand Amy had some initial involvement along the way with your associate, Mr Price, before you got involved, is that right?"

Hussein's cut-glass English accent took Ryan by surprise, but he pressed on and added a little small talk, "Feisal, yes, and a pleasure to speak with you also, I trust you're well? I presume you're calling me from your Paris office or has the necessary evil defeated you once again today?"

"Yes, I'm in Paris, Declan - so I'm winning today. This is my home these days, and what's not to like about Paris, eh?"

"I can't argue with you on that Feisal, although you sound as though you may have spent more time in England than France?"

"Well, I blame my father for that, London was my birthplace, and he decided where I went to school – in England. He held romantic notions of me becoming prime minister one day, but it didn't quite work out. So, Declan, they tell me you and your associates are in the leisure industry, with plans for a themed leisure park on the side of a mountain in Wales? Sounds good to me."

Ryan and Price ensured their facts and stories aligned before Ryan's telephone call to Hussein. The bogus premise to buy the mine and the land was to build a mountain bike park and leisure village, with a ski resort type chair lift for the mountain bikers.

"Feisal, yes, we have many plans in lots of places, although we are targeting Blaenavon for this particular project of ours. Some of the global marketing is already in place for us, I mean it is a World Heritage Site after all. So, you could call it a bit of piggyback marketing, riding on their coattails, and then we hope our mountain bikers will be riding on the local trails. We are also thinking of a zip-wire attraction once we get fully established."

Ryan's chat seemed more plausible by the minute, and Hussein sounded enthusiastic, "Then maybe I should keep the mine and rent it to you Declan, and take a stake in your business idea?"

"A thoughtful gesture Feisal, but we have all the investors we need on board. All we need is a hub, a base. Your old mine is just one of a few locations on the side of that mountain we can adapt to suit our needs.

But right now, your asking price is much higher than we had anticipated, and we do have other options."

"Declan, as you may have seen, I retained the asset as a part of my portfolio for a long, long time, and I am in no rush to dispose of it. I have declined offers for it several times. We know our price of €960k is a good market valuation. I will let it go to you, but only if the deal is good."

"The deal can be good for both of us Feisal - depends on how much tax you intend to pay on the sale of it. Why give a huge chunk to the British taxman if we can both pay less tax – legally? I'm talking about tax avoidance here, and not tax evasion, there is a big difference. One is legal, and the other isn't."

Ryan knew Hussein would not bat an eyelid at his suggestion to avoid paying anything to anybody, hence his Cayman Islands shell company and bank accounts. The two men continued to talk for another forty minutes and struck a verbal agreement - with the understanding that Ryan was a man in a hurry with plenty of cash.

Ryan agreed he would meet Hussein in Paris at the office of Hussein's lawyers and would legally buy the mine and its land for a fraction of the asking price, he would pay €160k. There would be a full 'paper trail' with ownership transferred to Ryan. The €160k would be worth twenty times that when the rare earth discovery made it into the newspapers and TV news – a superb investment.

What no one else would ever discover was that Hussein would also receive, with its negotiated discount, a further €700k, in cash – a total of €860. What he chose to do with the cash, where he dispersed and deposited it was his business. He was a Jordanian, connected to the Royal family, with half a dozen dodgy bank accounts in the Cayman Islands, Turks and Caicos, and the British Virgin Islands. If you know the right kind of *wrong people*, there are plenty of countries in the world where a person can purchase property, Ferraris, almost anything, with cash - no problems, no questions asked - cash is still king. Especially, if you have some royal blood in you.

~

€700,000 in €200 notes, weighs less than 4kg, similar to a couple of bags of sugar. The notes fit with ease into a medium-sized messenger bag, with room to spare for two packs of sandwiches. Declan Ryan had the bag slung diagonally around his chest when he and Michael, the younger and biggest of his cousins, stepped off the TGV high-speed train, at Gare de Lyon in the centre of Paris.

"That train ride was grand Declan, luxurious, and fast - 300 km per hour - but why didn't we fly up?"

"Mikey, by the time you piss about in the airport, then get through check-in, it takes the same time to fly as the train takes. Besides if you thought I was going to march through the airport, and through their check-in X-ray machines with the best part of a million quid on me, you had another think coming."

Ryan used a large law firm in Barcelona for his regular business, and they provided a Parisian legal representative. He met them off the train and hailed a taxi to take them to meet Feisal Hussein at his lawyer's *Ohleyer's Avocats*, in Rue du Cygne. The short journey hardly warranted the €20, but Ryan felt flush and in a good mood. He was about to do the job his dead money launderers would have taken a year to do in less than an hour.

Ryan had seen online images of Hussein, although nothing prepared him for the slender, bearded, and diminutive man whose hand vanished inside Ryan's. He came up to Ryan's shoulder and held his gaze during their brief handshake. Ryan spotted Hussein offer a noticeable glance towards the messenger bag - he knew what the bag contained.

With pleasantries exchanged, the two lawyers exchanged a few polite words in French to each other. Everyone, including Hussein, looked surprised when Ryan asked, in perfect French with an Irish accent, "Gentlemen, would you prefer to conduct the meeting in French or English?"

Hussein wrongly assumed that Ryan's French was as poor as Jason Price's, who had struggled with the language not so long ago. Hussein intervened, "That won't be necessary Declan, I don't think my French is as good as yours by the sound of it. You're a man full of surprises."

"Thank you, Feisal. Yes, I'm a man full of surprises, and with a bag full of money. Let's crack on with it shall we?"

The lawyers counted the money, signed it off, then moved it to one side, whilst Ryan and Hussein signed and exchanged the necessary documents. Last, of all, a €160k bank transfer went through for the official transparent sale. Hussein's lawyer explained he would notify the authorities in Wales immediately of the change of ownership of the drift mine.

"Congratulations Declan, you now own a mine or a leisure park or whatever you are going to build."

Hussein harboured several doubts about Ryan's intentions for the old mine, but he didn't care. The dilapidated asset was off his spreadsheet and onto someone else's. €160k seemed a plausible, defendable, sum to anyone asking questions. A problem solved. The lawyer placed the money in a safe, with Ryan preferring a glass of cognac in favour of champagne offered to him.

The French can be rather fussy when it comes to raising a glass and toasting a success or a special occasion.

Declan Ryan offered the traditional toast, and one familiar to him, *"Santé."*

Everyone, responded in good spirit, although, the stuffy French aficionado lawyers noticed a few discrepancies in Ryan's toast. They didn't mention a word, until later, when he was out of earshot and about to leave. They light-heartedly concurred that he had overlooked one or two of the golden rules of

French toasting - ensure that you toast everyone else before you drink, and do not put down your glass between the toast and the first sip.

Many years had passed since Ryan had toasted anyone in France, an easy mistake to make, for the rusty Ryan.

The discreet jovial French banter concluded between the lawyers, "Seven years bad luck for your client due to his poor toasting technique. But I'm sure he will be fine."

Hussein overheard the lawyers and pondered, *"Something makes me unsure about him being fine? An instinct? Or an omen? But something will be out of sync – and perhaps for him, not so fine?"*

Chapter 19

The Homecoming

A mild, sunny, early Spring afternoon welcomed Jason Price as he approached the sweeping moorlands at the north end of the valley a mile or two up from Blaenavon. The rugged hills and solid mountains, either side, ran for miles and funnelled him along the exposed road, with not a tree in sight.

"Bloody hell, it's been a while. Stunning. Looks like a movie set - come to think of it, I heard it was in a few."

He slowed down as he rounded a bend and passed over a brow, then pulled over to take in the view. Even Price needed a moment to fully appreciate what he could see. The view of the landscape improved further, spectacular in its unique way. Tucked away, he could begin to see the outskirts of the town and some of the industrial developments, including the winding wheels of the 'Big Pit' mining museum. Along the side of the mountain, he spotted a few old drift mine sites, and one rambling dingy establishment in particular, now in the hands of the consortium. Well, more precisely in the hands of Declan Ryan.

"Jesus, how much did he pay for that pile of rubbish?" Price didn't have the full picture concerning Ryan's purchase and that laundered cash paid the lion's share to Feisal Hussein. Seen as a sound investment, or at least a good utilisation of his dirty cash by Ryan – understandable – but still a risky investment, the fat lady had not yet started to warm up, let alone sing.

Price realised he had arrived at the edge of where the main coal and iron mining took place nearly two hundred years ago. He didn't need reminding that the ironmasters back in those early days were the equivalent of modern-day slave drivers, with boys and girls as young as six working in the pits and losing their lives. Miners pay only came in the form of tokens, redeemable at the company shop, with homes for many miners and their families rented from the ironmasters. The ironmasters controlled a greedy monopoly for a long time.

"Looks great to me. Now it's someone else's turn to make a big pile of money," he muttered to himself.

The 'humps and bumps' to his left were not natural hills, they were imposters, formed from the dumping and scattering of the unwanted coal and iron spoils back in the day. The tell-tale black colour of the tracks and paths made it obvious. Further on ahead to his right, he could just make out the base of what was once a huge cone-shaped slag heap, close to where Savvas had revelled in taking some of his samples. The 'chopped off' cone - there were more than one – decapitated, and reconstructed, to look to the untrained eye, as though it blended in with the rest of the countryside. But there was no escaping its heritage, and how it came about. Most local people Price's age remembered how it once looked and some gave it a nickname - *Little Egypt*. Many of those could remember the coal spoils spewing out on top of it, making it bigger and bigger, as the filthy work of friends and family continued underground well into the 1980s. But this entire area was where the new riches of Blaenavon lay, waiting for someone to uncover them and make themselves a huge fortune. Price and his cohort of fraudsters would stop at nothing to ensure it was them.

After well over forty years, Price mused, *"You can take the boy out of Blaenavon, but you can't take Blaenavon out of the boy - so they used to say. Yeah, nice, and things are going to get even better before long with a bit of luck. Now I need to go and round up a few farmers."*

When they were in school, some kids broke their arms playing football, got bloody noses in the schoolyard, or needed stitches in their knees from playing netball. As those youngsters grew and progressed into adulthood, they remembered their bumped and bruised events vividly. Jason Price was responsible for the most traumatic event any child could ever imagine - the death of another child – his younger brother Rhys. But somehow, Price had managed to erase any memories from his mind.

He and his parents left Blaenavon months after the incident. The so-called accident remained a mystery to the police and his parents, although rumours abounded in school and around the town. Price was not traumatised by what happened, he simply carried on with his life, aware of what he did – for a while – before choosing to forget it, as an unimportant day in his life, like it never happened. Ironically, in later life Price made significant donations to various children's charities in the UK and Spain.

Now returning fifty years later, gazing across the landscape, Price stood there, not thinking for one second about his childhood, his parents, or his brother. The horrific event of that freezing cold day at the *Keepers Pond* never entered his mind. All he could see was the potential in the lucrative soil, a means to an end, and the next steppingstones in his plan – the pivotal landowners and the tight-knit, cautious local council. His confidence flowed; he did not anticipate any hiccups from here on in. A week or two and everything would be in place – simple.

Price drove for half an hour, circumnavigating the town, in ever-decreasing circles. Parts of the town were unrecognisable to him. Satisfied that he had managed to reacquaint himself with his bearings, he stopped at the bottom end of town and found his way into a coffee shop he had passed earlier. The coffee shop in the building, which was once his old junior school, was now a trendy café alongside a heritage museum. Price cautiously wandered through the doors, half expecting a greeting party and his old headmistress rather than a latte, *"Yes, things have moved on around here."*

Price settled down with his coffee in a far corner and started flicking through his notebook. He came well prepared and had compiled a 'to do' list to accompany a small map which he laid out on the table. In assorted colours, he had carefully highlighted the boundaries of four areas. Ryan's new mine and its relatively small portion of surrounding land, and three large nearby sections of farmland. Price saw an approximate configuration of them when he drove in earlier, planning a closer inspection later. Each of the three pieces of farmland had a farmer's name written on his map and the same names written into his book.

The book also contained more details - a thorough profile of each of the farmers. At least as much as was possible to glean from public records and the local community Facebook group pages that he had joined. The farmers were not captains of industry with a personal Wikipedia page or even LinkedIn profiles. No, they were middle-aged, hard-working, normal men and women, with families. Two of them worked part-time, as well as working the land to make ends meet. One tried to make a full time living from the farm with sheep, horses, cattle together with providing an open-air winter storage rental area for small caravans.

Price was not familiar with checking out potential vendors at such a macro level, certainly not for smallholdings worth peanuts. As a rule, he worked at much higher levels, in both the UK and Spain, his small team carrying out the research and donkey work for him. Not this time, he wanted to keep his cards close to his chest. Land registry flagged up a few other avenues to explore and he then drilled right down to the 2001 census. Although, his final piece of detective work involved outsourcing private credit checks to an associate. She provided him with one for each of the farmers by using the soft inquiry method. Sometimes known as a *soft credit pull* - a regulated financial process and illegal without permission to do so – and still illegal even if there were £150 in it for someone.

A smirk spread across Price's round face with the excitement of reading the credit reports again. "All but one of them would struggle to obtain a car lease agreement, let alone get a mortgage from a bank. It doesn't get much better than that, does it? Perfect."

Almost licking his lips in anticipation, he took another long, meticulous look at the book and the map, *"David Davies, aged 57, Maggie Powell, aged 42 and Robert Carter, aged 46 - it's your lucky day."*

An irritating distraction came from Price's iPhone, vibrating and pinging on the table. His eyes widened when he saw two missed calls and a voice message from Declan Ryan, *"Call me."*

The 4G came in and out in some parts of town, and the calls had gone to voicemail.

Price did not mess about when he needed to win, and he had learned over the years that surprises often arrived with a negative sign on them. An old boss of his used to say to him, *"Give me the good news, give me the bad news - just don't bring me any surprises."* The mantra stuck with him and looking at Ryan's message he had the unpleasant feeling a surprise could be on its way.

The drift mine deal took place less than a week earlier, and the lawyers acted swiftly, notifying the necessary authorities about the change of ownership to Ryan. Now he found himself officially on the council's radar, and easy to pin down. Unlike the previous owner, Feisal Hussein, who along with his shell companies, hid well behind smoke and mirrors in the Cayman Islands.

"What's up, Declan? I only just picked up your message - there isn't much of a signal around here."

"I'll tell you what's up. Feisal *Fucking* Hussein. He is what's up. The bastard has shafted me."

Price, could feel himself sinking lower into his café chair, and whispered, "What do you mean? How? What has he done?"

"*Restoration and regeneration to original condition and aesthetic.* Does that ring any bells, Jason? I had an email from the council. Not just an email - a fucking bill, for over £200k."

A couple of hikers, not much older than Price, sat on the adjacent table. There was nothing wrong with their hearing and they both flinched at the tirade leaking out of Price's phone.

Price would have put his head in both hands had he not been holding his phone with one of them. The terms rang bells, though he was more familiar with dilapidation costs on office blocks, to make them fit for purpose and back to the original appearance and function.

"Shit Declan. I didn't see that one coming."

"No, but Feisal did. I spoke to the council, they said they had tried and failed for years to get him to pay it. Now it falls on me to pick the bill for the work the council have already carried out to tidy it up and make it safe."

Thinking on his feet, Price chirped up, "OK, OK, I have an idea. *We* pay the bill at the end of our financial year, almost a year away and longer than that by the time we get the accounts done. I'm sure we will be fine."

"So, are there any more surprises in store for me, Jason? I'm the only one who has forked out any money on this bloody venture so far. Well, you had better read the legal jargon, there are reams of it, and looking at it, I think *we* need to pay the bill upfront before *we* can do anything else. I'm sending it over to you. You told me you're the expert, right?" Once more, Ryan's voice had risen to a shout, causing the hikers to glance again in Price's direction.

Price watched his iPhone react as moments later an email notification from Ryan pinged in. *"And today was going so well. Why, oh why, did I ever get involved with that poxy Irishman in the first place? Damn it."*

For years, Price's decision making, and risk-taking track record did not have a blemish on it. There were the inevitable handful of close calls, but nothing ruffled him. Now every step of the way he found himself running into problems, *"Two more weeks and we will be on the other side, through the crap and sorted. I know we will - otherwise I'm up against a huge problem. An Irish one."*

Chapter 20

The First Milestone

David Davies and his sheepdog, Bea, had experienced better days than this one. His sheep were a couple of weeks late lambing this year, always a hectic time for any farmer. Day and night shifts, trying to keep an eye on five-hundred sheep seemed to roll into one irritable, tired haze. To make matters worse, David needed to shoot a stray dog that morning, as it was attacking one of his pregnant ewes. He tried to scare it off, but the uncontrollable, stray dog gave him no alternative.

"Why don't the owners read the bloody signs! More to the point where is the bloody owner."

The shooting meant notifying the police, a laborious form filling exercise, and worst of all a confrontation with the dog's furious owner. He hated what happened, and mercifully, shooting such dogs was a rare occurrence, but a harsh reality existed – healthy sheep and lambs paid the bills. Wealthy farmers were few and far between, and there were none of those in Blaenavon.

Price hoped to have chosen well by singling out David Davies as the oldest and perhaps the most influential of the trio of farmers that he needed to get on board. It was a risky decision. Davies worked full time on the farm, and he was the farmer with the best credit rating, with the potential to turn his nose up at an attractive financial opportunity. But Price realised a decent credit rating did not automatically mean someone was rolling in it, it only meant that they could pay their bills and make ends meet. Another imponderable nagged him - farmland - in particular, farmland handed down through generations could sometimes be a touchy, personal subject. Outside interference is often unwelcome - shunned, and you never get a second chance to make a good first impression - a crucial introduction loomed.

The search to find Davies began, hardly a big challenge, and the opportunity presented itself sooner than expected. A battered old slate grey Land Rover came towards to where Price had parked up, off a side road on the moorland, a popular starting spot for dog walkers. The potholed, single-track road led to David Davies's family cottage, one of a handful, all not far off listed building status.

The well maintained old house, displayed a large log pile stacked to the side of the front door obscuring part of the cottage's whitewashed walls. The chimney produced visible signs, suggesting the inside of the cottage was warming up, and a cold gentle breeze drifted the smoke a few hundred metres back up the track, towards the open window of Price's black Range Rover. From two hundred yards away, he watched the tall, grey-haired Davies, park and wander up to his front door. A 'broken', unloaded 12-bore hooked over his shoulder, and with a sheepdog scurrying through between his wellingtons the moment the key opened the door.

"So, you're the guy Nick Savvas met in the local pub not so long ago, are you? I'll give you fifteen minutes before it gets dark."

A knock came on the farmhouse door, "Who the hell is that? I'll get it."

David Davies's red-haired wife Elizabeth answered the door, TV remote control in one hand, fending back a barking dog with one of her slippered feet. Still hunting for clothes after taking a shower upstairs, David called the dog back. Elizabeth gave a stern up and down look at the figure of Jason Price who stood at the door in his 'fresh out of the box' *Hunter* wellingtons, and a *Barbour* gilet on top of his tweed jacket. An out of character *look*, purposely chosen by Price.

Before Price had a chance to open his mouth, he found himself interrupted by an indignant, "Are you looking for David?"

Again, the word *yes*, barely left his lips before he nodded and listened to a deafening shout directed upstairs, "David, someone for you. Lord

Monmouthshire is here by the looks of him," she winked at Price as she said it. He smiled in return.

The diminutive woman, raised her chin and looked up to the shorter than average Price, and asked full of attitude and confidence, "What's your name love?"

The forthright question had Price on the backfoot, "Jason, Jason Price. I'm here to..."

"OK Jason, he'll be a minute. Sorry, but it's cold love," and the door closed in Price's face faster than it opened.

"Welcome back Jason," he thought to himself, as he waited there like someone trying and failing to sell double glazing.

A minute or so later, the door half opened again. This time David Davies stood there, dressed in a sweat top and jogging bottoms, with his grey hair, damp, but combed. The curious dog also nuzzled its head through the small gap in the door to listen in.

"Hello, how can I help you?"

Price made a conscious effort to detune his more refined accent, adopted over the years, "Mr Davies, I'm sorry to trouble you. My name is Jason Price. My associates and I run a small mining company and we have recently acquired the old drift mine up on the side of the mountain adjacent to your land. We have plans to renovate it and improve the land around it – as you must know, all left in a bit of a sorry state by the previous owner."

"What? You mean your you're going to start mining coal again? You must be nuts."

"Well, technology has moved on and new processes will make it more viable and a profitable operation. And that's the reason why I called to see you - with your neighbouring land. We have a business proposition for you if you're interested. An excellent one. You could make some good money without lifting a finger and without investing a penny. Can we have a chat about it?"

That was Price's rehearsed pitch, short, succinct, and interesting enough for Davies to want to know more - he hoped.

"Where's the catch?" Having paused the TV, Elizabeth chipped in from behind David Davies.

"Alright Liz, give the bloke a chance, will you. Let's listen to what he's got to say for himself. Look, Jason, my tea's on the table. Give me an hour and we can discuss it over a pint at the Whistle. Is that OK for you?"

Jason Price held out his hand and David shook it, "Great, thanks. Ok, I'll see you in an hour, David, meanwhile here's my number if there are any problems. By the way, there is no catch, simply good news, I can assure you. Cheers. Goodbye Mrs Davies."

The door closed, and Jason Price walked back to his car, a relieved and excited man. He didn't expect rejection, but sometimes things don't always go to plan as he experienced from recent events. But no problems with the Davies's - not yet anyway.

During his patient hour of waiting, Price noticed the Whistle pubs' steady flow of regulars, hikers, dog walkers and hardcore mountain bikers covered in mud and wearing headlamps. All of them converged on a beneficial distance of the big log fire whilst he went through a few additional pieces of information in readiness to show David. But his hidden agenda was to persuade David to open up about his relationship with the other two neighbouring farmers, and to find out if David was the leverage Price hoped he was.

One hour later, on the dot, David Davies walked in with his dog Bea. She headed straight for a favourite dog bowl full of water and avidly lapped whilst Price ordered his new acquaintance a pint of lager.

They moved to a quieter table away from the heat of the fire, and Price said *cheers*, acknowledged by David, with a subtle raise of the glass.

"A beautiful looking dog David, a proper working dog by the looks of her?"

"Yes, she is, working but still learning. She's almost the finished article. So, what's on your mind? Tell me what's going on with the old mine? This has all been a bit sudden, and I'm a little bit concerned to tell you truth. We don't need any more mess around here, and it's peaceful most of the time apart from the motocross boys making a racket now and again."

Price, responded in an empathetic, logical manner, "I understand your concerns, David. But let's be honest the old mine has left a right mess, a genuine blot on the landscape. No one has ever tidied it up. Now that we own it, we have a legal obligation to pay for reparations to the landscape, which we will do.

We even got a bill from the council yesterday and my colleague is dealing with that. All of that will happen, in time. Meanwhile, we have plans to widen our scope for a short period, make some money for two or three years with an open-cast mining operation, and after we finish our mining, we will close everything down and landscape the area. This is where we would welcome your help and pay you a handsome fee."

"Handsome fee? Wow, the best news I've had all day - well all year to tell you truth. I'm listening."

Price sensed the opportunity to press on with the crucial points. "We would like to pay you to *borrow* your land from you, for a couple of years, maybe three, and then hand it back to you just as we found it. A bond would be in place, upfront, to ensure the condition of the land met any conditions we might agree. For each year, we would pay double the income you presently make from the land, with an inconvenience bonus paid up front when we begin work, to enable you to move your livestock to a temporary piece of land in the area. I'm sure there are plenty to choose from for the right money, aren't there? A legal covenant would be set up to ensure adherence to everything we promise. If you do the maths, we are offering you more than twice what you earn now for three years, that's the bottom line, and yes there will be mining on the land and some noise. But hey, a heck of a pay rise, isn't it? How do you feel about it, David?"

David took a long slow sip of his Stella, and wiped his mouth, "Well I wasn't expecting that. A bit of a bombshell that is. I thought you were going to tell me you wanted to fix the fences, repair the roads, and sort me out with a few quid. Bloody hell. A lot to take in there, a lot to think about for sure. But like Liz said earlier, where's the catch?"

"I assured you and your wife earlier there was no catch, and I meant it. But I would like to show you something if I may?"

From the inside poacher pocket of his gilet, hung over the back of a chair, Price produced a map. Identical to the other map he had already marked up with the farmer's names and their property boundaries. This map was clean and unmarked. He showed it to David and pointed out the land associated with the drift mine, together with the other farmland nearby, including that belonging to David.

"So, David, here you can see the mine and the land we own and here is yours." Price carefully marked on the map in blue biro David's land.

David agreed, "Yes, that section is my land all right."

Price continued, this time producing a red biro, "And here is some other land owned by someone else, I presume this is your neighbour? Can you help me out with this one? I don't have that information. It was a real struggle to track you down David, I had to ask around." Price lied. He knew exactly who owned every square metre of the neighbouring land, but let the conversation run.

David helped him out, "Well, the other land is owned by two people, not one. Robert Carter and

Maggie Powell. Maggie is my cousin. Why do you need to know?"

This was another small milestone moment coming up for Price, and he watched for David's reaction to it, "David, my company can work our drift mine and our piece of land and nothing else if we need to. But the way *we* can *all* make a lot more money involves an opencast mining operation, and to do that we need all this land, not just yours. If everyone is on board, we can do the deal I described to you for both Maggie and Robert. But I would need to discuss that with them. So, this is not a catch, but an opportunity if everyone will agree to it. Depends, if all the people concerned would like to make a pile of money - or not. What do you think?"

"OK, look, I'll tell you where I stand. In principle, I am interested, if the money is right and all the other things are as you say they are. But I need to give it some thought and speak to Liz. Like I said this is all a bit quick to take in."

"Thank you, David, I appreciate it. In the meantime, do you have contact details for your neighbours? Maybe I can give them a call rather than knock on their doors. Oh, and apologies for turning up on your doorstep unexpected earlier. I didn't have many options - Blaenavon is a bit of a mystery, isn't it?"

"No worries, I understand. Look, I'm happy to give you the mobile numbers for Robert and Maggie, I don't see much of them, but I know they will be fine with that. Tell them you spoke to me. I might even send them a message myself later to give them a heads up. So where are you from Jason, do you live around here?"

"No, not anymore. I have a home in Wales, but I live most of the year in Barcelona. My family were originally from Blaenavon, but we moved away when I was a kid."

When David Davies went home later that evening, he opened his laptop. He wanted to find out as much as possible about the entrepreneurial randomer who turned up, out of the blue, on his doorstep earlier. David had lived in Blaenavon all his life and had gone to school there. He thought something didn't add up about Jason Price, who was only a few years older than him. They may even have gone to the same junior school together. Something rang a bell somewhere in his head.

Chapter 21

Found Out

Nick Savvas finished filling his dishwasher late evening in Sitges when a WhatsApp message from Jason Price pinged into his iPhone.

"I met your old farming buddy David Davies earlier. Nice dog. Not keen on his wife though, a bit of a feisty handful. I didn't pass on your regards to him for obvious reasons. But we had a beer and a long chat. He's not stupid, and he can see that there's nothing to lose and everything to gain from the offer, and so he should. Looks like Davies is up for it, and I think the other two farmers will follow suit. Meeting the councillor tomorrow. Catch you soon."

Savvas looked up from his phone, and glanced at Mia, "Jason has met the first farmer, David Davies, remember I told you about the guy I bumped into in the pub with his sheepdog - decent bloke. Sounds like he's up for it. Shit – this is happening for real? I'm getting nervous and excited both at the same time."

Mia took off her reading glasses, placed them down and looked back, "Are you still OK with all of it? I know how much it worried you."

"Yeah, of course, I'm OK. We will have to pay Jason for a stake in the farmland in a month or two. A hefty chunk from our savings accounts, but we can afford it. Besides, the return on that investment will eclipse everything, won't it? I'm not entirely comfortable with how he is going about it. He says we aren't breaking any laws, but I'm not so sure. Now that Declan is on board, the three of us are officially directors of the new mining company set up by Jason and I should have a say in things further down the line. We'll see how that goes, they are the businessmen, not me."

Mia displayed her underwhelmed look, "Hardly reassuring, is it?"

"But I'm the one with the technical knowledge, they will have to listen to me, won't they?" Savvas's voice didn't inspire confidence when he said it.

Mia was also aware of Dee Munchetty, and the rekindled interest in making a documentary, which had carried over from the aborted project in China. Mia realised how much it meant to Savvas, "What about the woman from National Geographical Nick? Is she still keen?"

"Yeah, she is. I decided to keep her in the loop and well informed. I'm almost more excited about her than the mining profits. Blaenavon is a unique location - hard to put into words what it might mean to the scientific community when the news breaks, things will go crazy. Which reminds me, I need to check on a few more pieces of information for her. She said she might be in the UK when I go to Wales. She might even come down and check it out."

"Have you told Jason about her?"

"Not exactly."

"What? You mean not at all?"

"Not yet, I was meaning to tell him, but I forgot. When I tell him, he'll be bang up for it, you know what he's like. Especially if he thinks they might interview him. On the other hand, maybe I'll do the interviewing - after all, Blaenavon is my discovery, not his."

Once again Mia shook her head in disbelief at her husband's conceit, "I think you're getting a bit carried away with yourself - again. Besides, no one has done a deal with anybody yet. Many a slip and all that. Oh, and by the way, I think that Jason put you onto Blaenavon in the first instance, and not the other way round? Or am I wrong? He discovered it didn't he?"

Mia's, harsh, but fair words, stung. But they fell on deaf ears.

Savvas shrugged his shoulders and changed the subject, "I've got stuff to do. Then I'm going to bed."

~

The following morning after breakfast Savvas wandered off into his study, pulled out some lever arch files and opened his laptop. Overnight his head had filled with innovative ideas to share with

Dee Munchetty, ramping up in readiness for *their* documentary. He wanted to check on some facts and find some new contrasting comparisons with other rare earth mines - big profitable mines - that would pale into insignificance alongside Blaenavon's eventual remarkable statistics. He wanted added impact, she needed impressing, and he intended to ensure that she would be.

He logged on to the NSW University intranet. Next came the intricate series of navigation steps to the geology department portal and the files he had saved there almost a week ago. The plan was to refresh his mind with what he had researched and saved on previous occasions. He looked at the familiar portal page, with his login profile not requiring his password because he never bothered logging out. That was when he spotted an anomaly. He stared at the top line, in a bold, blue font, alongside his profile picture - and shuddered.

Nick Savvas - You last visited this page and these files two days ago.

"No, I bloody didn't. What the hell? Who did then?"

He knew immediately that the date showing as the previous viewing date of his files did not tie in with when he knew for certain he last visited them.

"Someone has been nosing around. For Christ's sake, are you kidding me?"

Savvas slammed the side of his fist onto his desk. The thump bounced the keyboard, along with several pens and pencils which hopped out of a desk tidy, scattering across his desk before they cascaded onto the oak floor.

Mia heard the commotion combined with a bunch of expletives coming from her husband's study and poked her head around the door. A worried look from Savvas suggested he had encountered an IT problem.

"Mia, can you give me a minute, please? I think it might be important and serious."

Mia built websites, ran international digital marketing campaigns, and often found herself assisting Savvas with technical glitches, more often than not of the self-inflicted variety. After a brief explanation concerning his alarming discovery, Mia sat for ten minutes at the laptop, as she made some simple backup checks to see if she could uncover anything.

And she did, explaining in her calm and collected Spanish accent, "There we go, Lauren Eaves. She is the person who viewed your stuff. Does that name ring any bells? Do you know her? Because Lauren certainly knows you. She is either a lecturer or a student, or at least someone affiliated with the college and with an active login. Oh, and Nick, I'm sorry to tell you, she didn't just stumble across it with one click. Lauren Eaves has viewed it several times – at length – and saved exported copies of the files for herself."

"What? Downloaded my files? Are you sure?"

"Nick, I'm sure, 100%. I do this for a living. She did it. I'm telling you she did. OK?"

"Jesus. So, who is she? I don't recognise her name, certainly not a lecturer in the geology department, or any other department as far as I know. Can you look at some of the student registration information? Start with some of my lectures, maybe she latched on to me from there?"

With some diary checking and verbal guidance from Savvas, Mia, tapped away at the keyboard, with an answer moments later, "Yes. Yes, there she is. One of your former students. I can't access her personal or contact details, even if I could, you might get into serious hot water with HR or the Dean. Why don't you check your social media? Most of the kids follow you, don't they?"

Savvas stepped away from his computer monitor and began scrolling through his social media accounts on his phone. He generally used them for business and even then, only on the odd, rare occasion, "OK, I found her. Lauren Eaves, from Westonia - wherever that is. Looks as though we connected via a few of my accounts. Including my Facebook of all things. I keep telling myself to tighten my settings up on this stuff. And damn it, why the hell didn't I log out of my NSW portal?"

With some simple digging around between them, he and Mia soon formed a picture of Lauren. Mia commented, "She is living in the UK, in South Wales, studying for an MSc in geology. Her family are mineral miners from Western Australia. What are you going to do Nick? What if she suspects you're onto something in Blaenavon? Although let's face it she already does suspect something, doesn't she? More a question of what she intends to do with what she has found out?"

"I don't know what I'm going to do yet. I need to think about it. She could ruin everything, and we haven't even started yet. Jason's going to hit the roof and Declan will go ballistic - probably with Jason to start with and then with me. He won't be a happy man. I need to nip this Lauren Eaves thing in the bud. I am going to have to speak with her. I can contact her using Facebook Messenger, or what the hell, I can somehow get her number from the University and ring her direct."

Alarm bells started ringing inside Nick Savvas's head, which was at that moment shrouded by his hands.

Chapter 22

Old News

Years of experience told Price that the first meeting under his belt with David *Dai* Davies went well - it went far better than he had expected. Following the meeting in the pub, Price managed to resist the powerful urge to make a call to Robert Carter and Maggie Powell on the same evening. Instead, he slept on it. He decided to wait until lunchtime the next day, by which time he hoped they might have received a positive message from Davies, providing him with some additional leverage.

Thinking to himself, *"There is no substitute for a personal referral."*

Price would know in a few hours. A breakfast of scrambled eggs on toast and a preliminary meeting with a local councillor awaited him during the morning.

A prompt response email had arrived from the Coal Authority, confirming the mining licence. The change of ownership purchase of the drift mine, with an existing thirty-year agreement, made it a quick and easy formality. A complete contrast to the frustrating 233 days to wait, due to the Native Title issues experienced by Harry Eaves on the other side of the world to obtain a similar licence.

Price felt chuffed with himself and muttered as he double-checked the Coal Authority email, *"We are now in the mining business. All we need next is a nod from the council to get our hands on the farmers land."*

Price had arranged the informal meeting with the local councillor and mayor, Augusta Mertens, just before he left Spain. She owned a local law firm but dedicated a considerable proportion of her time to serving the local community. A brief email exchange between them included a summary of his intentions, which outlined the prospect of some local investment providing local jobs and his hopes to meet as soon as possible. He needed to tick things off his list, and waiting for other people to make up their minds on certainties like land or coal licences meant not taking control. All Price could visualise was succeeding and he intended to get there in a hurry.

They met late morning in a smart little hotel in town just before the busy lunchtime period. Price spotted a woman whom he assumed was Augusta Mertens, as soon as she arrived, bang on time. For some reason, he expected an older woman, not the slim, navy trouser suited blonde woman with her hair in an immaculate bun, who strode with purpose in his direction. She smiled and acknowledged a few other local women as she breezed through the hotel lounge.

Price didn't get the chance to fully rise out of his seat to greet Mertens. She took the initiative, and held out her hand on the move, from two metres away and shook his as he hastily managed to stand, "Jason? Well, you're the only man in the room so a good guess. How are you?"

"Augusta, a pleasure to meet you. I'm good thank you and thank you for seeing me at such short notice. I have business in town this week and I'm so glad you could catch up with me. I thought it important that we should meet. My business partners and I are keen to make a start on our ambitious project within the next month if we can."

"Please, call me Gussie, everyone does. And I'm always pleased to move things around in my diary if a meeting might lead to some positive developments for the town."

Price organised two coffees and made some small talk which included a summary of his entire rags to riches story, not attempting to obscure the dazzling and expensive Swiss timepiece strapped to his wrist. His extravagance, worth more than many of the houses in the county, did not go unnoticed by Mertens. She was beginning to wonder why she was there. The normally more circumspect Price had let his guard slip back into his natural mode. An unusual oversight for him - he had not stayed *on message*.

Mertens wanted to learn about job creation, the longevity of the business, promoting the success of the town, its history, and a possible PR spin story. Despite Price presenting some facts about the new mining business using his laptop, she only got glimpses, intertwined with segments about his splendid Spanish lifestyle and the trappings of success.

Mertens felt rather underwhelmed with Price and what he stood for. She harboured strong reservations about whether he intended to deliver on any of his promises. *"Is this guy really into dirty coal mines to scrape in a small profit?"*

His message to her didn't add up. He said he wanted to return to his roots, but his only connection appeared as no more than a geriatric uncle, who lived in a nursing home in town and once worked in Big Pit. Price's true local boy story didn't add up either - yes born in the town, but left at eleven years of age and had never returned.

Mertens pressed him on the 'jobs promise' and what he hoped to achieve after their meeting, "What is it you need from the council, Jason? How can we ensure you provide the long term jobs you just alluded to? And with the minimal environmental impact?"

A minor wake-up call from Mertens. Price had a sudden realisation that he needed to raise his game, "Augusta – *Gussie* – I beg your pardon. Perhaps my excitement of arriving back in town and seeing our project unfold has caused me to drift off the subject and get ahead of myself. I think one indication of our commitment will become apparent when we honour an outstanding fee for reparation work already carried out by the council. I agree the remainder of the land around our new acquisition is a mess. Image and perception are important to us. After all, we are building a brand and intend to promote our new venture not run it down."

"Thank you, Jason. Good to hear. A positive step in the right direction."

Still thinking on his feet Price continued with his insincere sales chat, "Gussie, I see so much potential for the town. We have ideas to develop the mountain area alongside our mine working into a mountain bike park and zip line called *Adrenalin Central*. Blaenavon could attract a much higher percentage of leisure visitors if we get this right. Look it won't be Disneyland, but it will be a terrific attraction."

Mertens nodded in appreciation, "Adrenalin Central. Sounds like an adrenalin junkie destination and a great idea. But I'm afraid you may need to back off on the zip line and show some caution. We are a UNESCO World Heritage Site here in Blaenavon. We are not a theme park. UNESCO removed Liverpool's World Heritage status last year; so I can assure you we will not risk that happening to us for the sake of a zipline."

Her remark stunned Price for a moment, so he digressed and pressed on, "An excellent point Gussie - the zipline isn't integral to our operation. We are in this for the long term," he began ticking things off on his fingers, "We possess all the right credentials. We have high profile mining experts invested in the business who run the old drift mine and my team now own a mining licence. Whilst we appreciate the council's approval is not a deal-breaker for us, it would make life easier for us, as we start to recruit and commit further investment – if we have full support and cooperation from you and your colleagues. No special favours, or anything like that. Just a good old fashioned, open book, collaborative approach."

What Price meant, was that if the council gave a nod of approval to the project, their reassurance would boost confidence with the farmers, encouraging them to want to come on board.

Mertens body language appeared more amenable than a few minutes earlier, "Jason, please send me a copy of the slides you presented to me today. I will share them with colleagues at the council. I'm impressed by the ideas you put forward. I wish you every success with the business. In principle, I see no reason for us to put any hurdles in your way. Now, I need to get going I have another meeting in half an hour. Nice meeting you, Jason. Please keep in touch."

They stood up and shook hands. Mertens disappeared through the lounge and out into the car park, Price's face was a picture - smirking with clenched fists gently pumping.

Mertens did not have another meeting, she did have another busy day ahead of her but simply didn't wish to continue the discussion any longer than was necessary. She had met dozens of chancers over the years, and something about Jason Price and his hasty approach to the project bothered her. Most businesspeople would take several months getting an operation up and running, yet he was going to start almost immediately. She remained open-minded, although not convinced of the integrity of the man and decided to ask around about him and his background.

Back at her office, Gussie Mertens turned to Steve, a senior colleague, hammering away at a defenceless keyboard on a nearby desk and asked him, "Steve, if you don't mind me asking, you went to junior school in town in the early '70s didn't you?"

Steve looked up from his spreadsheet and smiled, "The grey hair - what's left of it. A dead giveaway isn't it. Yes, I did, Blaenavon man and boy."

"You don't look a day over sixty Steve. But didn't you have a significant birthday last year or the year before?"

Steve, looked bemused, "A long way off retirement Gussie, but I'm sixty-one. I know that comes a bit of a shock, but I put it down to a good moisturising regime. Why do you want to know?"

"Cast your mind back fifty years. Yes, fifty years, sorry, work with me on this one. Someone called Jason Price. Maybe you went to school with him?"

The playful banter stopped, and Steve's bemused look changed to a sullener expression, "Bloody hell. That name is a blast from the past, a long, long, time ago. I remember him, or at least I remember the name, vaguely, although he went to a different junior school in town to mine. I knew of him before he and his family left town after what happened."

Gussie's, eyes widened, "*Happened?* Kettle's on Steve - what's the story?"

Steve sat with Gussie for ten minutes and shared the facts he could recall and some of the rumours surrounding what happened to Rhys Price back in 1973.

"But you know what people are like, neighbours, and friends of friends, before long half a dozen, horrific, morbid stories began to circulate. Most of it rubbish, but there were some common themes."

Gussie remained intrigued to know more, "Themes? Like, what?"

"From what I can remember, he didn't tell anyone for hours where they were playing. Most kids play together, don't they? How come Rhys went on to the ice on his own? Maybe because his brother, *Jason*, threw his bobble hat across the ice and told him to go and fetch it? And then pelted him with rocks - allegedly. He also bullied his younger brother remorselessly as well – hated him - so people said."

Gussie asked, "Was any of it true, do you think?"

"They reckon his parents spent more time in the pub than at home - his father had a violent reputation – then Jason confided in an auntie and told her what happened. Did she divulge anything to anyone? No one will ever know, she passed away years ago. Only one person can tell you for sure what happened that day, and it sounds as though he just reappeared here in

Blaenavon. Bit of a shock to hear about him popping back up on the radar - so unexpected. From what you say, he hasn't come anywhere near this town since it happened. Don't blame him. Awful thing to deal with."

"But the police didn't intervene did they Steve? So, therefore, it was an accident with some gossip attached. He didn't kill his brother, did he?"

"Who knows, something bad happened with a lot of background gossip surrounding it. Perhaps, there was more to it. Sickens me to think about it. Let's give the guy a break, shall we?"

Gussie's curiosity got the better of her and after her conversation, she went online and accessed some old local newspaper archives. A few pictures of the family emerged, including one image of the two brothers together, shoulder to shoulder, sitting on a park bench holding ice creams.

The features were the same, the lack of hair and a fuller face didn't disguise who she could see in the image. One brother smiling, happy and playful licking his ice cream. The other staring straight down the lens of the camera, with a stern look - unmistakable - Jason Price, the millionaire land speculator.

Mertens viewed every grainy pixel of the old black and white digital image, *"Another bad penny turning up. I suppose every small town has them, and now here's another one, come back to get his hands dirty again by the sound of it. Maybe he's come back to make amends for a tragedy - a freak accident? Or maybe if you're born round, you don't die square? And I'm supposed to help him get his shit together - great. He had better be squeaky clean, otherwise, this could get interesting."*

~

The same day, before Price had met Gussie Mertens, Elizabeth Davies and her husband David had sat around their breakfast table debating the pros and cons of their random visitor from the previous evening.

Elizabeth, had seen and heard it all over the years, nothing ever shocked or surprised her, and her suspicious nature didn't take long to manifest itself over the bacon and eggs, "Love, you and I both know, if something sounds too good to be true, then guess what? Yeah, Jason Price and his cronies are up to something - that's what I think. Coal mining, my arse. We need to see the colour of his money first - before we agree to anything."

David didn't expect anything less from his wife. She was often the voice of reason and didn't take crap from anyone, "Liz, I know, it sounds like a scam, but the guy is on the level. Google him - he's minted. He owns all kinds of property and land businesses, and he comes from Blaenavon originally, he's done well for himself. What's your problem? Is it because he turned up as if he stepped off a page from a Sunday supplement? Is that it?"

Elisabeth would not let it go, "No. Listen, get real. This is Blaenavon, not London, or Las *bloody*

Vegas. People don't turn up around here *waving wads of money* around under other people's noses. That doesn't happen, neither does winning the lottery."

"OK. I get it. We need to tread carefully, and we will. *I will.* I promise. Besides, he wants to speak with Maggie and Rob to make them the same offer. I've already tipped them off to expect a call from him. Let's see what they think. But they sounded dead, keen, and I don't blame them. And Rob hasn't got a *pot to piss in,* has he? He'll bite Price's hand off. Look, I need to crack on, see you in a bit," David and Bea headed off in the old Land Rover.

Twenty-five minutes later David's phone rang on its usual loud setting, in his coat pocket, "Alright Liz, what's up? Won the lottery, have we, babe?"

Elizabeth had some news, "Very funny. You bloody wish. No, not exactly. I've been busy, doing some research and asking around. I told you Jason Price was bad news."

David's smile vanished when he heard his wife, "Why? What do you mean?"

"Remember when you were in junior school, and that young lad drowned in the Keepers Pond. All the fuss about it at the time, you told me about it a few times years ago. You probably can't remember it happening it was so long ago. I'll bet your mother told you more about it as you were growing up. Rhys Price, he was in your class in school. Well, guess what, Jason Price is the older brother. Yes, *that* Jason Price."

Chapter 23

Contact

Lauren reached for her headphones and settled in on QF8001 for the long flight from Perth to London via Singapore. She somehow found herself upgraded to business class on an Emirates *partner* flight instead of the original Qantas.

She smiled to herself, *"I mess them around – twice - and this is the thanks I get – an upgrade."*

A few hours earlier, another emotional family farewell left everyone bleary-eyed, with promises all around to keep in touch more often than before. Harry seemed fully recovered, firing all cylinders, and making plans for the transition to his rare earth mining. Everything depended on it, the family needed the money and the security that came with it, but they had a tough nine months ahead of them until they could start in earnest. Even then there remained a small element of uncertainty whether everything would go to plan and the venture would be a profitable success.

Harry wanted to share Lauren and Jack's optimism, instead, he kept a more circumspect lid on it.

Meanwhile, a resolute Lauren had a full itinerary for when she arrived back in Wales – get to the bottom of the Blaenavon project, and find out if there was a business opportunity there to help take the pressure off her father. She sensed the excitement building - something might come of it - something big.

She welcomed the free inflight Wi-Fi and charging point. After take-off, Lauren's phone resurrected itself from the dead. A bunch of messages pinged in from friends and family, even a few friends in Wales looked forward to her return, *"Where are you?"- "Have you emigrated?" - "Let's go for a 'two for one Wednesday' when you get back."*

Her chuckling came to an abrupt stop when she scrolled down to a Facebook Messenger message from a familiar name, Nick Savvas. *"Hello Lauren, how are you? I can see you're now continuing your studies in the UK. Please can you contact me as soon as possible, it's important. Here is my mobile number... – Best wishes - Nick Savvas."*

Lauren's stomach somersaulted the moment she read it, "Shit, *shit.*"

She knew. She realised straight away that Nick Savvas had caught wind of something. But what? How?

Lauren squirmed a little as the sumptuous seat became far less comfortable, then she decided to front it up, and pondered, *"Play it cool, maybe he doesn't know too much."* She typed a reply to delay him for a while and buy herself some thinking time. *"Hello, Nick, nice to hear from you. I'm fine. Yes, I'm still studying - doing an MSc in the UK. Sorry can't speak right now, I'm about to get on a flight from Perth to the UK – I just went to a wedding. And I think it's the middle of the night with you. Bye for now. Lauren."* She clicked send, *"There, done. That should do him for a while. Why should he have all the fun and make all the money, that's if there is money, sitting there in Blaenavon. One thing's for sure if there is any, and he's not on top of it, then it will be fair game."*

Lauren's grit and determination would not subside. She had the bit between her teeth, and one way or another she would find some answers. She also expected to come under a bit more pressure from Savvas before long but thought she would deal with that when it arrived.

Savvas picked up the message and turned to Mia, "She replied. She says she is on a flight back to the UK from Australia. I'm going to give her a day or two, and if she hasn't called me first, I'll chase her up. But first I need to call in a favour from someone and get hold of her number."

He had an old friend in the admin department at the University, who once received a glowing reference from him whilst applying for an internal position. An innocuous-sounding request via email, purporting to need the number for an urgent intern placement, soon provided the contact details he needed. Not standard procedure, but nothing ever was with Nick Savvas, and the request caused no ripples or questions.

Thirty-six hours passed. Lauren had made the journey to her accommodation in Cardiff - rested, slept, ate, battled with the jet lag, and rested again. She called her friend, managed to borrow a battered little VW beetle for a couple of days and planned to go to Blaenavon the following day with all the kit borrowed from Uncle Jack.

Savvas had heard nothing from Lauren. Unable to wait a minute longer for a reply he picked up his mobile and tapped in her number.

Under most normal circumstances, Lauren would not answer an unknown number on her mobile. That day, her body clock was still out of sync, with a lot happening at home, and she needed to get up to speed back in the UK. College work and finding a weekly pay cheque needed some attention - she took the call.

"Hello?"

A vaguely familiar Australian voice spoke, "Good morning Lauren, this is Nick Savvas from the University of New South Wales, long time no speak. I hope you're well. How is your course going?"

A startled Lauren responded, "Oh, *Professor*, I mean Nick, gosh. I mean hi, I meant to call you. So sorry, jet lag and everything else. You know."

At the back of her mind, Lauren expected Savvas to contact her again, either on Facebook Messenger or even an email. With either of those, she would have digested his words before giving some thought to her answer.

Savvas's phone call out of the blue stunned her, but she didn't wilt and gathered her thoughts. "Well nice to speak with you again Nick. Although I'm surprised that you have my number? There must be an emergency or something?"

"Well, not exactly an emergency, but something important. That is to say something personal concerning my business activities has come to my attention and I hoped you could help me clear it up. Before I take it any further."

Savvas had complete confidence that what Mia showed him was correct and that Lauren could only be bad news. So he took the strong initial stance and hoped for a nervous reaction.

That stung, and Lauren's tone slowed and quietened, "Further? Take what further Professor Savvas? I'm not sure what you mean?"

"Lauren, you *do* know what I mean. You've nosed around my private folders and files at the University. You must know I can see that you downloaded several files. Would you mind explaining yourself? This is your opportunity to tell me why you took them."

"Oh that...I'm sorry, Professor Savvas, I had no idea it was an issue. I didn't have your contact details and I was in a rush. You know I'm working on a rare earth dissertation, and I stumbled across a few things on the portal. Nothing encrypted, so I presumed the information was fair game for anyone to look at. Is there a problem with that?"

"The problem Lauren is that the files belong to me. In my personal and private folder. Pretty obvious to anyone, don't you think? Or maybe you don't?"

"Well obvious to some people perhaps, but not to others by the looks of things. I mean I had no idea they were private. Anyone could access them, just like I did. They were just there, and helpful to me."

"Lauren, you need to know, that I have clients who have paid a great deal of money for the work involved in those files. These people will not tolerate interference in their business. They have investments at stake, and you could be jeopardising those investments. Do you realise that you have broken the law?"

In the space of one minute, Lauren's emotions switched from tentative apprehension to annoyance, "I don't think accessing files available to anyone with genuine access to the Uni portal constitutes breaking the law, do you? Oh, and I don't know where you got my phone number from, but I did not give it to you. Isn't that a breach of GDPR or something? Also, the college takes harassment from a male member of staff towards a female student extremely seriously. So maybe you need to back off."

Savvas remained silent, letting Lauren's retort sink in for a moment.

Before he could respond, Lauren kept the pressure on and rolled the dice with a gamble, "While we are on the subject of the law, do the local town council know what you are doing in Blaenavon? Or is that one private too?"

Savvas lost his cool and replied in a threatening tone, "You listen to me Lauren, you don't know what you're getting yourself into. These are serious people you're dealing with. You're the one who needs to back off and mind your own business."

"Nick – do one."

The line went dead. Lauren ended the call and sat on the sofa in her lounge, trembling, "Oh my God. What have I said? What have I done?"

Late that evening, and early breakfast time *ahead* in Western Australia, she decided to call her father and Uncle Jack on a three-way group call. She felt more in control and calmer than she did earlier in the day and had spent several hours reflecting on the situation. Lauren was a thick-skinned terrier, but Savvas's attitude and words had rattled her. The strange thing about his anxious call was that by doing so, he had validated everything.

Lauren had no doubts in her mind, *"He is doing something he shouldn't be doing."*

The video call opened up and Lauren explained to Harry and Jack what Savvas had said and how she retaliated.

Harry expressed his concern, "Lauren, how many times have you got yourself into trouble with that hot head of yours. He might report you."

"He won't. Not a chance. But he's not happy. I'd say on a pissed off scale of one to ten, he might be maybe at a nine right now. When I mentioned the local council, I could tell it spooked him, he sounded shaken. Dad, I'm going up there tomorrow morning. I've got all the gear, so let's find out where we stand after that. The results won't lie, and they will be instantaneous on the spectrometer."

Jack, wished her luck, adding, "Just be bloody careful Lauren. Hope you find the *good stuff.*"

"I will be careful. Remember, he more or less admitted the significance of Blaenavon, and didn't tell me we are too late, did he? So no doubt everything is up for grabs, and not enough people in authority know what he is up to, maybe including the farmers. But we can change that and help them out. I can't sit around and watch Savvas rip those people off, they are sat on a fortune, with no idea. They are entitled to a fair share, and then if they look favourably on me for helping them, then that's great too."

The next few days were going to change everything for a lot of people.

Chapter 24

Cold Feet

When the phone line went dead Mia could tell by the look on her husband's face that the conversation did not go according to plan. He glanced back at her before avoiding further eye contact, instead, he gazed at the floor tiles and shook his head from side to side, muttering a broad selection of expletives.

Irritated and confused, Savvas broke the silence, "She couldn't give a shit. I pushed her hard, and she bounced it straight back at me."

Mia comments, "I picked up a few words and comments coming from the phone. She's got some balls – I'll give her that. Christ sake I would have run a mile if I were her."

"Yeah, I wish. She even suggested we are doing something without the council's knowledge. I mean where did she hear that one from? That bloody girl is a threat to everything now. I don't know what to do

I need some fresh air. Grab a jacket, let's move out of here, take a walk and come up with a plan. My head is spinning."

Mia and Nick Savvas found themselves walking hand in hand for miles along the Sitges seafront and promenade with its bars and large luxury homes. The sound of gentle surf pulling on the sand soothed the tense atmosphere that existed.

"Nick, how the hell did we find ourselves in this situation? One minute we were gliding along effortlessly, everything was easy, and all of sudden we are stressed to the max."

"Jason's bloody sixtieth party, and me and my big mouth, that's how it all started."

It was a late Mediterranean spring morning, cool, and sunny, with most of the bars and cafes open for lunch. Savvas said he could eat something, "Never too early for a tapa, is it?"

As they sat and talked Mia probed her husband for genuine answers, "Nick, every time I ask you all I hear back is a fob off. You seem happy to keep going with all of this, yet you could walk away from it tomorrow, today even. One phone call to Jason, to tell him you don't need the hassle. And Declan Ryan sounds like a nasty piece of work – why not leave him to Jason? What's holding you up?"

"Mia, we've got enough money. *Enough*. We're content, right? I thought I was until now. Look around you, can you see those yachts down there in the marina? Can you see all these properties behind us worth millions? This is the moment to keep going and have some of that, all of that is within easy reach. There, for the taking."

"Aren't you forgetting something Nick?"

"What?"

"National Geographical, the TV documentary and all the plaudits in the scientific community you mentioned that go along with this project. You said it wasn't all about the money. So is that the main reason? Or isn't it? Or is it both? You need to make your mind up."

"I suppose the TV thing is important. Of course, it is. I spent twenty years lecturing about geology and then consulting claiming I'm some kind of an expert. Great, now here's the cherry on the top. Why not, I worked hard, I know my stuff. Some recognition would be fantastic. Yes, that's what I want. Sorry, does that sound big-headed? Athletes and footballers win medals and cups, film stars win Oscars, and academics win gongs. But the money is also recognition, isn't it? Payback for all my years of hard work."

"I don't blame you - I completely understand. But there is something else to consider. Something you keep overlooking."

"Go, on?"

Mia looked serious when she said the words, "Fraud. Prison."

Savvas, shuffled in his seat, "I know. I think about it every day. What we are doing is wrong, it *is* illegal. Fraud and deception are illegal the last time I checked.

I know it is, I'm not stupid. I didn't need to check - I already knew that for God sake. As much as Jason Price claims it will all come out in the wash when the open cast coalmine suddenly discovers rare earth minerals under false pretences, is all bullshit. All he needs to do is tell the farmers about the true value of their land and cut them in."

"Then why doesn't he? What's stopping him? Then everyone can relax and not worry about anything."

"He won't for two reasons. First of all, Jason Price is a greedy bastard. If Jason cuts the farmers in, we have to dilute the value of the profits between various farmers, their wives and anybody else claiming some entitlement. Maybe even the council too. We can't be certain. And if we tell the farmers upfront, the land belongs to them, so we won't receive an equal share. They might offer us peanuts. Half a per cent? One per cent? Who knows? The second reason is if we tell the farmers now what their land is worth, who's to say they will even agree to partner with us? They could say thanks a million, pardon the pun, say cheerio to us, and sort it out with another organisation, like the Chinese or the Americans. I could end up getting side-lined and wouldn't get the same recognition. We'll all have nothing. Mia, if we do it, then there is only one way – I hate to say it - Jason's way."

"There is a way, Nick. One which keeps you out of prison if it ever got that bad. You insist to Jason and Ryan that you tell the farmers in advance. You don't want any part of it otherwise. The farmers see you as the genius that makes them all fortunes and they look after you. And you can go ahead and make the Nat geo documentary. Jason and Ryan need to take their chances?"

"Ryan's just paid a small fortune for the old drift mine. He won't go for it, not a chance. He is now fully committed and wants everything. Maximum returns."

Mia, persevered, "Nick, have you seen the TV documentaries about the inside of British prisons? A man of your age, with no criminal past and no vicious bone in your body - the other prisoners would humiliate you and eat you alive in there. Get real, will you? This is serious. You need to find a way out of this before it gets too late. This Lauren girl is sharp, she will not let go. I'm telling you. By the way, someone will take the mine off Ryan's hands, someone will need it for the same reason you do. He owns an asset."

"OK, I need to think about it. Please give me some time…and you know the worst thing about all this is the farmers? They'll end up with next to nothing. They are decent hard-working people. I hate myself for doing this, everything about it is wrong and illegal."

Early evening Mia had some work to catch up on, so Nick Savvas decided to go for one of his regular runs. For hours, the conversation with Lauren Eaves, her snooping and veiled threats had been eating him up. He had looked back at his original message to her and even considered calling her again, but didn't. If it weren't for her, he would have been calm and in control, prepared to push on with Price and Ryan and see it through.

The call earlier on with Lauren, and Mia's heartfelt opinions, forced the realisation and magnitude of the risks to sink in deeper. The project scared Savvas. He was out of his depth - his conscience and heart were no longer in it. Yet he wanted the kudos for the Nat Geo programme. A huge dilemma. He had a big ego and never lacked confidence, but deep down he realised he could not under any circumstances do criminality. For any normal human being, serving a sentence in an overcrowded, hostile British prison is an awful and unpleasant experience to endure. Price would argue it would never come to that, but the thought of it terrified and sickened Savvas. Unthinkable. With his mind made up, he knew his next move meant an uncomfortable, and unpleasant discussion with Price.

Chapter 25

Full On

There were two names and numbers written in blue ink on a page of Jason Price's *Moleskine* notebook - with a bold line drawn under each of them. Price had also saved both numbers into his mobile phone, and couldn't decide which one to call first.

Early afternoon, his shift at the local supermarket ended an hour ago, and Robert Carter and his spaniel were enjoying a walk near the river when his phone rang. He had been expecting, hoping, for a call from *someone*, and answered it without any hesitation.

Jason Price introduced himself and explained that fellow farmer David Davies gave him Robert's number the day before.

"Yes, Dai's been in touch with me. He said he had spoken to you, and met you in the pub. He told me a bit about your plans and said you would call."

"That was kind of David to let you know. Yes, there are a lot of exciting things happening, and I just came out of an extremely positive meeting with one of your local councillors, Gussie Mertens. I explained our business proposition to her, and she says her team will give it their full support. However, my colleagues and I would welcome your involvement in the project. We can offer you a profitable suggestion, along the lines of what we offered David. I assume he mentioned something to you. I should say that I also need to get in touch with Maggie Powell."

Robert responded, "Don't worry about Maggie, we've already had a chat. Dai told her what's going on. She's interested to find out more about it too. Same as me."

"Thank you for letting me know Robert. Then perhaps I can meet you and Maggie if you are both available. Today? Later this afternoon? Unless either of you is working or you have something else on? I appreciate this is short notice."

"I'm OK to meet up later, I'll check with Maggie and call you straight back."

David had been in touch with Robert and Maggie, although since then David had discovered another piece of information concerning Jason Price's childhood. Rather than rock the boat, David decided to keep the knowledge to himself, for now, and let things play out.

Sure enough, two minutes later, Robert called Price back and arranged a meeting at a coffee shop in town. Robert confirmed Maggie would join them, "I also called Dai. He says he can't come - he's got something on, a bit too 'last minute' for him. So just the three of us Jason is that OK?"

It was more than OK. Later that afternoon Jason Price found himself meeting two of his three potential meal tickets in a trendy café. He went through the same information that he had with David Davies and made both Rob Carter and Maggie Powell the same offer. Loads more money for doing nothing, other than some inconvenience for a year or two. On the face of it an excellent offer, if all he intended doing was to scrape up some old coal dirt and make some money from it.

Price excused himself to visit the gents, as he wanted the pair to take a few minutes without him to share their thoughts.

Robert spoke first, "Well, Dai was spot on Maggie. But I wanted to hear it direct from the horse's mouth. I can't believe it, can you? Double what we've been making plus a bonus, and then they tidy it all up when they finish. Am I dreaming?"

Maggie's beaming face gave her answer, "I feel the same. Pinch me. What happens next? Did Dai tell you? He hasn't said anything to me. And where is he? What's more important than this? Sometimes I think he's on another planet. Honest to God."

Robert nodded, "Yeah, I wondered why he didn't come too. Just went a bit quiet if you ask me. What's he worried about? Everything will be legal. And what did Jason just call it, a covenant? Like a guarantee? Speak with Dai for me, will you Maggs? Check he's OK with all of this? I mean he's your cousin. He's been a bit strange with me on the odd occasion."

Maggie agreed, "Don't worry. I'll call him later when we are done here."

Price returned, he sensed from the body language and the residual hints of smiles that the pair shared some positive comments, "How are we doing? Another tea or coffee?"

In unison, both farmers politely declined another drink. Then Robert asked a question, "Maggie and I just had a little chat, and your offer seems like a fair one Jason. What happens now? When will things start?"

Price held back for a moment, rather than pounce with an excited reply, "I'm pleased you approve of the offer. I don't blame you. Yes, David asked me the same thing about the next steps. I will ask my legal guy to draft something up tomorrow, and we'll need a couple of signatures and witnesses. You may want to run it past a solicitor in town and ask them to handle it. If you do, we will reimburse you for whatever the legal fee is. I'm sure it won't be more than a few hundred pounds. If you're happy with everything, we would like to get our contract agreed upon as soon as possible. Within a week if we can, as my associate is getting access to the old drift mine handed over this week. Keys to padlocks and a bit of a briefing from the property management agent that sort of thing. I think they'll be glad it has a new owner - I'm sure you feel the same about it."

The trio exchanged email addresses, shook hands, and agreed to speak again over the coming days, before going their separate ways. Price now had a verbal agreement from all three farmers, and signed contracts would soon follow – or so he thought.

Maggie and Robert continued their conversation along the path back to their cars. When she sat alone in her car she called her cousin, "Dai, we just met that Price bloke. Exactly as you said, brilliant, and now he's getting some legal stuff together for us all to sign. I expected to see you. What's up?"

"What do you mean what's up?"

"Why didn't you come? Washing your hair, were you?"

"Yeah, funny. Besides, I met him last night, he told me everything then that he told you a few minutes ago."

Maggie sensed some reticence in her cousin, "So are you up for it then or not? He wants us to sign contracts this week. Me and Rob are happy."

David's answer was not the one Maggie expected, "I might be. Me and Liz are still talking about things. No rush after all is there? Make him sweat a bit. Might even get a better offer out of him if we push him harder. He's the one who is desperate to sort it out in such a hurry."

Maggie couldn't believe her ears, "Are you serious? Do you want to piss him off before we start? He might turn around and offer us less, instead of more. You should think that one through? Rob thinks all his

Christmas's just came at once. He's skint remember. And I'm not exactly loaded, am I?"

"I know Rob's skint. His bloody fault for being an idiot and spending half his time down the betting shop and the other half in the pub."

Agitated, Maggie's voice got a little louder, "Then you need to call Rob and tell him. Because I'm not going to explain it to him. I can't believe you sometimes." She ended the call in a huff and tossed her phone onto the seat next to her.

Maggie was not the only person having communication problems with David Davies. In the hour after he met with the two other farmers, Jason Price called him twice and left him one voice message. He did not get a reply, and could sense his blood pressure rising a few increments, *"Bloody farmers."*

By the time she got home, Maggie, decided she needed to call Rob and not rely on David to do it. She explained what David had said in their conversation.

A shocked Robert told her, "One of us needs to go around there and talk some sense into him. I think it should be you. Because if I see him, I might end up saying or doing something I regret. Bloody idiot. What's he playing at?"

"Rob, he said he would call you, and tell you what he's thinking himself. But you know what he and Liz are like, by the time they finish arguing about things, that could take days. If he calls you – *if* - stay calm, don't fly off the handle. You could make matters worse. I need to pop to see him after tea and get to the bottom of it. Leave him to me, Liz is OK with me."

After tea, that's exactly what Maggie did. The lights were on, David answered the door, "C'mon in. Where's Rob?"

Maggie said a quick hello to Liz, then answered David, "Same place as you were earlier - having a good think about things. That's when he calms down a bit. What's on your mind Dai? One minute you're all excited the next thing you go stone cold."

Over a cup of tea, David explained his reason for going cold. Liz interjected every other sentence until Maggie managed to obtain the full picture.

Maggie responded, "OK, fair enough, he's got a bit of history. I remember that story now. Hard to tell the truth from all the bullshit though if you ask me. Why can't people accept it was an accident? Instead, all the local busybodies had to make up some cock and bull story into something else because they didn't have satellite telly and mobile phones to play with back in the 1970s. That's all it was."

David shrugged his shoulders. Liz stayed surprisingly silent, but added, "Well it came as a bit of shock when I found out. He marched in here bold as brass, like lord of the bloody manor."

Maggie, looked up from her tea, "So what you're saying is you want to cut your nose off to spite your face? If the bloke's offering us good money, on a legal contract, I couldn't care less if he was Hannibal Lecter. We aren't giving the land away, are we? We are lending it to him. Look, what happened when he was a kid could have happened to anyone. Kids are kids. Let's move on. And to tell you the truth - I need the money - and Rob needs it more than me."

David looked more sympathetic than he did minutes earlier. His wife had other ideas though. She sat there impassive, poker-faced, with her arms folded and looked happy to stir the pot at any moment. David continued, "Maggie, let's not fall out over this. I wouldn't mind the extra money the same as you. I just don't like the bloke, something about him is not right. I want to think about it. Give us a day or so and we can sort it out. Price has rung me twice and left a message. He can wait."

Price's impatience became more evident, manifesting itself in a text message to Maggie later that evening, *"Can't get hold of David? Not returning any of my calls. Is he OK? Any ideas? Can you speak to him by any chance? Thank you, Jason."*

Maggie had a dilemma, whether to tell Price of her cousin David's second thoughts and jeopardize the contract or do nothing and let everything unravel, to the annoyance of Price. She realised something needed doing, so she took the initiative to keep him *on-side.*

Price answered the call before the second ring, "Maggie, hi, how is your evening going? Everything OK?"

"Hi, Jason, yes I'm OK, Rob's OK too, but Dai's playing silly games though. You met his wife, Liz, when you went to his house didn't you?"

Price could feel a *red flag* emerging, "Yes, I did meet David's wife. A bit of character. What's happened?"

Maggie used a ploy to deflect the issue away from David, by suggesting Liz was the fly in the ointment - true to some extent. But she decided not to disclose the knowledge of Price's childhood accident as a factor.

"Look, Jason, Dai and Liz are always cautious with money and taking risks. That's maybe why they have more money than me. This is another one of those situations. I spoke to him earlier on. He wouldn't tell me everything, but I know when he's holding back. I think they are just thinking it through. You need to show some patience. Leave it with me and I will try another approach with him and Liz tomorrow."

"Maggie, thank you for letting me know. I don't want to alarm you, but you *do* realise we need all three of you onboard - or the deal will be off the table? We need David to say yes – and soon."

With her head spinning, Maggie took a deep breath, "I will speak to him again in the morning. I can't promise anything. He is a stubborn so and so when he gets something into his head. But he's bound to realise this is a good offer and get his act together."

"Maggie, let me help you out with an extra incentive, for all three of you. As part of the contract, I mentioned a bonus payment. There's four grand each, in cash, for you and Robert. I'll give you two grand each first thing in the morning, eight-thirty, and the other two when David says yes and signs up. Let's call it a goodwill advance payment of your bonus.

Nothing that isn't already in your original offer - just a bit sooner for you that's all. I can see you in the morning with it."

"OK. Thanks, I appreciate it, so will Rob. Tomorrow, see you first thing. Do I tell Dai about the bonus?"

"If you need to. See how you go first without telling him. Then let me know. If we can't agree on a contract, then you will appreciate - there is no more bonus - there is nothing at all for anyone. So, do your best Maggie."

Maggie looked at her phone. She couldn't decide who to call next. Robert or David. She couldn't decide if ringing either of them would make much difference. David and Liz might not change their minds for a while, and maybe even not for two grand. "Shit, what am I going to do?"

Chapter 26

The Right Thing to Do

As agreed, the next morning Jason Price met Maggie and handed her a small white envelope. It contained £2000 in £20 notes. She thanked him and said she would speak with him later that day. As she started to set off to go to her part-time job Price commented, "I'll hang on to Rob's early bonus then shall I Maggie? I can give it to him when we get a result. Same for David."

"Rob knows about it. I told him last night. But yes, OK then, you keep it for now. No pressure, eh? Better sort out that feckless bloody cousin of mine."

Price started to feel agitated with negotiation slipping out of his tight grip as he put his trust in Maggie Powell. But he accepted that she represented his best option for the present time.

As he walked back to his car the heavens opened. By the time he sat inside soaking wet, he had a call coming in from Nick Savvas. "Hi Nick, good morning my friend, how is the Costa Brava sunrise this morning?"

Savvas's reply followed a moment's hesitation, and Price sensed in an instant that things may not be going to plan.

"Hi Jason, yeah the sunrise is as good as ever on the Med. Listen, mate, I need a long chat with you." Savvas could make out what sounded like heavy rain bouncing on the roof of Price's car and windscreen wipers going nineteen to the dozen, "Is now a good time?"

"Well, I'm parked up, wringing wet, and the weather is atrocious. So now is as good a time as any. A few moments ago I saw one of the farmers I met yesterday. We are still trying to sort out a few minor contractual issues. Nothing serious – I hope. What's on your mind, Nick?"

"Jason, I appreciate how much work you and Declan are putting into this project. Not least the significant investment already outlaid by Declan. But things are happening over here in Spain, behind the scenes and with Mia. My head has been spinning for a day or two to tell you truth. But I made a decision earlier, and I want to make it clear to you where I stand on the project."

A confused Price, let Savvas's words hang in the air for a moment, as he watched Maggie speed past on her way to work, giving him a cursory wave as she did. All of a sudden, his lower back was sticking to the leather seat, *"What the hell is he talking about?"*

Savvas's pre-prepared message rolled on, "I might need to formally step out of our arrangement and leave you to find another consultant. There are plenty out there and I can recommend some good ones to you. I'm sorry but I just can't carry on like this. This is wrong, deceitful, and bloody illegal. You know it is. I'm sorry mate, but I ain't taking one for the team."

"Whoa, hang on a minute, Nick. What do you mean *out*? Why? What's happened?"

"Jason when we all end up in a police station, with the detectives interviewing us and a fraud charge hanging over our heads, what do you expect me to say to them? 'I had no idea there were billions of dollars of rare earth minerals in the ground that we just bought for peanuts after we shafted those farmers.' They'll piss themselves laughing - so will a jury. But that isn't the worst of it and not the main reason why I can't go on. These people - these farmers – they deserve a right to the money sitting under their feet. Why should we steal it from them? Even if we dodge a bullet, and don't end up in prison, my conscience won't let me do it, Jason - it won't. We need to tell those farmers about what we know from the get-go."

Price could hear the panic and concern in Savvas's voice as the pace of his rant increased. "Jesus, Nick, where the hell did all that shit come from? Five minutes ago you were full-on, ready to join the Sunday Times rich list with me and Declan - or whatever Rupert Murdoch's version is back in Australia? Are you losing your mind?"

"No. I know what needs doing – the right thing. And now is the time."

Price's attitude switched in an instant into a more threatening one, "Well you're too late Nick, we can't back out - not now. Ryan has sunk a small fortune into that bloody drift mine in readiness for when we get our hands on the farmland, you don't know the half of it. The farmers are more or less ready to shake hands on a deal. We own a mining licence, and the council is right behind us. What do you expect us to do? Throw it all away?"

Savvas remained unmoved, "Declan and the farmers can all use the mine when they realise what their land is worth. The drift mine buildings are an asset, he won't lose any money."

"Nick, there's more to it than you realise. He paid more for the mine than you think. A huge chunk of change – in cash. Declan is expecting a quick return on his investment, a massive one."

Savvas had no idea of the final amount Ryan paid and didn't want to know. He had no intention of getting dragged into any more detail that would add even more to his pressure.

Price tried to advise Savvas with a few sage worthy facts, "Nick, let me spell it out for you, *mate.* Here are the scenarios. If we tell the farmers now, they might find someone else to work with them and not us. Even then, if they work with us, they will give us a tiny fraction of the main profits – next to nothing. If we own the rights to the land, start mining and find rare earth, technically what we find belongs to us not them. The farmer's contract small print states *coal and any other minerals retrieved during the mining process* – we are safe."

"Jason, I don't know. My head is spinning, and my stomach is churning. I can't do it. Nothing of what you said is new to me. The fact remains my conscience won't allow me to carry on without telling the farmers. Neither will Mia's. And that is what I intend to do in 48-hours if you don't tell them before I do. You need to explain to them what's going on before I do. And there's another complication you need to hear about too. Something important."

Price could feel himself on the verge of exploding but held back because he realised the real reason for Savvas's sudden change of heart would soon come out. "What's more important than that fucking bombshell you just dropped? Go on, I'm listening."

Savvas explained to Price the entire story concerning Lauren Eaves. Managing to avoid divulging how Savvas's online carelessness was the sole reason for the problem.

"She figured it all out. And she isn't going away Jason. She also knows about something else I am working on."

Price couldn't believe his ears, "Today started so well, then suddenly a huge shit storm just descended on me, caused by you Nick. So, what is this, *something else,* you are doing? We may as well get it all on the table before I speak to Declan. By the way, if you think I'm pissed off, wait until he hears about all this. He will be incandescent. My God."

Savvas explained his intentions to make a National Geographical documentary with a producer called Dee Munchetty, "We were going to do it in China, then COVID stopped us. Now, this came up which is an even better story. Of course, you would be involved Jason, you're part of the story. The documentary can still go ahead - nothing's changed."

"Nick are you for real? You ring me say…no to tell me…that you've suddenly found a conscience and you are quitting, then to cap it off, you're making a bloody movie? Oh, and you're dishing out a forty-eight-hour deadline for me and Declan to fall into line with your demands. Who the fuck do you think you are? I'll speak with you later - after I talk with Declan. You need another long hard think about this Nick. Listen carefully, the farmers must not find out about this until we complete our deal, and we are locked in. Otherwise, the project will finish before we even start, that's what happens when you lose control of these things. I'm warning you. Oh, and it sounds like you developed more of a conscience after the bloody Lauren girl caught you out and not before."

The line went dead. Earlier, Savvas had felt sickened at the thought of the deception with the farmers and that some young student had managed to push him into this position. Now he felt sick with panic and wondered if he had made a mistake speaking with Price as he did. Had he been too strong issuing a deadline? But he persuaded himself his only choice meant telling Price and it was the right thing to do. He always did have a conscience about the farmers. He also realised Price got it spot on - Lauren Eaves had pushed to find it and make his big decision.

Mia sat next to Savvas with her hand resting on his knee in support, listening to every word. A relieved look and a hint of a smile returned to her face, unseen for several days as her husband's uncertainty and concerns had mounted.

She squeezed his leg and said, "Thank God you did it. Relieved is an understatement. I still feel like crap, but now we need to see it through. The ball is in Price's court now. Maybe he will surprise us both and get his act together?"

"I wouldn't bet on that Mia. He and Ryan are a ruthless pair of bastards, well-matched if you ask me, and if Ryan says jump, Price asks him, 'How high'? I can expect a load of shit coming my way from them over the next few days. A worry, but I can manage it, I must."

Mia looked across and gave a supporting look back at Savvas. Deep down inside she wondered *how* bad things might get if Price refused to alter course. Despite feeling apprehensive and anxious, she had every intention of riding out the storm and seeing it through. She just didn't know how big the storm might be.

Chapter 27

The Drop

Declan Ryan's logistics business leased their offices and freight yards in numerous ports across Europe, with Barcelona as the main hub, by far the most prestigious and close to where he lived for most of the year. He still put the hours in, although playing golf, or wining and dining clients in fine restaurants, all accounted for an ever-increasing proportion of his time. His eldest cousin Michael spent most of his time wearing the Hi-Viz and hard hat, whilst he screamed at the Spanish forklift truck drivers and crane operators who shifted steel cargo boxes onto articulated lorries. Ryan's Barcelona distribution hub would meet Karim Nasri's special shipment when it arrived from Taiwan within a week.

Michael realised something dramatic had taken place in the nearby main office block. One of the supervisors came outside, walked past him, smiled, thumbed backwards to the office, and gesticulated with his hands and arms opening wide above his head. The supervisor signified some kind of explosion – meaning Declan Ryan had detonated with rage - an occasional occurrence.

Ryan possessed a serious temper. Staff tended to wander off to the farthest corners of the office block or leave in a hurry when he lost it. Under normal circumstances, Michael would stay far away but decided to venture inside the building and approach Ryan's office to find out what had lit the fuse this time. Michael walked through the open plan, white bench office area, where one brave soul remained, working away wearing headphones, ignorant to the torrent that just occurred. Another employee sat discreetly, in a secluded, tall-sided meeting booth space.

Ryan's sumptuously appointed, glass-walled private office sat at the end of the office area, partially tucked away behind some planter boxes. He stood with one hand holding his mobile phone, the other hand rubbing the roots off his cropped grey hair, as he stared out of his window towards the ocean.

A red-faced Ryan caught sight of Michael, and waved him inside his office, "Good timing. Shut the door, grab a seat. We are up against a massive problem. *Massive*."

Michael knew his cousin well, he recognised serious bad news brewing, and struggled to get the words out, "What is it?"

"The problem is not *it*. The problem is *he*. That fucking Australian, Nick Savvas. Well, him and his

Mrs, that bloody Mia. The pair of them. Jason Price called me a few minutes ago to say Nick Savvas wants to pull out of the operation in Wales unless we come clean with the farmers. He's bottled it. Got cold feet because of the farmers. He wants Price to tell the farmers everything and thinks they might give us all a fair share before we do a deal with them. Yeah right - never in a million years."

Ryan went through everything Price had told him and added a few other comments and observations of his own.

"I just spent a bloody fortune in Paris with a Jordanian *thief*, and now someone else could end up using the place. Because it might not be us the way this is all panning out. We are supposed to go to Blaenavon tomorrow to see the agent and gain access to the thing. I feel like setting it on fire when I get there and throwing Price and Savvas on the bonfire whilst I'm at it."

Michael sat down opposite Ryan and asked him, "So what are we going to do?"

Ryan gave Michael a piercing look, "We need a little chat with him - Savvas. On the phone to start with, and we see how that goes shall we?"

Ryan composed himself, made the call to Nick Savvas, on speaker for Michael's benefit. He needed to persuade Savvas to change his mind if he answered the phone. He answered, "Nick, good morning my friend. How are you doing? Can you spare me a few minutes for a chat?"

"Good morning to you too Declan. You were on my list to call this morning - I'm sorry you beat me to it. I guess you spoke to Jason earlier on?"

Ryan's initial voice appeared calm and with a conciliatory tone, "Yes, Jason called me twenty minutes ago. Nick, this is devastating news if what Jason told me is correct. Although devastating is an understatement. What's going on Nick? Talk me through it?"

Savvas explained the thinking behind his decision and reiterated everything he told Jason Price. Ryan interjected a few times, but it fell on the adamant Savvas's deaf ears.

Savvas then added, "I'm sorry Declan. I realise the timing is poor. But this is all new to me. I'm a lecturer, not a land speculator and I'm certainly not going to break the law. I don't care what Jason says, breaking the law *is* what we are doing - we were – but I'm not prepared to anymore. There is a way through this for you. You can still make a huge success of this project, and I am happy to stay involved if you do as I ask. I told Jason ages ago that I was unhappy doing things this way, and that I wanted the farmers involved. I told him straight, but he fobbed me off with some bullshit. Your old drift mine may be a relic, but it is an asset. If for any reason you don't go ahead with the project, you can still make good money on that if you sell it on. The mine's in a desirable location for anybody's rare earth mining operation. But there's nothing to stop you from doing a deal with the farmers is there?

I made up my mind earlier. I'm out if you don't involve them."

A long silence filled the empty space after Savvas finished his nervous retort. Savvas sensed Ryan listening to him. All he could hear was the exhalation of air through Ryan's flared nostrils as he waited for him to speak.

Ryan broke the silence, a controlled tone masked his growing venom, "Well Nick, you turned into a real spineless bastard didn't you, eh? You're right on a couple of things and wrong on others. Yes, your timing is poor, as you put it, and I'm not sure if Jason has told you what I paid for the drift mine, but it sure as hell isn't much of an asset. Listen carefully, one way or another the deal is going through - without the farmers on board knowing the ins and outs. Not with - *without*. Jason and I are up to our necks with investment in this, with millions on the line here. His casino project cock up needs paying for, so does my drift mine. Why do you think *my* stake in *our* business is so much bigger than yours and Jason's? Are you stupid as well as spineless? You can make millions and millions out of this deal you prick. Seems to me like you've got a big careless mouth, Nick. What with this young Australian woman sticking her nose in, and the TV presenter, Jesus. Why couldn't you keep your big mouth shut?"

Ryan's words stung Savvas, but from somewhere he summoned up the courage to respond, "Declan, I told Jason, two days to sort it out with the farmers.

Find a way. Come clean with them. Otherwise, I'm going to do it for you."

Savvas hung up and Ryan looked across his desk at his cousin, leaned in, and spoke to him in a quiet voice, "That went well, didn't it? Where's that brother of yours today?"

~

For the rest of the morning, Savvas and Mia had decided to park the topic of Blaenavon and went to their usual work zones at their home. She had a marketing campaign to finish for a client, and Savvas needed to catch up on some of his outstanding college responsibilities. They re-emerged for coffee on their front patio, shared ideas for the coming weekend, and a potential trip in their VW camper van. Neither of them wanted to voice their concerns about their decisions and actions, so they skirted around each other with small talk. Savvas chose to ignore the unpleasant tone of Ryan's earlier lambasting, not wanting to worry Mia any further.

But the subject of Price hung in the air like a bad smell, and Savvas mentioned to Mia, "I need to see this thing through, contact David Davies and get it out of the way before we go away for the weekend. What are the chances of Jason listening to me – zero?"

Mia replied, "Jason must listen to you. He has no choice, does he? Can't he see sense when it's staring him in the face? He's overreacting, the farmers will be fine with him."

At that moment, their doorbell chimed, "My Amazon deliveries," Savvas stood up to collect his parcel. He walked through the lounge, kitchen and hall leaving Mia to her coffee and music on the back patio.

Savvas opened the door with an expectant, welcoming smile. Instead of receiving a parcel, on his secluded tree-shrouded porch, he found himself staring at two stocky, masked men. Both men arrived dressed in black, both with automatic pistols pointing at Savvas. He had never before seen a pistol suppressor, other than in movies, and immediately recognised the terrifying object as one man thrust his gun towards Savvas's face, whilst the man's other latex-gloved hand grasped his neck. After freezing with shock for half a second, he resisted, making an instinctive move back inside his door. The second gunman blocked his path and punched him hard under his ribs. The winded Savvas dropped to his knees, gasped for air, and received a heavy boot to his abdomen. Incapacitated and stunned by the onslaught, he saw the blurred image of a masked man place a hood over his head, and sensed zip ties securing his hands and feet. He heard the sound of a roll of heavy-duty tape unravelling and wrapping around his head, over his mouth and ears, on the outside of the hood. As he lay there, the only thought entering Savvas's confused and terrified brain was, *"Mia."*

Less than forty-five seconds after he opened the door, the men hauled Savvas over his threshold onto the hallway floor and closed the door behind all of them. Before the minute elapsed, at the other side of the property, they had dragged Mia inside from the patio and forced her face down on the lounge floor, with a gun at the back of her head. Immobilised and helpless to assist her, Savvas could just about make out his wife's initial screams from where he lay with his hearing muffled by the tape and hood.

One of the gunmen uttered the word, "That," to his accomplice, gesticulating with a pistol to the heavy square *Rubik's cube* like ornament, on the coffee table.

He picked it up, and in a pre-planned move, he crashed the object onto the rear of Mia's head, twice, carving open her skull. She lay lifeless in a pool of blood, expanding itself onto the porcelain tiles from under her dark curly hair. One of the men walked out of the room to the prone Savvas, wiped the bloodstained object onto his clothing and tossed it onto the white leather sofa, smearing it with blood.

Another instruction, "Keys to his car or even better, his VW. Any one of them. Quick, c'mon."

Moments later they dragged Nick Savvas outside his front door and flung him through the awaiting already open sliding side door of his camper van.

The drive, in two vehicles, took them less than ten minutes, east along the C-31 main coastal road, close to one of Savvas's popular jogging loops at Cala deVallcarca. But they were not close to the beach, they drove high up above the road, along a track near a cement works. All Savvas could hear were his van's indicators, a rumble of rough ground crunching under tyres, the handbrake, and the faint voice of one man speaking and receiving instructions from a mobile phone.

Savvas knew the men were not opportunists but organised professionals. He also realised why he found himself in his desperate situation, and who had orchestrated it, *"Oh my God - what did I do? Why did I say it? What are they going to do next? Maybe just scare me? Mia? Are they hurting her? Is she hooded? I'll kill Ryan - I'll kill him."*

In between his terrifying thoughts, he tried and tried to scream to make himself heard, but to no avail - no one could hear him. Flailing and kicking also proved a futile, energy-sapping, oxygen draining exercise, in his hooded and hog-tied position.

A noise, another voice - outside the van. The door slid open and clunked to an abrupt halt close to his ear. They pulled him to the doorway and even through the sweat-soaked hood, he could smell some kind of vegetation, along with a hint of cement dust in his throat.

A finger pointed to the distance, and another instruction communicated between the men, "Two minutes."

Savvas heard the snap of a pair of pliers and experienced the relief of the wide heavy-duty zip-ties releasing from his ankles. The men pocketed the discarded zip-ties. Next, they pulled him, disoriented, to his feet and marched him hooded, resisting their doubled handed firm control under each of his biceps. He continued to struggle from their grasp and attempted to scream, which agitated the men, resulting in yet another punishing blow to his solar plexus. The punch sickened him, forcing him to drop to his knees, causing desperate nasal sounds, as he tried to suck in the scarcity of oxygen that barely existed inside his damp hood.

They dragged him to his feet one more time. Once again, he enjoyed the strange pleasurable sound and accompanying release provided by the pliers snipping at the restraints around his wrists, *"Thank God. Are they done with me now?"* He pleaded, "Can I go? I get the message – please just let me go home and see my wife. Please?"

The tape began to unwind from around his head, and then his mouth was free to suck in lungful after lungful of the precious unfamiliar air, rejuvenating his lungs.

A hand whipped the hood off Savvas's glistening head. He blinked and squinted as the bright sunlight burned into his eyes. All he could make out ahead of him was a skyline and void below it. A final sensation involved a hard shove between his shoulder blades. The vicious push sent him somersaulting from the precarious escarpment the men had stood him on. He flew through the air, and crashed onto a train track one hundred feet below, into the perfectly timed path of an oncoming high-speed passenger train as it emerged from a tunnel.

Chapter 28

Is This for Real?

An intelligent, resourceful, high achiever. Those words stuck in the back of Harry Eaves's mind for years after reading one of his daughter's final school reports.

He reminded his wife, Margaret, of them as they wondered how she would fare when she arrived back in Wales - spectrometer and test kit in hand, "She'll be fine love. No point trying to hold her back. You know what she's like once she gets something into her head. Like a dog with a bone."

Her parents and schoolteachers had made a fair assessment. She loaded up her friend's battered little car in Cardiff with the kit, a packed lunch, and set off on her private mission to Blaenavon - full of optimism and undeterred by the words of Nick Savvas a day earlier. Her priority involved a future for herself and her struggling family.

On arrival in Blaenavon, she followed a condensed version of Savvas's week-long well-executed expedition, using his pre-planned sample *roadmap*, hoping to achieve some good results within two or three days. After that, she would enter uncharted territory and if necessary, call on the remote guidance and skills of her father and uncle. The first test site meant the boring into the ground adjacent to the Coity tip spoil heap. The same spot that Savvas made his initial startling discovery, followed soon afterwards by Declan Ryan's cousin Michael, validating the same thing.

As Lauren started her first bore through the fine black shale, something crossed her mind, *"Bloody hell. Forty-degrees and T-shirt the last time I did this. Now I'm here in wellies and a puffa-jacket, freezing my butt off. Different clothes same result."*

The moist Blaenavon soil proved kinder than the arid Westonia crust, enabling her to produce her first sample in a fraction of the time she had anticipated. No sooner than the first black dirt sausage emerged from the ground, Lauren kicked and spread the muck, then prepared to zap it with Jack's spectrometer.

"C'mon Blaenavon, what can you show me today? Do your damnedest. Let's make this little adventure interesting, shall we?"

Over the next ten minutes, with adrenalin pumping, Lauren's emotions replicated those experienced by Nick Savvas during the first morning of his recent visit. - astonishment.

Several times she gazed at both ends of the spectrometer, then checked and double-checked the simple procedures she learned less than a week earlier, ingrained into her, thanks to her Uncle Jack, "You are kidding me? Is this for real?" She muttered.

Part of the training and real-world practice of the process imparted by Jack also included outlining some parameters. Quick, realistic comparisons, similar to distillery tests to check a good whiskey, which should show 40% proof - a 90% proof for example would show an error somewhere. Lauren knew that the rare earth and similar 'noble' or 'precious' metals she expected to find should show 6 - 8 ppm.

Lauren looked down at the black muck smothering her hands and wellies in stunned silence, uncertain of her next move, she quizzed herself, *"Uncle Jack, told me 6ppm, 7ppm, or 8ppm at best. He did. I know he did. This is ridiculous. This is 121ppm, twenty times those numbers. I'm standing on a fortune. I don't care what the time is in Western Australia, I need to talk to Dad and Jack. No wonder Nick Savvas was so touchy. This is crazy. Madness."*

A surprised Harry Eaves answered the group chat first, moments later the three-way conversation included Jack Tennison. Harry commented, "You keep forgetting we are ahead of you Lauren, not behind you. Your mum and I just finished washing away the dinner plates."

Everyone laughed, then Jack's booming baritone voice resonated through all their internet connections, "You look like you've been down a coal mine Lauren,

I didn't realise you were using your nose to scrape the ground?" Referring to the dark smudges across her forehead and chin.

"Well some things are worth getting dirty for, and today is one of them. Dad, Uncle Jack, I checked the kit. The batteries are new, and I'm in the same spots that Savvas came to. Jack, you wished me luck and told me to, *go find the good stuff*, didn't you? Well, guess what? I did find the good stuff. Better than good, amazing stuff, 121ppm stuff. Yes, I know, you heard me right. Averaging 121ppm for Iridium and Caesium, plus some other hits. I tested two spots already, but I need to go check other locations. I realise they could be freak locations, but I doubt it, I just want to check and be certain."

Despite the few hundred kilometres between Harry and Jack, they seemed to look at each other on the video phone call - dumbstruck. Then Jack spoke, "Let me help us all out here with some simple mathematics. A reading of 121ppm means that if we dig just over eight thousand tonnes of soil, in lay terms, a volume equal to about twenty decent sized swimming pools, it could contain one tonne of what we are looking for - which is worth more than gold. Before processing and refining fees, at £62,000 per kg, which equates to around £62 million. Why has everyone stopped laughing? I'm not joking," he laughed, "I'm serious. Those are the gross numbers, but what's £30 million in processing fees between friends."

Harry didn't hesitate to intervene, "Bloody hell. We thought we were in a race. Now we understand the reason why. Let's hope the race is still running, and we have a chance?"

Jack, agreed, "Yes, I reckon the race is on Harry. But our element of surprise is gone. I think we may be approaching the last lap, and in with a good chance. Finish off today and tomorrow Lauren and then we have some serious questions for whoever will listen to us - or should I say listen to you? We don't need to wait for official lab results guys, we know enough, and we need to set the cat amongst the pigeons after tomorrow, sooner if we can."

Lauren had an idea, "Won't take me long to get things in motion guys. Blaenavon is a small town, no doubt everyone knows everyone. A few questions in the right places will give me some names of the landowners on Savvas's location map. Farmers by the looks of things, and I can check out the local council to find out what they think is happening."

Lauren's instincts proved correct. An hour later, whilst wrapping up for the day, loading the boot of her friend's car, a tall fair-haired man in his forties, carrying a small backpack, binoculars and a long lens camera came striding towards her. He looked like a serious hiker.

He smiled as he approached, and tried to avoid staring at the coal and mud-covered young woman, still finishing off her loading up, "Afternoon, how are you doing? Have you had an accident or are you practising for one of those *Tough Mudder* endurance events?" Chuckling in a hospitable manner as he said it, "Need a hand or are you all done?"

Lauren smiled back, "You're not far wrong about the muddy endurance event. No, thanks I'm all good here, you turned up five minutes too late. Yes, I know, I must look a state."

"Sorry, I don't mean to intrude. If you don't mind me asking, what have you been up to? Foraging for something by the looks of things? Apologies for my nosiness. Oh, and I'm Luke, by the way, Luke Adams. I'm a local wildlife photographer in my spare time if you're wondering what all this gear is."

"I'm just doing some research, I'm a geology student. I don't normally end up covered in mud, only on special occasions. I'm Lauren, by the way. But maybe you can help me out with some information Luke?"

"Sure, I'll have a go. What is it?"

"Who owns the land around here? It would help me with my college report."

Luke explained to Lauren about the three farmers, whom he knew well from his hobby, and that the council, the Coal Authority, and a small mining company owned other bits and pieces of the pieces of land.

Lauren, pressed Luke for more information, "How can I contact the farmers and someone at the council? Any ideas?"

Luke provided Lauren with an address for two of the three farmers, although he didn't have any of their phone numbers, "Then, maybe Gussie Mertens, or someone at her law firm office might help you out, either with her or with one of the other councillors. The council in town is on the ball, and always pleased to help people." He explained how Gussie's office was an easy first point of contact, or she could try via the council website or Facebook page. "Good luck Lauren, nice to meet you."

"Same to you Luke, and thanks for the info."

Lauren put a sheet on the driver seat and drove back to Cardiff, *"I'm stinking dirty, and cold. I need a shower before I do anything."*

Showered, fed, singing to some music playing in the background and in a great mood, Lauren scrolled through her regular multitude of social media messages. One particular WhatsApp message caught her eye, from an Australian friend whom she studied with back in Sydney. *"Lauren, have you seen your Twitter, feed? Remember Nick Savvas, the lecturer from our course? He's dead - yesterday, in Spain - where he lives. Suicide. Jumped off a cliff – and under a train. OMG. Can't believe it. He was a decent bloke. All a bit confusing. They think he murdered his wife first, then killed himself."*

Lauren read the message twice, then immediately started searching for more information concerning the tragic incident. No mistake, several of the news feeds in Spain and back in Sydney had a story and picture of the man she had spoken to only a couple of days ago – Nick Savvas. Some stated murder-suicide, other later stories, suggested his Spanish wife, Mia, had survived a brutal attack in their Sitges home and remained in a critical condition at a hospital in Barcelona. Police said they were not seeking anyone else in connection with the crime.

Lauren turned off the music, then sat stunned at the news, *"Oh, my God. Nick Savvas. Murder-suicide? He sounded edgy the other day, but OK. Is it to do with Blaenavon or something else? Shit. Oh, why now? Why me? Why?"*

Following a couple more hours of contemplation, evening time in Cardiff meant the middle of the night in Westonia. Not a great time to call the *Intrepid Trio* hotline and not the kind of news a mother and father might want to hear at that time, *"Why spook them? I'm sure there's a good explanation for what happened to Nick and his wife. He always gave me the impression of a highly-strung bloke, running around all over the world, living out of a suitcase - a long way from home. Who knows? Maybe his marriage had problems? I can find out more tomorrow about him. But I need to finish what I started in Blaenavon first. Oh God, I just had a churlish thought about what Uncle Jack said about the competition - there's one less now. That is so sick. I hate myself. It's not that late, but I'm tired and stressed. I'm so, sorry Nick. I'm so, so, sorry. I'm going to fix it."*

She dabbed her eyes for a second time, turned off her light and fell into an exhausted deep sleep.

~

Awake long before her early start alarm, Lauren arrived in Blaenavon before most people had left for work, and way ahead of any school run movements.

CHAPTER 28

She decided to keep a lid on the Nick Savvas news for the time being. She would bring her family up to date with a complete picture of her blitz sample testing, and the eagerly anticipated, excellent results, later on - around lunchtime - with luck.

Consistent, perfect results, time and again throughout the morning - matching yesterday's, from every new test site sample location. A relief, but not a surprise. The extra precautions of towels and a change of clothes, together with more controlled enthusiasm meant a more human-looking Lauren Eaves emerged from the rugged landscape. With all the emotion and excitement of the previous day, she had overlooked her flask and packed lunch, so drove into town to the little heritage museum and café.

As she waited in the queue, with two people ahead of her, Lauren picked up on a woman's foreign accent. Not unusual amongst the regular, eclectic flow of overseas visitors to the famous historic town. Lauren paid for her coffee and soup, then wandered through the busy café with her tray, searching in vain for a spare seat. She spilt everything on her tray when she came to an embarrassing, abrupt halt.

Moments earlier, the woman ahead in the queue, who had since taken a seat, offered a sympathetic look up towards Lauren, picked up a soup spoon that had clattered to the floor, smiled and said, "Are you OK there? Let me get that for you."

Lauren recognised the dazzling smile, short black, straggly hair, combined with her confident American accent, and in an instant knew that the woman speaking to her was the same woman she had Googled several days earlier - Dee Munchetty.

After a second or two of looking like a rabbit caught in car headlights, Lauren gathered herself and replied, "So clumsy of me, I beg your pardon. And thank you so much. I'll grab another spoon."

Munchetty looked around the packed seating areas of the café, and with another smile, suggested, "Hey, grab a seat, I have three spare ones here, and there are no seats anywhere else in here."

Only on rare occasions did Lauren go red in the face with embarrassment or awkwardness, this time was one of them, "So kind of you. I'll try not to spill any more, or knock the table over," Lauren added, with her own bright smile.

"I'm Dee…Boston...as in from there," gesticulating with a gentle sweeping hand, in a general direction 3000 miles away.

"Hi, Dee. I'm Lauren, my friends call me accident prone…only kidding. I'm from Western Australia, near Perth - but studying in Cardiff at the moment. Nice to meet you, and thanks again."

The two women made some more small talk about Wales, Blaenavon, and its history. For a while, as Lauren finished the remnants of her soup, she wondered whether or not to pretend she did not know who Munchetty was, and why she had arrived in town. In the end, she decided to come clean and explain herself.

CHAPTER 28

"Dee, I have a small confession to make. I think I recognised you when I dropped my spoon. Coming in here today is sheer coincidence, if you believe in coincidence, some people don't. But we have something, well, we *had*, someone in common, such sad news…about Nick, Nick Savvas. You and I may both be in town for the same reason."

Dee's eye's narrowed, and the smile vanished, converting her face into a sharp focus, "You know Nick and what he's working on? Sad news? What sad news? Please, you're gonna need to explain that one to me?" Her voice receded several decibels as she asked the question.

The embarrassing awkwardness returned, *"Shit, she doesn't know. Oh, no. Oh, my God. Me, and my big mouth."*

Lauren broke eye contact for a moment looked away, regrouped, and continued, "Dee, I found out last night from a friend back home. I'm so sorry to tell you, but Nick killed himself two days ago. The news of his death and what happened is online in Australia and Spain."

Dee's head dropped and Lauren could see the colour draining from her face, which hid behind both her hands as they raised to mask it, "Oh my God," Dee whispered between her fingers.

After a few seconds, she dug out her iPhone, did a quick search, and gasped. She looked back at Lauren, lost for words, before asking, "Lauren, would you mind if we went somewhere a little more private?"

They took their coffees to a quiet, research area, adjacent to the interactive museum. Dee shook her head in silence. Lauren didn't appreciate how much the death of Savvas, not much more than an acquaintance, had affected her until that moment, her emotions triggered by the woman she met only two minutes earlier.

After a few minutes of meaningless chat, the conversation drifted into focus. "Nick knew I would be in town," Dee explained, "I told him I wanted to come down from London and check it out. The project looked like a perfect substitute for a documentary that we scrapped in China due to COVID. He told me he would meet me here. I must have called him a dozen times but got no response, and now I know why - incredible. This whole project sounded a bit hush-hush though. We talked a lot, but he wouldn't tell me everything, although he did mention needing to meet the council before anything could kick-off. I did some digging around myself and figured out who his partners are, *or were*. Although, I had no idea he had problems at home, or that he had the capability within him of… killing someone. His wife, *Mia*, for God sake. I mean I knew her."

Both women said nothing for a moment. Then trying to make sense of everything, Dee looked at Lauren and asked, "So, Lauren, tell me about you and Nick. How did you know him? Were you one of his students?"

Managing a true, yet diplomatic answer, Lauren explained, "Yes, he taught me in Sydney a couple of years ago. We kept in touch with things when I came to the UK, Cardiff, for my MSc. Then, by accident, I discovered something about Blaenavon and Nick's involvement in it. He wouldn't tell me much, but I know he wanted me to keep a low profile until he finished his work here. Now I know we were both working on the same thing, a bit awkward. So, now I need to carry on, for myself and my family, they need the money – if there is any here - so do I."

Taking the initiative and striking, whilst the iron was hot, "So what do you know about Nick and Blaenavon, Dee?"

Dee told her everything she could think of, including about the business friendship between them, and Nick's aspirations, "I had known Nick for years, but this time, with this project - I had never seen him so excited." She also filled in all the gaps concerning what she knew of his business partners, Jason Price and Declan Ryan.

Both had the same burning question for each other, Dee went first, "Do you think, *he* did it, and then killed himself? I mean - Nick? Really?"

"I wanted to ask you the same thing. I wish I knew the answer. They say his wife is still alive – unconscious - with serious head wounds. Who knows what that means? But she will know the truth."

Dee added some final observations and detail, "There is a huge amount of money at stake here. Many, many, millions if Nick's assessment is correct, which it will be. These two guys Price and Ryan are powerful people, and I have a feeling Nick didn't like the way they did business, just things he said about them. Then some of the things he didn't say – they often speak louder," the older woman looked at the young Australian woman in front of her, touched her arm and said, "Be careful Lauren."

As Lauren let that one sink in for a moment, Dee asked her another question, "So what are your plans to make money here?"

Lauren explained, "I now realise this land is worth a fortune. I confirmed that with my samples earlier today. I intend to speak with the local council, first of all, I suspect they haven't got a clue about the magnitude of Nicks discovery."

"And then what?" Dee probed.

"Then I am going to see the landowners, some farmers, I know who they are. Dee, I have a strong suspicion Nick and his partners have not informed them of the true value of their land. That's the worrying thing. Now you tell me Nick had concerns, and look what just happened to him. The whole thing stinks. I might even go to the police, although the mayor of Blaenavon runs a law firm, all the more reason I go and see her first - today with luck.

Dee, nodded in agreement before stating, "I agree, and I'm coming with you - if you don't mind some company, OK?"

Chapter 29

In Transit

The germ of an idea for the deadly 3D printer weapons manufacturing process started following an innocent visit to the *Intelligent Asia Exhibition* at the Nangang Exhibition Centre in Taiwan, less than six months before Nasri met Ryan for lunch near Barcelona. The future of 3D printing for the whole world to see and admire, ground-breaking concepts, making the impossible possible.

The 3D printing concept had existed since the early 1980s. These days, startling new advances appear almost every month. Modern armies and F1 motor racing teams often take 3D printers and raw materials with them to battle or races, to manufacture broken components when needed. Remote hospitals around the globe can make simple life-saving components within minutes given the appropriate training and technology.

The inevitable, worrying step, became a reality, when a misguided mechanical design engineer, living and working in Devon, decided to take her idealistic vision for the world to another level. The engineer and her brother, Karim Nasri, both ascended to become senior members of the ISIL terror group, Wilayah al-Jazair. Their deadly plan made its way by sea from Asia, only a matter of days away from reaching fruition in the UK, and a new campaign of attacks and violence.

Hacking and theft of detailed digital designs, from a careless Swiss subsidiary company of the famous Austrian gun maker, Glock, renowned for manufacturing their unique composite pistol, notched the campaign up to another level. The terror group converted the designs to a perfect STL format (standard triangle language) to enable 3D printing, within weeks. Thousands of rounds of 9mm ammunition, ordered and delivered months earlier, awaited the weapons in the UK. The group had further plans formulating to obtain the necessary information to manufacture fully automatic rifles.

All that remained was to obtain the appropriate high tech plastic raw materials, a sophisticated high capacity industrial 3D printer, and someone who could programme and operate the machine. The task of getting the innocuous-looking machine - the size of a small van, and its authentic paperwork to the UK fell to Nasri – and Ryan. Under normal circumstances increasing numbers of the machines found themselves procured for projects in the pharmaceutical industry and a straightforward shipping process ensued. The big challenge required the programming, commissioning, testing of the machine and passing off the expensive, performance-plastic raw materials, as something other than stocks, butts, clips, and barrels for guns.

Nasri's programmer waited for the call and arrived in Barcelona, at Ryan's logistics centre, when the ship docked from Taiwan. Ryan took an instant dislike to the geeky young man, who marched into Ryan's office as if he owned the place. For no apparent reason, dressed head to toe in black, with a thick black beard, ponytail, and a pair of full sleeve tattoos.

Ryan, led him to a secure bay to carry out his work, "So you've come to fix the machine, eh? Best crack on with it. Then you can head off back to the mosh pit with your mates."

Less than an hour later the task of uploading the pre-prepared STL file completed, the 3D printing machine stood ready for the final leg of its journey, to the UK. The planned route would take it via Zeebrugge, mixed with another container consignment, for shipping to Immingham and transportation on a wagon to a farm in Devon.

Standing with his cousin, Ryan watched the upgraded consignment leave his distribution yard and reloaded back onto a freight ship, ready for a slow four day multi-stop trip to the UK, and told him, "That there is the shittiest job that Nasri has ever handed us. I told him - I'm sticking to shifting drugs in future. No more like that one. Never mind the money, that's the last of those. But if things go to plan when we get to Wales, we will never need to shift any more of anything."

"Sounds good to me Declan"

"Oh, and I've got a little idea about those guns. I need to mull it over and then we can have a little chat about it."

Chapter 30

Every Cloud

Jason Price and Dee Munchetty both experienced the same communication problem - neither could understand why Nick Savvas had dropped off the radar. Despite his few cold words, Price expected at least a response to a progress update text, but nothing appeared. Then Price's wife sent him a message, followed with a conversation, to explain the dreadful news. Even the thick-skinned Price felt a jolt of utter disbelief when he found out. *"Bloody hell – Nick - Mia. Jesus."*

Declan Ryan and his cousin Michael landed in Cardiff from Spain and were on their way to Blaenavon to check out the drift mine. Not the first property or the first business enterprise he had ever purchased unseen – just another asset - a necessary and valuable one in the wider scheme of things. They also planned to meet Price who anticipated an imminent conclusion of dealings with the farmers and a celebration. Price expected Ryan to arrive in town at any minute.

Moments after getting the message about Savvas, Price called and spoke to Ryan, expecting a solemn response, but got something in between, "Yes, I heard. Such sad news, and so unexpected from such a nice guy, I met his wife - a lovely woman. But Jason, Nick's gone now, we have important business to attend to and every cloud has a silver lining. It appears that poor old Nick won't be saying anything to anyone, least of all the farmers - looks like he did us a favour and we dodged one there my friend. I suppose we are back on track, and I already checked out where we can hire a replacement geology consultant, so relax. Now, tell me more about this nosy Australian girl and the American woman. What else do we know about them? How concerned should we be? And where are we with those farmers – have they signed yet?"

Price and Ryan were well aware, the biggest threat to their project could come out of the blue from Lauren Eaves and they realised the project could still be on a knife-edge. Dee Munchetty had a different agenda and remained an irritant - rather than a threat. Although, Price hoped to meet her, and saw himself as a stand-in for Nick Savvas in any documentary she might end up making. Both women remained worrying obstacles.

Price tells Ryan, "The good news is I know who they are and what they look like. The bad news is

I saw them both together, in town earlier, around lunchtime, getting into a beat-up old pale blue Beetle, outside the post office as I was going in. I heard the American's voice then an Australian accent and heard the name *Lauren* - not rocket science, is it? This is a small town. They are here, *together* for God's sake. What's that all about? Nick Savvas has a lot to answer for. Bloody idiot. Good riddance if you ask me. As for the farmers, we are getting close, I can talk you through it when you arrive."

Price had no intention of disclosing that one of the farmers may have gone cold for some unknown reason and that all hopes rested with Maggie Powell. Price hoped for a positive update before meeting Ryan.

Lauren's similar assessment of Blaenavon as a small town proved more accurate than she could ever have imagined. Only the day before, she told her father and uncle about the compact town and everyone knowing everyone else, and now of all people, Jason Price almost bumps into her, and he recognises her on the main street.

Ryan and his cousin Michael arrived in the valley town, met the property management agent and a talkative part-time caretaker, who took them to the location of the drift mine. All four donned some PPE before embarking on a brief tour of the drift mine and its buildings. A run-down handful of buildings, with a few broken windows, and keep out signposts. Some rusty conveyor belts, water pumps, air compressors and heavy-duty machinery all littered the site.

Ryan commented, "I've seen worse - but not much worse. You're gonna need more than a few cans of WD40, and a bit of elbow grease to sort that lot, Mikey. At least the roof is in one piece."

Michael Ryan, looked unimpressed, "Thanks a million cuz. One minute my tobacco break is overlooking the Med, on a bikini-clad beach in Barcelona, the next minute, I'm covered in crap up the valleys in freezing cold Wales, surrounded by sheep."

Michael always did as his older cousin told him, and never questioned it. The logistics business acted as a convenient front for drugs, extreme violence, and large amounts of money - that's all that he knew and all he cared about. Diversifying and making even more money sounded like good news - whatever the cost.

By mid-afternoon, Price needed to know if Maggie had made any progress with David Davies and called her, "Hey Maggie, how's your day going? Any news from that stubborn old cousin of yours?"

"Jason, hi. He's still taking his time, and I've been at work all day. I tried calling him a few times, he's useless. I managed a snatched conversation and all I got from him sounded like his dog barking, plus a few swear words. I think he wants more money or a better deal. So, I'm going to call in on my way home later."

"Then why don't I come with you, and we can discuss it together? If we need to improve our terms, then let's have a proper conversation about it. I'm sure we can figure something out between us."

Maggie had got more than just a few swear words. David told her much the same as the day before. Despite her pleading with him to stop being a selfish bastard and think of other people's circumstances.

"OK, Jason, let's pop and see him together. If there's a problem with that, I'll let you know and put you off. Aim for five at David's then."

Price's original offer to the farmers was a sensible one, or so he thought. Offering them a ridiculous amount at that time would have aroused their suspicions. Now, if he needed to up the ante, then he would. As much as needed, the farmers could name their price, as long as they signed his contract.

At the back of Price's mind, doubts began to grow. He thought hard about the sudden, unexpected death of Nick Savvas near Barcelona, and the huge positive significance it had to Price and in particular, Ryan, who by coincidence just arrived - from Barcelona, *"No way? Ryan? Savvas, and Mia? Would he? Shit."*

For one worrying moment Price began to wonder what might happen if the farmer's contract failed to get over the line – a tiny glimmer of doubt appeared. The casino project remained at a standstill back in Spain, haemorrhaging money - most of it Declan Ryan's money. Price wondered if he had imagined things, or had he given himself a stark reminder of the potential ramifications for failure with David Davies and the others? He began to realise that failure was not an option.

Chapter 31

A Wing and a Prayer

A man unfamiliar with pressure or nerves could feel his shirt sticking to his back, yet the chilly late afternoon temperature outside and a hint of air-con did nothing for Jason Price. He endured an anxious wait to meet Maggie, up the road from David's house. Price had £2000 in cash in his pocket, and a significant improvement on the original contract value offering in his head. All in readiness for the biggest negotiation of his life – with an obstinate Welsh sheep farmer who earned less in a year than Price did in a bad week.

Dogs are perceptive animals and can sense when someone isn't welcome. With her tail stuck out straight, accompanied by a low continuous growl, David's intelligent sheepdog, Bea, made her feelings known when Price walked over the threshold of the farmhouse with Maggie. The dog's eyes and growl targeted Price, rather than Maggie, before David, sent the dog away.

Despite the intensity of the pressurised situation, a fleeting thought entered Price's mind, *"Can't decide which I dislike the most, boxer dogs or sheepdogs?"*

David offered Maggie and Price a seat and the obligatory cup of tea. David stood up to put the kettle on, but Liz stopped him, "No, I'll get it – you speak to these two." Her feisty attitude hadn't mellowed since the last time Price met her.

Maggie did her best to disguise the wringing of her hands inside the overhanging sleeves of her coat, whilst avoiding eye contact at all costs with Liz.

As he began speaking, David looked at Maggie initially, but with words intended for Price, "Jason, Maggie wanted to see me and said you should come too. She said you had some new ideas. I know she told you I had a few last-minute doubts about doing all of this, but her and Rob are dead keen and if I'm not in then nothing's doing. So bad news all around and I don't want to ruin things for them if we can avoid it. What's going to change my mind then Jason?"

The critical moment Price expected just arrived, *hoped* would arrive, at least it was an opportunity. The possibility of a *yes* and not a firm *no.* It appeared a chance to make an agreement did exist.

Humility didn't come easy to Price, but he did his utmost, squeezing every drop from himself choosing a softened dialogue, "David, Liz, thank you for allowing me to see you again. I realise Maggie has spoken to you for me, and I am aware that all three of you have differing opinions and strong views about going ahead. But you may be pleased to hear that our offer has improved. The terms of the arrangement might not change too much. We still need to work the land - over the timescale that I explained the other day - and we will make good the land when completed, hence the bond. The main improvement is in the commercials – the finance part. The first point that you may recall, I explained that we would offer a bonus. Well, that is still the case, but I can now bring that forward - to today. A goodwill cash advance bonus of £2000. The main improvement is that we will double the offer we made for all the parts of the deal – double – but that is a final offer, for a quick contract agreement."

Even Liz looked shocked and made a startled, yet approving look at her husband from the kitchen door. Maggie didn't realise that she had been holding her breathe and let out a silent sigh of relief.

David's rigid shoulders and back seemed to relax as if someone had removed a great weight from them. Everyone has a price, and the new offer exceeded what he wanted, "OK, Jason, sounds good enough for me. How about you Liz? Maggie? Both of you OK with that?"

Liz nodded, "Fine, let's get on with it. Oh, and where's the cash?"

Maggie could at last release the self-inflicted grip on herself, "Perfect for me, and Rob, he's in. He was in the first place. So he will be dead chuffed when I tell him about the new offer."

Jason Price held out his right hand, David offered a callused palm and responded with a firm shake. Liz also shook hands, as Price passed an envelope into her free left hand, with a hint of a smile and a nod of acknowledgement shared between them. He made arrangements to bring the revised contract with him later the next day for signatures.

Price sat in his car for twenty minutes, long after a gleeful Maggie had driven off. He had never felt so relieved in his entire life. He knew from experience the climax of such agreements often took less than a couple of minutes, even long, complex commercial business deals. The stating of the crucial sentences and the verbal agreements that followed with clients often happened and fell into line in minutes once all parties aligned their thinking. Those few minutes inside David's house were the longest he could ever recall.

Declan Ryan's day had not gone as well as he had hoped. The mine was just about OK, no worse than expected, a rough old building needing a lot of work. But Ryan's biggest problem was Mia Savvas, and he couldn't get her out of his head. He had not stopped haranguing his cousin since the day before, when official news reports broke, "You told me she was dead?"

The deep discussion and Ryan's mood lightened when he took the call from Price, "Declan, I just left a meeting with the farmers. We shook hands, and they all agreed on the new deal - it's done. They promised to sign tomorrow when I get the paperwork changed and sorted."

~

Lauren's day had also gone well. The samples were all perfect, she had an unexpected encounter with Dee Munchetty and found a welcome sense of camaraderie with her. Together they wanted to get to the bottom of the Nick Savvas mystery - at least his involvement in Blaenavon. They concluded a cautious acceptance of his death as an unfortunate coincidence, with everything else that may have been happening in his life. Both women suspected there was a race of some sort taking place regarding the secretive rare earth mining. They had called into Gussie Mertens's law firm office, but she was out of town, so they made an appointment to see her first thing the following morning. Based on what Dee mentioned about Savvas and his associates, saying they *needed to see the council*, the women talked it through and agreed they should see Mertens first, before approaching the local farmers. Lauren decided not to knock on their doors and risk an embarrassing conversation if a mining contract already existed. However, she remained optimistic that time was on her side for a little while longer.

The following morning the temperature dropped, re-freezing a recent thawing snowfall, and compounding it with a murky fog. Just another unpredictable late March morning in Wales.

Meanwhile, in the small Welsh valley town, a multi-award-winning international American TV producer and an enthusiastic, young Australian geology student, waited in silence outside Mertens' austere oak-panelled office, with its frosted glass windows. Mertens concluded her previous engagement, then emerged - full of vigour, introducing herself as Gussie, before inviting them in with an offer of refreshments.

She opened the discussion, smiling and looking over her bifocals, whilst referring to a note on her desk, "My associate has provided me with some basic information about the reason for our short-notice meeting. *A new mining operation and queries associated with it*? I'm curious, I was under the impression the fascination with coal mining had evaporated decades ago. Mining appears to have made a resurgence in Blaenavon in recent weeks - or should I say days? Please enlighten me, and tell me how I can help you today ladies?"

Dee had plenty to say but managed to restrain herself allowing Lauren to speak first, "Thank you for seeing us at such short notice, we do appreciate it. Gussie, I come from a family in Australia with a long tradition in the mining industry, not coal, but other more valuable minerals. That combined with my geological studies has brought me to Wales, and now to Blaenavon."

Lauren, politely paused, allowing Dee to explain her presence, "Oh, and I'm a TV producer with an interest in mining documentaries. We are kind of working on a special project together." She stopped, and smiled, sensing a degree of intrigue in Mertens, before letting Lauren continue.

"Yes - we are. Gussie, you mentioned your awareness of another mining discussion, or operation taking place? May I ask is that an official start-up? Going ahead for coal mining or are they mining something else? I only ask because I may have astonishing news for you. Something you may not yet be aware of."

Without breaking any confidences, Mertens explained her awareness of a new coal mining operation under consideration in town, which the council intended to rubber stamp. She emphasised the term, *coal mining*, "I don't think this is a secret. They claim they have a recent coal mining licence and to have received a notification from the council planning team concerning fees for reparation works? Perhaps I am over-stepping the mark here, but they say they are in final discussions with local farmers to operate on their land - to excavate coal. What can you tell me to the contrary that will be so astonishing?"

Lauren went on to describe at length to Gussie, her suspicions concerning the mining operation, run by a man called Jason Price and his associate Declan Ryan. She also provided a comprehensive explanation of the term rare earth, its high value, applications, and scarcity.

"Gussie, the Blaenavon land Jason Price is trying to acquire from the farmers will not be used to mine coal. He is going to mine rare earth metals, tonnes of them, worth millions, and millions. I have evidence of the astronomical value of the land around Blaenavon, because of what I - and Jason Price - have discovered in the soil. Let me show you something. Please bear with me, I'll try not to make a mess."

Lauren produced a small electronic device from her backpack, like a child's elaborate water pistol, with an LCD screen, and a freezer bag containing a handful of dark grey dirt. Using some of the soil spread on a piece of paper she activated the spectrometer until it pinged seconds later.

She explained the reading, "There we go. This is just a fraction of one of the numerous scientific samples I took from the area we discussed. We have tested this one and many others just like it, and they are all loaded with the same remarkable saturation of rare earth particles. The whole area is worth a hundred times more per acre than central London – millions."

Gussie looked from the sample to Lauren to Dee and back to the sample in disbelief, "Can I keep this sample?"

"Of course you can, that little piece is probably worth £5 - just kidding. I'm sorry, I beg your pardon – that was flippant of me, and this is a serious business. From what you just told me, neither the council nor the farmers have any idea about the land value. Forgive me, Gussie, I'm not a lawyer, but isn't that fraud?"

The furious look on Gussie Mertens face provided the answer, she then offered a suggestion, "I don't know how close the farmers are to committing, but I think we need to intervene as soon as possible and tell them what we know. I know Maggie well from the school PTA, and I know where she works. I think a visit is in order. I have her mobile number - I'll call her first to hear what she knows."

Gussie tried to call her in front of the women, but there was no answer, "She works over the mountain, in Abergavenny, ten minutes away. I can't get away right now, I have back to back meetings this afternoon. I'll keep trying her phone when I get a chance, but maybe you can go and see her. This is the place where she works..."

Lauren offered to drive, but first returned with Dee to her hotel to grab a warmer coat and her other notebook. The fog had lifted a fraction, and the snow turned into sleet, but the gritters had done a fine job on the roads. As the Beetle crested the pass over to Abergavenny, two hundred yards from the top, a cautious Lauren, more familiar with dust storms than snow, didn't see the white pick-up truck approaching at high speed behind them on her cautious decent. Neither did she see the pick-up truck pull up alongside and barge into the side of her car until it was too late.

The Beetle left the grippy surface of the road, finding zero traction on the grass verge, before sliding a bumpy thirty feet, through bracken and gorse bushes and coming to a stop under a double telegraph pole. The front end of the Beetle slotted in neatly between the poles, which ran in sequence all the way up the mountain. If Lauren had skirted either side of the telegraph poles it would have resulted in a serious accident. As it was, both occupants had a narrow escape, just minor bumps, bruises, and a jarred thumb as the steering wheel spun like a top catching Lauren's hand in the process. They were lucky, the car didn't roll, and the posts stopped the car from going hundreds of feet further down the steep slope. The battered car hung there by a wing and a prayer.

Two hikers, three hundred yards away saw the final moments of the nasty skid and came to assist. By the time they reached the car, the women had emerged from the front passenger side door, both covered in the chalky airbag dust. Shaken up, Lauren and Dee managed to scramble their way to a sheep track and walk through the crusty snow back up to the road above, with the aid of the hikers. They stood surveying the scene below, staring at the gouged track created by the Beetle's sideways skid. Both women were in reasonable shape but realised the incident was no accident.

On the road, a passing car stopped and offered to take them to local A&E. Still shaking with fright, anger and cold, Lauren thanked the driver and replied, "No, we are both OK, but instead of hanging around in the bitter cold here for a police car, a lift to the police station in Abergavenny will be great. We can make our way somewhere else straight afterwards."

Following their visit to the police station, to report the incident, Dee used the mobile number given to her by Gussie. Maggie answered and listened carefully to what Dee had to say. A little over an hour later, all three women met in the reception area where Maggie worked. The fifteen-minute break she had taken ended up extending into the most valuable forty minutes of her life.

Lauren listened to Maggie's update on the situation, "None of us have signed anything yet - just made verbal agreements. Price expects to meet us at some point late this afternoon with the new contract when we all finish work."

Taking her time, whilst rubbing her sore thumb, and still sprinkled with remnants of airbag dust, Lauren went through everything she had discussed and demonstrated earlier with Gussie. She then expressed her serious concerns about the *land grab deal*, as she described it. The deal still teetered on the verge of them signing it over. Lauren also told Maggie about the sudden death of Nick Savvas, and the earlier car incident. An alarmed Maggie, told them, "I need to make some urgent phone calls."

She returned having spoken first of all with Gussie, responding to her missed call from earlier, and then with her cousin David, "I never thought I'd say so, but David and Liz were right all along. They told me not to trust that Jason Price. Do you know about the rumours of when he was a kid? A tragic accident, or maybe worse. It happened not far from where you went off the road earlier."

~

CHAPTER 31

After lunch, Declan Ryan spoke to Jason Price, "We've had a busy morning Jason, what with one thing and another. Have they signed yet?"

"I'm heading up to see David Davies, at his house right now. He's expecting me, and he can make a start with his contract if the others aren't all there when I arrive. They can act as witnesses for each other's signatures. I'll bet they can't wait to see me, - and I feel the same about them."

Ryan sensed the excitement building. Curious to get closer, rather than stay on the fringes, he asked, "Why don't I join you? I'd like to meet them, or I can stay in the car, and play it by ear until you're done if you prefer?"

"OK, I'll pick you up - are you still checking out that mine – I'll come over? But let's not complicate things and crowd them with a new face, not until we have everything signed – then I can introduce you, OK?"

Having picked up Ryan, Price pulled up, outside David's cottage and almost leapt out of his car with excitement. The dog barked louder than ever as he knocked on the door. Expecting a cordial invitation to step inside, Price smiled to himself. Instead, the door swung open, and David took one step forward, grasped him below the collar of his Barbour and punched him on the bridge of his nose. Blood streamed down Price's face as he fell backwards into a filthy, icy puddle, with blows reigning down on him from David's furious fists. Ryan watched from the car, scrambled to unbuckle his seat belt, and stepped out to intervene, but the nasty episode was over and finished in seconds.

Liz dashed out through the door behind her husband, "Stop it Dai! Stop it! He's had enough." She battled to stop David's right arm issuing further punishment to Price's battered face.

"Here's your two grand you bastard. You can shove it right up your arse."

David tossed the cash onto the torso of a confused and semi-conscious Price.

"Have that from your brother Rhys. We've all got long memories in this town, mate. You won't be digging any of that stuff out of my land. What is it called Liz - rare earth? Yeah, we know all about it. Might as well be unicorn shit, cos you won't be getting your hands on any around here - we're done. And for the record, Gussie Mertens has already been in contact with the police, they are onto you and your mates."

Price had a vague recollection of a few keywords in the melee - *your brother Rhys - rare earth.* As he wobbled and struggled to get himself back to his feet, he saw Declan Ryan standing in the road. At that moment Price wanted the world to end.

Chapter 32

Revealed

Two days after the altercation between David Davies and Jason Price. Augusta Mertens felt a sense of leadership, and moral responsibility to Lauren, Dee, and the farmers. She decided to invite them to come together, so they could discuss a process to resolve the 'unsavoury incident' they had all found themselves exposed to. She had already spent some time with the police and offered her strong views on the matter. The police wanted to have a conversation with Jason Price and his associates, but they could not be located.

Mertens met the group of people after what local, uninformed social media described as *that car crash*, and *the scrap.* They gathered for a late sandwich lunch at the council offices in the Workman's Hall, a convenient and private location for all.

~

The day before the council get together, Lauren ha a long and honest conversation with her parents. Sh reassured them that the whole worrying saga had passed and all her instincts had been correct. Now, thanks t the support of Uncle Jack, there could be the 'rare earth family business opportunity in Wales that they had al hoped for. What they once thought of as pie in the sky now existed as a genuine business venture.

"Mum, Dad, meeting them all tomorrow at th council offices, will be a big day for me - well for al of us. This is my opportunity to present a succinc business case to the council and the farmers. I hope t encourage them to engage with us and to help them capitalise on what they have within their land. Let' face it between Dad's, Jack's, and my knowledge, w have all the expertise they could ever need. At leas they know they can trust me after all this crap."

Harry asked a question, "So are they expectin something from you Lauren? A presentation - or is i off the cuff and casual?"

"Well Gussie, the deputy mayor, is doing me a bi of a favour. When she invited us all to get together a such short notice, I asked her if I could have twent minutes to talk to everyone, and if she could hook m up to a projector and a screen. If you don't ask - yo don't get, right? I know this is all a bit sudden afte yesterday, but come on, the people are desperate t know about the land and what to do with it. So, I' explain all that to them. Dee is coming along too fo moral support."

"Dee?" asked Margaret and Harry in unison.

"Dee...Munchetty, the woman from National Geographical, the TV producer. We ended up in the car scrape together. Remember? I thought I mentioned her name already. Anyway, she's great."

~

Before Gussie's meeting, more facts started to emerge providing a clearer picture. Lauren and Dee Munchetty pieced everything together, although more significant news would soon break.

The local trio of farmers and their partners attended the lunch, laid on by the deputy mayor, along with a slightly nervous Lauren and an uber-confident Dee who said, "Lauren, they'll love you, babe. After what you did for them? Whoa, are you kidding me – relax and name your price? Oh, sorry did I just say...price?"

Mertons introduced Lauren once again to the group, although most had already met her and thanked her. But this was a more formal situation and right that Mertens should build her up and give her this opportunity to cement the relationship with the important people she had recently met for the first time.

Before Lauren was able to speak, David apologised for interrupting and asked to say something, "Guys, and in particular, Lauren and Dee, before you begin, I'd like to offer our heartfelt thanks, for everything you have done for us. Without your smart, quick-thinking who knows what mess our families may have found ourselves in. Those rogues would have controlled us, whilst they stole our money. We are indebted to you. There, I said my piece - please carry on." Everyone cheered and applauded.

Laurens's nerves vanished in a heartbeat, she started her presentation with a beaming smile and took the group through a brief history of rare earth metals, noble and precious metals. Next, she explained their applications, how the Chinese dominate the market and how they mine and refine the commodity. Everyone's jaw dropped when she came to the slide which explained the value of the land in Blaenavon to comparative mines around the world.

She allowed a murmur in the small audience before continuing her talk, "Yes, those remarkable values are correct. We have great experience and expertise of mining rare earth in Australia which we hope to replicate here in Wales."

The remainder of her talk focused on the process, timescales and investment required to get the mining plant up and running, using her family business as the subsidiary company to run the operation at a fair and reasonable share option fee. "Investment will be easy guys, there will be queues around the block of financial institutions ready to work with us. Although, I do have an idea to form a co-operative, like a consortium, for the Blaenavon townspeople, offering them shares in the business at preferential rates. I have produced some facts and basic financial models which

I will email to all of you later. I'm also aware that some areas adjacent to the farmland is still owned by the local council, and if we can incorporate that land then there could be even greater prosperity for the town."

David took the lead one more time, "Thank you for your excellent presentation, Lauren. We expected you would explain everything perfectly to us and you did - you have some fantastic knowledge and ideas - we are so grateful. We also discussed between ourselves that we need a business partner to lead us through this erm'...minefield. As I mentioned earlier, we are indebted to you, and with the support of Gussie and her fellow councillors, we want you and your team to work with us as soon as possible."

Mertens looked delighted and rightly so, she had been instrumental in helping the group get to this point and the foundations of a mining consortium. Good news for them and great news for the town.

Dee Munchetty couldn't restrain herself any longer. Never wishing to miss an opportunity to lock herself in, she explained that Lauren had agreed to involve her and her company to make a documentary, right from day one of the new partnership.

Sandwich in hand, Rob looked at Maggie and asked her, "So will we be film stars or millionaires or both?" Everyone laughed, unable to believe their luck.

The partnership would go ahead spectacularly, so would the documentary, the first of many involving Lauren and Dee. Margaret and Harry Eaves' Australian operation would also find some new local prosperity.

But a far more sinister side to the story would emerge over the coming days and weeks. One that no one in the room of overjoyed people could have anticipated. The dark side had already started with Nick Savvas and his unfortunate wife Mia, who appeared as though she would recover from her head injuries.

For centuries hundreds of men and children died in the valley, due to greedy slave-driving coal and ironmasters. Now, a pattern was re-emerging - coal mining, greed, and death – in recent weeks history had started to repeat itself – and perhaps there would be more to follow.

Chapter 33

Game Over

Declan Ryan's head almost exploded with rage the moment he witnessed David Davies's unexpected and severe assault on Jason Price. He dragged Price back inside the car and drove him away in silence other than for moaning, groaning, and snivelling coming from the man in the bloodied passenger seat.

Ryan's truck was at the drift mine where Michael had spent the day continuing to prepare a schedule of works and taking an inventory. Water and electricity were both up and running so Ryan took Price to the small makeshift canteen zone, to clean-up up his blood-drenched, pummelled face. Followed by a one-sided discussion.

Seething with anger, Ryan talked *at* Price, "Well Jason, that little visit went well for you, didn't it? You weren't expecting that were you? Neither was I to tell you the truth. I expected you to call me in to celebrate the signing of the contracts. What the fuck is going on?"

Still bleeding, Price sat crestfallen on a cracked plastic canteen chair, pinching his nose with a shaky hand. He bore no resemblance to the confident multi-millionaire businessman who pulled up outside David Davies's home earlier, full of optimism, dressed to the nines. The bridge of his nose had a gaping lateral split, and both his eyes were closing. Michael Ryan had rolled up some lengths of toilet roll and shoved them up inside Price's nostrils to staunch the bleeding.

Price gulped in air through his swollen lips, and struggled to get the words out, in between breaths, "I think I need to go to a hospital? I think I need *ditches* in my *dose*?"

If Declan Ryan was not so furious at what he had witnessed earlier, and the huge financial ramifications associated with it, he might have smirked at Price's nasal pronunciation. Instead, he smashed his fist into Price's already swollen face, knocking him clean off the chair, stating, "That was a waste of good toilet roll, Mikey. He won't be needing anymore though, or a trip to the hospital." Tossing Michael a roll of duct tape from an open toolbox, he issued an instruction, "Here take this while I have a little think."

Michael understood exactly what to do with it and bound the hands and feet of the motionless Price.

The quick-thinking Ryan had made the essence of his decision an hour ago - the moment he dragged the injured Price into the car. He had crushed Price's mobile phone with his foot as they drove back towards the mine, and then threw it under a cattle grid. Price would not need his phone again.

"He knows too much Mikey. He's not as stupid as he looks, mind you that might be debatable. Look at the state of him over there." Ryan, glared at Price in disgust, whining in the corner trying to escape his new duct tape cuffs. "He mentioned the Savvas's to me earlier. He knows the score - well what did he expect? I saved us all a fortune by *doing* them pair. But in the end, we couldn't reverse the damage caused by that idiot Savvas. Now we'll be in the frame unless we take care of business here, once and for all, with *this one*, then we'll be sound. He's cost me millions Mikey, I mean millions. I should just slit his throat and leave him here to rot."

Michael knew there would be some more work involved with Price, "So what's the plan for him?"

"*Yer man*, earlier, that chatty caretaker bloke, he gave me an idea. Fetch that old builder's supplies one-tonne sand sack I saw from around the back of the boiler room. Now let's go and have some dinner, we have a busy night ahead of us Mikey. We need to kill some time and we need some food, then we need to hit the road straight afterwards."

Michael yanked out Price's toilet paper packing, jolting him, but enabling him to just about manage to breathe through the semi-crushed passageway inside his nose, which had stopped bleeding - only to block up his other airway by gagging his mouth with more tape. They left him moaning, bound, and strapped to a steam pipe, "He ain't going nowhere for a bit."

When they returned from the pub after closing time, they hung around close to a gas-powered space heater to stay warm and waited there until after midnight. Once again, the fog had descended over Blaenavon, and the temperature had dropped to below freezing. A cold, quiet school night in town, not a soul around.

Jason Price's wife tried twice to call and speak with him, but twice her calls went straight to voicemail. Little did she know, the problem was not a poor phone signal or a dead battery - his phone nestled, crushed, underneath the rails of a cattle grid on a backroad.

Declan Ryan walked over to one of the broken windowpanes, looked out, and looked at his watch once more, "That'll do us. Let's get on with it Mikey," his breath condensing as he turned and issued the instruction.

Feet and wrists duct-taped together, they shuffled Price inside the heavy-duty builder's sack and dragged it through the building to the rear tailgate of their white pick-up truck. The truck still bore the pale blue scratches and dents from the collision with Lauren Eaves' Beetle.

Price's moans had become muffled squeals of abject fear, as they hoisted the sack and its wriggling desperate contents into the open bed of the truck "Christ, what have you been eating Jason? You weigh the same as the sand did." Ryan emitted a cruel laugh

Ryan sounded pleased that soon he could enjoy scant consolation and retribution for his losses with the elimination of any risk of arrest for the attack on the Savvas's.

Price lay stuffed into a cold corner of the open-backed truck and heard the wind rushing above him, sensing gears changing as the vehicle's speed increased. The truck's metal structure dug into his back and shoulders as it braked and cornered then slowed down. His scrambled brain tried hard to release endorphins and make sense of what might happen to him next.

The truck stopped and the throb of the engine underneath Price disappeared. The breeze wafted the smell of burnt diesel fumes and heavy braking through the low foggy air to the inside his sack. He heard both the doors of the truck open, then the damp, smelly bag opened, and a phone torch shone on his face. As his blurred vision adapted to the light and his new surroundings, he immediately recognised the form of Ryan leaning over, staring down at him.

In his unmistakable Irish accent, he commented, "You look like a man who's struggled through a tough day, Jason. A tough struggle for all of us today, don't you think?"

Price wriggled desperately and pleaded for his life, squealing through his taped mouth. His face proved challenging for Ryan to distinguish between blotchiness, hypertension, and congealed blood.

Ryan's anger flared again, "Jason, you just lost every penny you ever made, and then you lost fucking millions of my money. Now, you ain't got two halfpennies to rub together, have you? Nothing. So where does that leave us, eh?"

Price's tearful eyes opened wide. His overloaded brain had lost its ability to comprehend anything other than fear and his entire body began the tremble uncontrollably.

"We did a bit of impromptu research on you earlier Jason. At the mine, we spoke to one of your old chatty schoolmates. Sounds like your mouth was as big then as it is now. Shouting it off to him in school, about how you killed your little brother. Rhys, was it? You don't look so tough now though, do you?"

Ryan turned off his phone light and turned away from the sack, "This is the spot, Mikey, then down the slope and over there," pointing with a finger into the darkness.

As an accompaniment, two heavy concrete blocks landed on top of Price adding to his pain. The Ryan cousins next task was to tightly tie together the bags fork-lift straps.

Jason Price lost track of how many minutes had passed since the truck engine went silent. His arms, legs, and back no longer spasmed, they were too numb. He could make out truck doors opening and closing. He was drifting in and out of an agonising consciousness

As the terrifying nightmare continued, he knew he would soon be a dead man. All he could do was wait.

For some inexplicable reason, at that point Price felt some regret for his dreadful wrongdoing. For the first time in his life, he experienced remorse over the death of his brother whose name David Davies mentioned to him earlier. Price recalled, the dreadful part he played in Rhys's death and more tears filled his eyes - because for the first time in five decades he recollected the breathless face of his poor brother beneath the ice.

~

Two mornings later, the fog had lifted and whilst Gussie and her group were planning to meet, local wildlife photographer, Luke Adams, parked up at a high, moorland 'trig point' car park. He grabbed his Thermos, backpack, and spare camera batteries before meandering the half-mile across the soggy mountain moor. Sheep tracks provided the only option through the rugged landscape. Luke's simple plan for the sunny morning involved photographing whatever nature brought his way. Mountain ponies, skylarks darting around, or perhaps 'Welsh black' cattle roaming free, although he was cautious of those after he had to outrun a herd of them, protective of their calves, the previous summer.

Within ten minutes he approached the Keepers Pond, found a comfortable spot beside the water's edge, and pulled out his laptop.

"What natural delights did the last couple of nights bring for me?"

Luke plugged the first of the SD cards, retrieved from his two discreetly positioned infrared motion-activated camera's, into his laptop. He had placed both cameras amongst the heather mounds, well hidden in a secure, elevated position two days ago. They provided perfect views of the ten to fifteen metres in and around the bank down to a deep edge of the pond.

The natural delights Luke hoped for didn't materialise. He saw the usual array of sheep, two rabbits, and then he looked at the screen and paused. Flicking backwards and forwards, the sequence of dozens of perfect still images showed two men. One of the men wore a dark sweater, the other a sweatshirt. Together they dragged a heavy large white bag - a builder's one-tonne sandbag, with a builders merchants logo, printed clearly on its side. They stood on the edge of the bank and appeared to swing the weighty looking bag and release it. A splash and ripples spread across the monotone pond as they walked back, passing the camera in the opposite direction.

Luke inserted the second SD card, from his Bushnell NatureView Cam HD. Positioned with a similar view to the first camera, this would show high-quality video and audio footage of the same images seen moments earlier.

A breeze caught his hood as he sat there, so Luke plugged in his headphones to ensure he could hear the audio at its best. Once again, the men came into view, dragging the large bag, passing the exact point where Luke sat. He sensed something sinister about to happen and continued to watch and listen.

CHAPTER 33

The video provided more detailed information than the stills. Something alive, maybe a person wiggled inside the bag. And then he heard it, quickly cranking up the volume he could hear desperate, repeated, muffled *nasal* squeals, and could see exaggerated movements masked by the walls of the sack. Horrified, Luke realised he could hear someone inside the sack - kicking and screaming for their life.

An Irish voice came through the headphones as clear as day, "He'll be quiet soon Mikey, permanently quiet."

Luke made a mental note of the name, *"Mikey?"* Then carried on.

The words came from a man facing the camera, five metres away, he wore a pale sweatshirt emblazoned with an anchor logo on the breast and Oceanside Bar Barcelona printed underneath the anchor. Even in the monotone infrared video a distinctive cropped head of silver hair, scalp scars, and a cauliflower ear appeared clear as day.

The men paused for a moment with the bag resting on the side of the bank, the same man - the most vocal of the two and the obvious leader - kicked the round bulge on the side of the bag with his hiking boots, viciously, twice.

"Guess what Jason, they say this is the spot, exactly where you killed your brother. Now, this is your turn for a swim you bastard."

The men shuffled close to the edge, positioned themselves, and heaved up the bag. They started swaying the heavy white bag, and made it look easy, "OK, on three."

"One."

Luke stared transfixed at what he witnessed.

"Two."

"Three."

The sack landed in the water, well over a metre away from the bank.

Luke again saw the splash and ripples he had seen moments earlier on the still images, but this time in full motion, with perfect clarity and sharp audio. With a heartless, "Get in there," added by one of the men for good measure, as the bag submerged beneath the surface within seconds. They walked off without saying another word, so close to the camera he could even see a Berghaus logo on one of the men's hiking boots.

Luke reached out a hand to turn off his laptop. His fingers trembled as he searched and found the tiny button on the edge of his laptop. He eventually composed himself, threw everything into his backpack and ran the ten-minute walk to his car in six. Gasping, breathless, and terrified, he locked the doors and looked all around the car park. He found his mobile, started the engine, and with shaking hands called 999, "I think I just witnessed a murder."

~

Within hours of Price's murder, the Ryan's had stuck to their hastily prepared exit plan. They drove for an hour, parked up close to Cardiff airport, then slept for a few more. After their nap, they arrived unscathed and unnoticed at check-in, long before sunrise. They had booked last minute seats on a budget flight and arrived back home in Barcelona not long after breakfast, just two more faces in the crowd, dragging suitcases and going about their business.

The men didn't say much during their long journey, tiredness and introspection eroded the hours. It was the same emotionless reaction, which followed all the other occasions in past when they had needed to *take care of business* – murdering with impunity.

As a result of their earlier than expected return to Spain, they made a decision to carry on with business as usual, straight back into the swing of things - at least for Michael, enabling him to catch up with emails, and with day to day logistics business issues.

Two out of two money-spinning projects, both with Jason Price, had failed miserably, and one of the projects left Ryan with a large unpaid outstanding council bill. He continued to fume in a venomous frame of mind. All the issues meant he needed to take stock of his circumstances and reacquaint himself with his regular revenue streams. His other hugely frustrating problem had not gone away – finding future alternative methods to wash what remained of his mountain of unusable cash.

Ryan decided the best thing to do required finding some space to think and calm down, whilst he left Michael to pick up on some of his pressing tasks. Ryan's preferred choice for relaxation involved taking his small cabin cruiser along with his wife, and his two dogs for a few sunny early spring days along the Mediterranean coastline, avoiding any interruptions.

Gwent Police's digital forensics team analysed the information provided by Luke Adams. They acted on it as soon as they saw the images and cordoned off the whole area surrounding the Keepers Pond and its adjacent car parks. As anticipated, divers located a one-tonne builders merchant's sack in deep water close to the edge of the man-made pond within minutes. Inside the sack, they discovered the body of a man later identified as Jason Price. A burnt-out car wreck a mile away tied in with Price. A murder hunt ensued.

The Ryans, both experienced 'professionals' - thought they had taken care of everything from the word go to cover their tracks. They even left the scene using a pre-planned sat-nav route of back roads and B roads for fifteen miles and avoided any potential main road junction ANPR, Automatic Number Plate Recognition, cameras. But their luck ran out - they had not bargained on a wildlife cameraman's hobby and his remarkable incriminating evidence. Facial recognition software, age profile, all narrowed down by Irish accents meant it did not take the authorities long to identify Declan and Michael Ryan as the men responsible for the horrifying murder.

Spanish police assembled an armed squad and raided Ryan's home and businesses. Due to the speed of the information exchange, and their swift response they thought they had the element of surprise and would capture their target. But they were too late, a frustrated Ryan had gone to the coast, long before they arrived. The police enjoyed greater success at the logistics centre. Michael Ryan stood in full view in the yard, overseeing shipments wearing his Hi-Viz and a yellow helmet. He couldn't believe how quickly the police had identified and arrested him.

Declan Ryan had started the second leg of his mini voyage two hours before the raids on his home. His phone started pinging with messages and he then received a call from one of his employees alerting him, "Declan they just arrested Mikey, and they're coming for you. That guy, Jason Price, is dead. They found him in a reservoir or somewhere. By all accounts, they found pictures of you and Mikey doing it."

"Pictures - what pictures?"

Ryan couldn't understand why he was under suspicion so soon after leaving Wales. He made a hasty return to shore, noted down some important numbers from his phone, dumped it, and went in a separate direction to his wife. Things were moving fast, and he needed time and space until he could establish what evidence the police had on him and his cousin. His wife made some Google searches before they went their separate ways and explained the news from Wales. Splashed across every news feed were images of the Declan and Michael Ryan as persons of interest.

He kept shaking his head, trying to convince himself the videos and pictures couldn't possibly exist, *"How could they? Impossible? Who else was there?"*

But it dawned on him, and the harsh facts stayed with him. He felt like a sinking man who could not swim, out of control, ironically, just as Price did. He realised if the police had irrefutable evidence - images and a video - with the evidence stacked against him, his only option was to go on the run, hide up and make some decisions from there.

Taking a necessary but calculated risk, Ryan would drive his car to a small, isolated *casita* ski chalet he had used in the past, with a key box next to the front door for easy access. He drove the 140km to the Pyrenees. He stopped for provisions on the way, including a couple of pay as you go phones, and a *Just for Men* hair darkening dye pack using cash - he always had plenty of cash – that was part of his problem.

Karim Nasri's phone vibrated, displaying an unfamiliar Spanish number, unlike most people, he always answered such calls, if he could, "Oui?"

"Bon soir mon ami - I've never been so glad to hear you pick up the phone my old friend. I need your help. Big time - Can you talk?"

Nasri had an intense discussion for almost twenty minutes with his trusted old friend. Ryan explained the urgency of his circumstances, what took place in Wales, and how he had no time to prepare to go on the run.

"I always thought I'd be ready if something like this happened Karim. But you never are - are you? To make matters worse I have nothing with me, just some cash. The police are all over my place and my *safe*. I need something to get me up and running fast, I have a plan - an excellent plan, but I need a false ID and a passport. Can you help me? How good are your contacts and how fast can you move?"

Ryan recalled a conversation a couple of years earlier when Nasri mentioned sorting out passports for someone in a hurry. Ryan didn't forget it, and promised to organise them for himself, *"Fix a leaky roof when the sun is shining."* He told himself - but he never got around to it.

"Declan, stay cool my friend. I need to make a phone call. Give me half an hour and I'll call you back. I promise I won't let you down."

Half an hour later Nasri called his old friend back, with the news he wanted to hear, "I have good news, my friend, I am a well-connected man. I will have a passport for you within 24-hours. I need a few headshots for the passport - take them and send them to me straight away. Then I can bring everything to you, I'll come and see you. Let me know exactly where you are."

"Wow, 24-hours – wow. I owe you one Karim." Ryan had never been so relieved in his entire life.

"I told you I am well connected - and lots of cash tends to speed things up, eh? Besides, my shipment is docking in the UK tomorrow then heading for Devon, I need you safe and sound Declan."

Nasri knew the exact location of Ryan. The dead Harrison couple, still missing persons - owned the well-equipped, luxurious *casita* chalet, once used as an Airbnb, and Nasri and Ryan had used it on rare occasions to meet in the past. The Harrison's would definitely not be needing it ever again.

Decades ago, Nasri and Ryan had been to hell and back, side by side witnessing all kinds of sickening sights. In a warzone, their lives depended on the trust they had for one another. Now, time had moved on and priorities had changed, people keep in touch but drift apart - both of the old friends had hidden agendas.

Chapter 34

The Hunt is On

BBC Wales live news feed, "An international investigation is underway, and it all started here in the former mining town of Blaenavon. Police believe the killing of a man at a local beauty spot has a connection to a massive fraud scandal. Quick thinking by some local people and two visitors from overseas thwarted the gang, one of whom is under arrest in Spain. Augusta Mertens is a spokesperson for the local council and the deputy mayor of the town. She joins me now. Ms Mertens, we have already heard from the police, but what can you tell us about your involvement in this incident? And who are the visitors who assisted you and the police?"

Mertens looked at the camera, composed herself and chose her words carefully, "Thank you. The first thing I want to do is to offer our condolences to the victim's family. I also want to reiterate what Gwent Police stated earlier, and reassure the local community that as dreadful as this is, it is an isolated, targeted incident. Police are now looking for someone in connection with this crime in Spain, not in the UK."

The reporter continued to press, "Mrs Mertens, we understand that you contacted the police on a matter related to a separate incident earlier in the day and that two women escaped with light injuries after another car forced them off the Abergavenny road? We also hear that the women had just left your offices in town, is that true? Did the women know the victim?"

Mertens did not appreciate the forthright questioning, "We have just gone through a cold snap with the weather, yesterday morning the roads were atrocious, accidents can happen to anyone from time to time on the mountain roads. Yes, I believe I may have met the women you refer to earlier in the day, pure coincidence that they crashed, thank goodness they are fine. My understanding is neither had ever met the victim – there is no connection, no doubt just more speculation. People on social media sometimes like to put two and two together and make five, don't they? Thank heavens everyone else is well and that Gwent Police have resolved things. Meanwhile, as you can appreciate this is an active investigation and at the end of the day, I am a solicitor, so we must leave it there. Thank you."

Feeling safe and with Ryan in Spain on the run Lauren and Dee watched a re-run of the TV new from a screen in the privacy and comfort of Gussi Mertens home.

Dee commented, "Nice job Gussie – respect. That reporter guy just saved me the trouble of interviewing you for my show," Gussie acknowledged Dee's compliment with the hint of a smile, whilst Lauren managed a more overt chuckle.

Gussie asked the women, "What did the police say when they interviewed you earlier? What happens next?"

Lauren explained, "They carried out our interviews in a relaxed suite area at the police station, one at a time, then we both sat together and gave them the whole picture, filling in a few extra gaps. They were fine and grateful that we helped them. We told them everything we knew about the land and the farmers, our suspicions, and the facts. The police also spoke to Maggie, Rob, and David. Everyone realises now that Price and Ryan did not intend mining coal, but rare earth worth millions...and how I made the connection with Savvas...and then...how that meant... Price...and David."

Lauren's words and phrases slowed, then ground to a halt, as she started wiping tears from her eyes with a trembling hand. Her mind had taken control, blocking her ability to talk as the reality of every word dawned on her - that two men were dead, a woman remained in hospital fighting for her life. The whole traumatic situation could so easily have been much worse for Lauren and Dee, and Lauren could see that now.

Gussie touched Lauren's hand, as she took several deep breaths. With tears still streaming down her face, she continued to force the words out. "What if I hadn't been nosing around on the Uni computer? What if I hadn't contacted Nick Savvas? Maggie and David?" The names and their significance told the story and the impact they had on Lauren.

Dee comforted her new friend, "Lauren, I knew Nick Savvas really well. Deep down he was a good guy. Some of the things he told me over the phone, and in some of his messages, lead me to think his main driving force was to back out and not shaft the farmers. He couldn't do it. I'm convinced of it – so don't fret about what you said to him. He knew his actions were wrong and illegal. He brought it on himself. Maybe by the time he wanted to make things right with the farmers, it was too late, or maybe the others wouldn't listen. They were too greedy. Look at this, I showed the police earlier on."

Dee showed Lauren and Gussie a WhatsApp message trail between her and Savvas, she pointed out some notable messages where he expressed his concerns about his associates. "He didn't give their names, but no doubt in my mind now he meant Price and Ryan. I figured that out from the get-go. How he had reservations about how underhand they were, and that he needed to speak with them to sort it out."

Lauren appeared more reassured than she had moments earlier. "I'm sorry. This all just happened so fast, stuff going on back home, then over here. I need time to stop and think – take it all in. All I wanted was to make things right for the farmers, the town and try and help my family. What's so wrong with that?"

Dee smiled at Lauren, "Exactly, you did the right thing. Who wouldn't have made the same decisions you did? We all did the right thing. We are all in this together and thank God we were. There were some similar undertones in an email Nick sent me as well as stuff in his WhatsApps's. He may have been drinking when he sent some of them and said more than he intended. So, Lauren, the walls started to crumble down on his project long before you showed up, I'm certain of it. That's what happens to these people. Poor Nick, I hope his wife's gonna pull through. Jason Price and guys like him are never as smart as they think they are. Which is why most of them end up in jail."

Gussie added a polite warning, "You should both be aware, the world's media don't have your contacts details at the moment, do they? Well, guess what - registered on the town council website are all of my town councillor contact details. My inbox is practically exploding, and my phone hasn't stopped ringing with requests to speak with me. Sounds as though the murder is one thing, but the biggest story is the rare earth Klondike - as they are calling it. That story is still sinking in and reaching the news people like a second wave."

At that moment, Gussie's assistant called on Gussie's home landline to tell her people were queuing outside the solicitor's office in town, adding, "Town is going crazy Gussie, they are saying bookings for the museum, local hotels and Airbnb's are through the roof. What's wrong with people?"

Gussie explained she would be in the office in less than an hour, "Human nature and curiosity. Sounds as though Blaenavon is back on the map, for one reason and another, and things are not going to get any quieter for months or years from what Lauren and Dee are telling me. See you in a bit."

~

In Spain, the hunt continued for Declan Ryan. Interpol had all the details of the man they sought, and his cousin remained in custody – as expected Michael Ryan stuck to an old, ingrained mantra *whatever you say, say nothing.* Declan Ryan's wife was saying nothing as well. With suspicions aroused and more information available to them, the Spanish investigators started to assemble the pieces in their jigsaw.

Mia Savvas came out of her induced coma within days and started talking. Other than for the multitude of glue, staples, and sutures, with a few shaved patches, to their amazement nursing staff and the neurologist expected her to make a full recovery. Armed security guards in the hospital kept her safe whilst detectives hoped she could provide them with even more information than they already had.

The Barcelona police were no longer treating the Nick and Mia Savvas incident as an attempted murder-suicide, instead, they had a murder and an attempted murder on their hands. The main suspect was Declan Ryan, maybe with the help of others. The truth was that Ryan's two cousins had carried out the gruesome attack

CHAPTER 34

Whilst all the commotion took place in Wales and the hunt for Declan Ryan in Spain continued, a gigantic cargo vessel had left Zeebrugge in Holland, on its way to unload a cargo load of thousands of container boxes in Immingham in the UK. One of the boxes belonged to Declan Ryan, with its deadly contents the property of Karim Nasri.

Chapter 35

A New Direction

So much had happened in the four days since the pick-up truck forced the VW Beetle off the road. The battered, but repairable, pale blue car looked sorry for itself as it sat in a local car spray workshop. The car didn't even belong to Lauren, but she had a sympathetic friend, more concerned with Lauren's welfare than the car. Dee had already made an agreement with Lauren, the farmers, and Gussie to produce the TV documentary, and a car-less Lauren needed to stay in close contact with the farmers. So for the time being, Dee set her up in a hotel room next to hers and gave her use of her hire car whenever she needed it.

Dee and Lauren caught everyone's attention wherever they went in town, even in the hotel lounge. "Lauren, this whole TV thing we have going on is a big deal. I realise there is a difficult ongoing police investigation, still only four days since Price's murder but that will have a positive effect on everything you do from here on. You have no idea where this is heading. There is so much interest in you, people are bombarding me with requests every day. You must organise yourself and find an agent to deal with *stuff*. Well, to deal with *me* even."

They both laughed. Lauren responded saying, "We've only known each other a few days and I feel like we've been through ten years of strife. An agent? Gosh, Dee, an *agent* hasn't even entered my mind. Maybe I need to think about getting around to one of those. But my priority right now is getting this rare earth project off the ground. I need a few spare days to complete my dissertation, apart from that, nothing else is more important than the project with David, Maggie, and Rob. You know what, I think an accountant is more important to me than an agent right now – I know you'll disagree."

Dee smiled, "Sorry, Lauren, it's been a long, long time since I went to college. You're right, get that college thing out of the way and make yourself some serious money here. Then have some fun, and oh, I have a few ideas for you - if everything goes to plan."

Lauren looked confused at the 'few ideas' comment, her mind running with all sorts of mad ideas. She switched back on, in an instant when her phone rang, jolting her back to reality. It showed a familiar number calling – Uncle Jack Tennison.

"Uncle Jack, even I know it's the middle of the night back home, what are you doing calling me so late?"

"It might be the middle of the night in Australia, but I just landed in Heathrow – not far up the road from Wales. The way things have been going, and from what I heard, you looked like you needed a hand, so I thought I would turn up and offer one. But I reckon you could teach me a thing or two now by the looks of it. Do I owe you for batteries for my spectrometer, or shall we call it quits?"

Lauren laughed; Jack never failed to make her smile.

"When I told your mum and dad, I was coming over they almost pushed me onto the plane. How are you doing love?"

"Oh Uncle Jack, this is fantastic, amazing. I can't believe you're here. I'll come and pick you up off the train later. There's so much more to tell you. Things keep changing every minute. TV cameras everywhere - it's crazy. But to tell you truth, I could do with some calm, and common sense to get this thing up and running. Honestly, people are walking onto the farmers land with Tesco carrier bags and filling them with coal dirt – ridiculous."

Jack responded with his familiar deep chuckle down the phone, which caused a sigh of relief from Lauren. First Dee emerging from nowhere and now Jack. Things had started heading in a positive direction. The whole surreal series of events had happened so quickly, just a matter of a few weeks, then at the end, everything unravelled. Lauren found the situation hard to believe at times.

Jack couldn't resist a cheeky comment, "Lauren I know what coal dirt looks like, but you'll have to talk me through what Tesco is when I get there."

"Yeah right – but it's the truth. It must be less than a week since it all kicked off, and a bloke claiming to represent a Chinese mining company knocked on David Davies' door yesterday – just another 'chancer'. Oh, and because of the time zones, I haven't yet told you and Dad – there has been a development with the farmers and our consortium partnership. Or at least we will have one once we get around to formally sorting out the business side of it. Our *Australian sister company,* when we register one, has a 10% stake, we agreed it yesterday - handshakes all round. Jack, a 10% shareholding - have you any idea? They insisted we had a fair share, because of what I did for them – I wasn't expecting that. They are good people, and they will be dead pleased to meet you. I've already told them so much about you and Dad."

Jack's voice switched to a serious sensible business tone, "You and I can sit down and go through your original 'mini' business plan and put some meat on the bones of it. At the same time, we need to register a business in the UK, for the consortium, directors, shareholdings – that sort of thing - then we can start in earnest. Oh, and someone will need to think of a company name. So there is a lot of important stuff that needs doing, and I can guide you through all of those things. With the help of an accountant and a good lawyer - I heard you know one."

Jack proved invaluable over the coming days and weeks, he and David Davies became like long lost friends within no time. Even Liz softened when she met him.

The team needed some information concerning the ownership of the old drift mine and its buildings. Jack identified it as an ideal ready-made location to develop and utilise.

Two days after Jack arrived, Lauren took a call from Gussie, "Lauren, I have some good news from our planning department at the council. We will be notifying the new owner, Mr Ryan, of a compulsory purchase order on the mine buildings at face value, in his absence. My colleagues have discovered some *helpful* discrepancies in the recent procurement documentation for the building, compounded by defaults on the reparations fees. The council will want to speak with you concerning a change of use and joint ownership with the council. I hope that solves one of your problems."

It did. The face value compulsory purchase meant a fraction of the total unofficial price that Ryan paid Feisal Hussein.

Just over a week after the incidents took place and during the Sunday morning over breakfast a their hotel, Dee presented Lauren with a bunch o newspapers, "Have you seen these, Lauren? You'r in most of them. How many interviews did yo do? You're getting more column inches than most politicians."

"What *column inches*? Show me those papers."

Some of the story headers read:

"Welsh Klondike Murder Solved by Aussie Lauren."

"Australian Woman Rejuvenates Town's Local Economy."

"International Fraud Plot Foiled."

"Murdered for Black Gold."

"One interview on the TV news - that's all I did. They even found a picture of me in my cap and gown in Sydney. Where on earth did that picture come from? And here's one of the pair of us in town together Dee?"

Dee laughed, "At least, those papers should keep you busy whilst I head back to the *States* tomorrow. I have some planning and budget meetings. Our TV production investors are keen that we make this show a priority Lauren. You knew it was coming, I'm sorry, this is a distraction you can do without. If aliens had landed somewhere last week, then maybe things would be different. But they didn't – you did – here."

"Thanks a million, Dee. Aliens would be easier to deal with. But I'll be fine, Uncle Jack's here for a while then Mum and Dad are coming over. And come to think of it, I sometimes wonder if Jack's from another planet. Plus I'm popping back and forth to Cardiff - plenty going on."

~

Within weeks initial plans for the rare earth business were in place. Architect consultations to design basic roads and infrastructure, in collaboration with council teams had taken place. Alongside a recruitment drive for a management team and technical staff. Although nothing would happen overnight, things started moving in the right direction.

Jack had stayed on in Wales for two weeks. He explained to the farmers the process of excavation and refining, and how they would avoid completing the refining themselves but would ship the thousands of tonnes of partially refined soil to the Chinese for a premium, but well worth the cost. A full refining plant would cost them tens of millions.

The whole business enterprise came as an overwhelming shock to the landowners. They had in some respects won the lottery and needed to understand what to do next. Yet they had a role to play as directors in making important decisions in the early months ahead of them. They were smart people but acknowledged the need to employ professional teams, to put in place all the processes and procedures that a normal business needed. And that's what they agreed they would do, before stepping back when the time came.

Outside investors would bear the brunt of upfron capital costs. One of the more exciting initiatives anc innovative approaches involved launching a local shar ownership co-operative. Townspeople could buy small stake in the business at preferential rates. Ther were rumours of floatation on the FTSE small-cap index, one day, if things went well, which attracted even more interest in the scheme.

Well and truly enhancing Blaenavon's existing notable profile on the global map.

~

Lauren contemplated everything that had happened over the past eight weeks since she first arrived in Blaenavon. People had suffered violence, some had died, and the police had arrested others. Many people would argue it was *good riddance* to some of those - they had it coming. Those criminals made their choices and died indirectly because of greed and coal, *black gold*. Blaenavon and the history of the town made Lauren realise that sadly, over the past two hundred years, hundreds of other, innocent hard-working people and young children, gave their lives mining underground. They didn't have the luxury of a choice.

Chapter 36

Final Plans

48-hours after the murder of Jason Price

The same day 'on the run' Ryan arrived at the Pyrenean casita, the MSC Isabella docked in Immingham, UK. The giant container ship could carry up to twenty-three thousand steel boxes, each one measuring 6m x 2.6m x 2.4m. Computer-guided cranes worked for hours unloading and positioning the cargo boxes into designated grids and stacks in a specific sequence. Like a supersized Lego-fest crossed with Jenga, on steroids.

Only one steel box mattered to Karim Nasri, and men were manually unloading its contents with forklifts inside a warehouse. In most large ports, customs check less than 1% of containers. Regular shipments from large, reputable organisations receive a verified inspection and sealing of the doors before embarking, avoiding costly, time-consuming inspections at the destination. Declan Ryan's regular verified shipment, with all the documentation in order, literally sailed through customs checks in Immingham. A forklift truck loaded the innocuous palletised delivery, into a soft-sided wagon, ready for the final leg of its seven-hour journey to a farm near Plymouth in Devon.

~

Declan Ryan often wondered if the day would ever come - he had considered it, even planned for it - but never expected it would come. Neither did Bernie Madoff or Max Clifford. The day when Ryan needed to evade the police, get out of Spain in a hurry, cover his tracks, and find a new life. That day had now arrived. He should have expected it, he owned some shady businesses, but he wasn't well prepared. Instead, less than 48-hours after killing Jason Price, he found himself holed up in a remote *casita* ski chalet, at the tail end of a warmer than usual Spanish Pyrenees ki season, with no one else for miles. Staying on his mall cabin cruiser, with the crafts inbuilt identifiable ransmitter beacon, meant he could not contemplate he option of heading hundreds of miles to north Africa. For the moment, he needed roads and access o people – trusted people he could depend on to get him out of his mess.

Unlike some more ignorant criminals, he did ave the semblance of a plan, at least in his head. The lan involved getting to the UAE - to Dubai. For many years, Spain had a well-earned nickname of the *Costa del Crime*, but it lost that mantle ages ago. These days Dubai has assumed the role. Someone once said that certain bars in Dubai would offer up more British gangsters than a roll call in a London prison. All Ryan needed was money, contacts, and a passport. The first two were not difficult; he or his family could lay hands on cash or access bank accounts, and he had connections in the UAE who would make things happen without too many problems for him. Karim Nasri would provide the third element - sooner than Ryan expected.

The promise of a quick passport turn-around timing from Nasri came as fantastic news for Ryan. Whilst the clock ticked, Ryan had some other urgent business to attend to over the phone, with an old associate in Ireland, it needed immediate attention.

The 24 hours promised by Nasri had almost elapsed, and he confirmed with Ryan everything was still on to meet and hand over.

His first night on the run, and Ryan had struggled to sleep a wink all night, his mind went into overdrive with all sorts of nonsense, most of it negative thoughts most of which involved Jason Price, *"If I could kil that bastard twice, then I would - he didn't suffer enough Same for that clown Savvas. Shit, I should have seen al this coming."*

One of the mobile numbers Ryan retrieved from his phone before destroying it on his boat, belonge to James Mee, a semi-retired lawyer in Ireland. A old friend of the family, he was also an *old friend* of several other close families in the Irish Republic and still practising.

Mee wandered down the road from his home, enjoying one of his regular rain or shine walks to his local newsagent to collect a daily paper when an unknown Spanish number called him, he paused, then cautiously answered the call, "Hello, this is James."

"James, it's been a while. How are the family, and that lovely wife of yours?"

"Why, Declan Ryan, as I live and breathe. What an unexpected pleasure this fine day. How are you?"

Ryan had been on the run less than 48-hours, and Mee had not yet heard the news of Ryan's plight.

"Oh, I've been better James, to tell you truth. You know how it is. But I'm hoping things are going to improve for me real soon. In the meantime James, there's something I hope you can help me with. Something special I need you to do for me. Do you have a pen and paper handy?"

For the next ten minutes, Ryan explained the task he needed James Mee to carry out for him. He listened to Mee's opinions regarding certain aspects of it and asked him to do his best, as he knew he always would.

As the call with Mee concluded, another call came in, Karim Nasri. He was an hour away, and ringing Ryan to arrange where they should meet, "Away from the chalet just in case Declan, you never know? What do you think? And where would be safest?"

"Yes, a good shout. I agree - *you never know.* Let's give ourselves room to manoeuvre just in case we need it. Keep the cars parked separate and out of the way, I'll leave mine here and walk to meet you. I know a good spot."

Both men trusted each other, but circumstances dictated, extreme caution - once a by-word for them - and old habits die hard.

Chapter 37

Blood, Boccelli, and Loyalty

Both men had become familiar with an ingenious location finding 'app' called *what3words.com*. The app divides the surface of the earth into three-metre squares, each square possesses a unique phrase of three words permanently designated to it. The tiny grid square and the words never change, for anyone. Users share the words, and the app pinpoints you to each tiny location - anywhere. Ideal for finding one tent among a hundred thousand at the Glastonbury music festival or for a clandestine meeting between two gangsters converging on the same spot for the first time, way off the grid.

In the case of Ryan and Nasri, a tiny piece of wasteland in a forest, near a firebreak track just a short hike from a road, made them both feel at ease and more relaxed. Ryan remained on edge, racing against the clock. The longer he stayed in Spain, the greater the probability existed of pursuers tracking him down or discovering him, no matter how careful he was – and the more the pressure and paranoia would creep in. Even after being on the run for just over one day, he could feel it. So far there were no blue lights, sirens, or helicopters. In reality, the police had no idea where he was, and Karim Nasri did not register as a local or regular acquaintance and had not pinged on the police radar as a known or close associate of his. Ryan had nothing to worry about from the law.

Despite the *casita's* location at around two thousand meters altitude, the warmer weather, lack of snow and forest terrain, ruled out the snowmobile as a transport option. Ryan chose to avoid the roads by hiking the three kilometres, through the woods to the what3words location - *postcards.bodes.scalped*. The altitude, adrenalin, and physicality of the walk were invigorating, but challenging for the out of shape Ryan, who arrived panting, sweating and surprisingly early for him, so he waited for his old friend to turn up.

On time, smiling, smoking, but not out of breath, Nasri wandered into the sunny location five minutes later.

"Nice look Declan." Nasri referred to the darker than expected fake hairstyle of his friend.

They embraced, sat on a log, and talked. Ryan reiterated the entire saga about what went wrong with his investment in Wales and how it all started earlier than that, thanks to Jason Price with the casino.

CHAPTER 37

"I keep having conflicting thoughts - should I have killed him? Maybe I shouldn't have killed him? No, that's not true, it was a huge mistake. I was wrong - but I was furious with him - raging. Once it was in my head, what with all the errors he made - most of them with my money, and the fact that he had figured things out about the Savvas's - he needed to go. I wasn't having that. The bastard."

"Declan you always did have a temper and a vicious streak. I saw it so many times. You never learn. But I understand, when things interfere with business, things happen – don't they? So where are you going? What are you going to do?"

Ryan explained his plans to get to Dubai and that his wife would join him at a later date. "We can manage for money, for a while. That won't be a problem. But I can't go anywhere without documents. What have you got for me, Karim? What's my new name and am I, Irish? Canadian? Australian?"

Nasri, stubbed out his cigarette, slipped off his backpack and reached inside. But instead of retrieving a fake passport and driver's licence, Nasri had something else for Ryan. The ever-ready smile on Nasri's face vanished as he took two subtle, premeditated steps back.

Selected from his mini arsenal at home, Nasri had pulled out of his backpack, a Colt M1911 semi-automatic pistol. He had loaded it earlier wearing gloves, with .45 ACP ammunition. A quiet subsonic low velocity round, almost as good as using a sound suppressor. Nasri wondered if the loading with gloves and quiet rounds were necessary, no one would find the ejected shell casings or hear the shots.

The moment Ryan spotted the pistol he realised what was coming and lunged for his life towards Nasri. But the Frenchman moved at a lightning-fast pace and had already anticipated Ryan's reach by giving himself the steps backwards and extra space he needed. He shot Ryan twice, in the face, from less than two metres away, then shot him once more in the back of what remained of his cropped fake dark-haired head as he lay at his feet.

Nasri stood and looked over Ryan's face-down corpse for a few moments, said a quiet prayer in Arabic, and then offered an apology, "I'm so sorry my friend, our lives have always been different. My family and my beliefs mean more to me than our friendship."

The morning before setting off to kill Ryan, Nasri gave a reassuring nod to himself - relieved when he received the notification on his phone, of his shipmen clearing customs and the bonded warehouse in the UK for onward forwarding. The only thing tha could go wrong with his shipment was if Declan Rya remained alive and ended up getting himself capture by the police. Ryan knew too much about Nasri' widespread cartel business empire and in particular th recent shipment. Ryan had made himself redundan - risky, dangerous, and superfluous. He should hav realised it, but he didn't, and now he lay dead in som melting snow in the middle of a Pyrenean forest.

Nasri had a few more important tasks to carry out before leaving the high mountains. He needed certainty that no incriminating evidence remained on Ryan or at the casita concerning their relationship and the shipment. Ryan may have left a laptop, handwritten notes, or another phone. Nasri, wanted nothing left to chance. The possibility of anyone finding Ryan's body for decades remained slim, so Nasri searched the body and took what he needed – some car and door keys and one of Ryan's pay as you go phones. He hid the body under some broken branches, no one would find it.

He knew the location of the casita and approached it with confidence that he would not encounter any company or law enforcement. But, as a precaution, he circled the small cube-shaped, smoked-glass fronted building and used his binoculars to look for any other cars or obvious activity in the building or the nearby woods. He saw nothing to concern him, an open downstairs window and just Ryan's car parked out of sight, outside, and the reassuring, long single tracks going in that the car made the day before in the melting snow. The car blipped open and Nasri made a thorough search inside it and inside the boot - no bags, no paperwork – a clean car and no worries.

By using one of the casita keys he had taken, he ecided to enter the property through a side door nto the garage, where he found a snowmobile that at there unused for months. A sensor-activated light artled him when it came on automatically, as he recalled it did when he visited on a previous occasion. Whilst inside the garage Nasri thought he could hear something, a noise coming through the adjoining door from the first floor of the building. He listened again, then realised he could hear music - operatic music - and recalled Ryan's passion for it. Ryan had set up some music to play on a loop and had not turned it off. He had also told Nasri he was going to the casita alone, *"I can't afford to take any chances, and risk meeting anyone else."* He meant it. Nasri relaxed and tucked the pistol inside the rear of his belt.

He walked through the garage and opened a door into a ski and boot room. He found an untidy area, littered with old bobble hats, gloves, boots placed over 'drying pegs', skis, and poles. With nothing of interest, he jogged up three concrete steps into the warm, south-facing main living space, into the natural light. With the music a little louder now, he closed the boot room door behind him. The moment he closed the door, he realised he shared the room with two large, agitated, boxer dogs. Both dogs had positioned themselves on either side of Nasri and the door. His brief moment of surprise turned to one o concern, Nasri disliked dogs at the best of times, and the intimidating boxers stood growling and staring a him as he fumbled under his puffa jacket for the pistol

As Savvas and Price once observed at Ryan's home the highly trained dogs rarely growled or snarled at stranger. Unless their master was under threat. Now *h* was dead and the scent of his blood splatter on Nas filled the nostrils of Alfie and Bow. The normally placid animals reacted as any faithful dogs would react. The pair of incensed, 70lb boxer dogs, attacked, overpowering the slightly built Nasri, flooring him before he could make a full grasp of his gun. He somehow managed to fire off two shots. The first which missed the dogs and embedded itself into the wall, the second went clean through the tip of Alfie's ear. The shots did nothing to pacify the fearsome, determined dogs, and they tore him to shreds to the beautiful sound of Andre Boccelli, the CD left playing on *repeat*, meant to soothe the dogs whilst alone, - *Con te partirò* - time to say goodbye.

~

Immingham to Devon is a long drive, slower in a truck with a tachograph requiring an appropriate legal rest stop on the way. Anti-terrorist police had received a tip-off the day before from a reliable source. The source indicated they wanted the UK police to consider the tip-off as a gift in the hope of a favour for a favour. The dismantling of a well-organised terrorist network preparing to arm themselves, in return for a comfortable sentence and prison location. If there was such a thing for murder, for Michael Ryan, and if it ever came to it - for Declan Ryan.

Lawyer, James Mee, had a long track record of negotiation with the UK and Irish police, though on this occasion he realised he was between a rock and a hard place. Murder doesn't often receive a great deal of consideration under any circumstances. Little did Mee realise, a plea bargain for one of the men, Declan Ryan, would be a waste of time anyway as he was already dead.

Before he found himself on the run, Ryan had huge misgivings about the Karim Nasri shipment. On previous occasions, Ryan had occasionally smuggled guns and ammunition into the UK for sale to drug dealers and gangsters. That was one thing, but arming a bunch of terrorists was another. The irony of his Irish Republican family's gruesome terrorist history, and some of the atrocities he had personally carried out such as kneecapping and murder, decades earlier, didn't register with him. This was different, *innocent* people were at risk.

Ryan's one and only night's sleep in the casita had been a poor one – the reason was the responsibility he couldn't hide from - the 3D printer. The guns and prospect of the lunatics who would run riot with them troubled and sickened him. By the time Karim Nasri contacted Ryan the following morning to say he was on his way, Ryan had already decided 'enough was enough'. He had spoken to James Mee, and Ryan's contrition came in part to try and get a better deal for his cousin Michael, and himself - if the police ever arrested him - but also to do the right thing. Nasri wouldn't know it had been Ryan who pulled the plug. The weapons interception could have simply been down to eagle-eyed anti-terrorist police, who foiled the plot. Neither did Ryan know that he would soon be a dead man. A violent, dead man, who died with the hint of a conscience - too little too late.

Police acted on the information provided by Mee. They made no promises but offered their gratitude in return.

The 3D printing machine and the shrink-wrapped pallets of hi-tech composite plastic raw materials arrived at their destination in Devon. A forklift truck unloaded and positioned the printer in a clean and dry, modern storage unit at the farm, fully equipped with three-phase electricity to run the energy-hungry machinery. Karim Nasri's sister watched the installation take place - with the initial commissioning and testing already completed in Barcelona. Soon, she and her accomplices would be manufacturing identical replica, high-performance semi-automatic Glock pistols. Thousands of them.

Nasri's sister could not understand why her brother had dropped off the radar. His mobile appeared active, yet he had received but read none of her messages or returned any of her calls. He told her he had some important business to attend to. If he was personally involved in *important business* and had not delegated it, then it usually meant he had something serious to attend to, and she gave him the benefit of the doubt for his temporary absence. But both Nasri and Ryan had been dead almost a day.

For the 24-hours after being delivered to the farm, the machine sat there, powered up, ready to go. Final checks and preparation all complete. Everything ready to work - including the listening devices and micro-cameras, built into the LED screen of the programming unit at the front of the machine, and swapped into the cooling system warning lights, by anti-terrorist technicians whilst the unit left Immingham 'in transit'. The police watched and recorded hours of discussions, compiling valuable information and incriminating evidence, waiting for the moment to move in when they had the greatest number of culprits in one place at the same time.

The curiosity of several key players in the weapons manufacturing plot got the better of them. They all arrived to watch the first Glock samples churn off the production line and snap together, fully assembled in seconds, just like the genuine guns. They were genuine guns. A young man laid out the magazines in front of them and produced a box of 9mm bullets. The young man's associates failed to get any closer to loading or firing the weapons - an armed assault team descended on the group. The plot ended without a single shot fired.

Chapter 38

Unexpected

Blaenavon - Six months later

Lauren had not long got home from the gym. As she stood in the kitchen about to launch into her first forkful of scrambled eggs, the doorbell almost caused her to miss her mouth - she wasn't expecting visitors.

"Great timing! Early evening? Midweek? Who is this? I'm not expecting any deliveries."

She could see no sign of a van outside. When she opened the door, it wasn't Amazon.

"I hope you're not going to try and toast me with that fork!" Lauren laughed as she immediately recognised the unmistakable Bostonian accent and a familiar face.

"Sorry I thought I'd surprise you, oh, and I've brought you these."

Dee Munchetty produced a box containing an expensive bottle of one of France's finest fizzes and in her other hand an equally enticing box of Belgian chocolates.

"Well you know, I didn't get to catch your graduation, so it's the least I could do, and you look like you have space for a few hundred cals."

Other than a handful of WhatsApps and a few Zooms the two women had not seen each other for almost two months, work had kept them both busy, preventing a physical meeting up.

"Dee! Come on in. I'll lose the fork. What a great surprise." Lauren went in for a hug with her friend.

They chatted, and Dee had some important news. "Everything seems to have spun out of control, Lauren. The bidding war for the rights to broadcast Rare Earth ended yesterday. I wanted to surprise you and tell you in person because you had such a huge involvement in it. They loved you. They loved *ou* story. They love Blaenavon."

Lauren put the fork down, ignored the eggs retrieved two glasses, began to uncork, and said "Amazing news. So what happens now? Tell me more."

Dee smiled and took a sip. "Apart from the extr syndication bonus you're going to make, what happen now is that *you*, well, *we* have a problem. They wan more of you. I'm receiving ideas for environmenta documentary projects almost every day. Rainforests glaciers, and seabeds - take your pick. You did say tha the consortium is running smoothly now didn't you

Thank goodness you took my advice and hired the agent at the same time as the accountant. They are both about to get busier!"

She handed Dee a glass of the Bollinger, and grinned, "I think this calls for a celebration! Cheers!"

About the Author

Mark's parents dropped the 'Jonathan' in favour of Mark almost immediately and he once forgot how to spell his Christian name several years ago - easily done. He is originally from the former Welsh mining town of Blaenavon, now a famous UNESCO World Heritage Site attraction.

As an apprentice, he survived electrocution, whilst drilling a hole in the floor of a flooded milking parlour, before going on to qualify as an aeronautical design engineer. He then spent most of his career in key accounts, designing and selling office interiors to blue-chip clients. His near-death experience decades earlier was almost surpassed, when he was nearly shot in the head at point-blank range with a Magnum .44 by an over-exuberant client whilst at a hospitality event in Sweden!

His award-winning short stories and other works can be found in national magazines and websites or published in his personal short story collection.

To relax he's recently cycled some classic Tour de France alpine climbs, hiked the 'Camino' across Northern Spain to Santiago de Compostela, snowboarded Mont Blanc's Vallée Blanche and once managed to outrun a herd of rampaging cows across his local Welsh mountains. He is secretary of the Hay Writers Circle and a dedicated yogi.

He lives in Wales with similar views to the characters in his Valley Noir themed books.

Acknowledgements

During my research, I listened to the excellent advice of all the people below and embellished where I needed to:

Roannah Wade Senior Policy Adviser – Land Access and Exploration, The Chamber of Minerals & Energy of Western Australia. Neil van Drunen Director AMEC (Association of Mining and Exploration Companies) Western Australia, Northern Territory, South Australia & Industry Policy. Adrian Wilcock Principal Planner Torfaen County Borough Council. Martin Pittuck CEng, FGS, MIMMM Corporate Consultant (Mining Geology) Paul Pelopida Finance Expert. Jackie Huybs Blaenavon Town Councillor (who also read the original short story in 2019). Andrew Ryan Sales Manager Labquip NDT (Spectrometers) Ltd. Blaenavon Historians: David Smith and Joyce Compton of BWHEG. Dr Amelia Pannett of CADW (the Welsh Government's historic environment service).Padraig O'Keefe and Ralph Riegel authors of *Hidden Soldier.* My editing and feedback friends. A bunch of amazing people who kindly gave their time to read my work and help me - Katy Stones, Alan Oberman, Margaret Vidler, Jean O'Donohue, Joss ajjada, D. D. Bartholomew, Gill Haigh, Jan and Phil Thomas, Liz and Rob Jelley, Rhiannon Chandler, Anna arrett, Candi Blakey. Not forgetting all my friends at the Hay Writers Circle for their constant enthusiasm and support.

With special thanks to my wife Anne, she has spent hundreds of hours listening to my ramblings, reading, and correcting my work.

Blaenavon

The town where I grew up, went to school, met my wife, and where I once fell through a frozen mountain pond - The Keepers Pond - as a 10-year-old. Fortunately, I survived to tell the tale. Blaenavon is a town full of great people, and interesting characters, with its fascinating industrial heritage. Well worth a visit, the town boasts coal and iron mining museums, a fabulous Heritage Centre, and an amazing landscape. And yes, Blaenavon was the original birthplace of steel. Once a small town with over 60 pubs, now there are barely more than a handful. I recommend you check out two of the oldest remaining - the fabulous old Goose and Cuckoo and the Whistle Inn.

To the best of my understanding and extensive esearch, the quantities of coal and iron spoil waste xtracted over 150 years are accurate. At its peak, Big it produced 250,000 tons of coal a year. This would ave produced three times as much waste to go with it, dding to the waste from dozens of other pits and iron vorks around the area in the previous decades. The iaduct across the valley mentioned in Chapter 10, is fact, although as stated, today it is covered in coal nd iron waste soil now. This small part of the valley ading to the ironworks would have required at least ne million cubic metres or tonnes of earth to fill the oid. Wembley stadium is four million cubic metres. n the many walks I make over the mountains it's easy to look around and understand the huge scale of the mining that took place on both sides of the valley. Hidden from view, underground are literally hundreds of miles of disused man-made tunnels which produced the coal and waste.

Commercial Property Development and Land Speculation

Throughout my career, I have worked with dozens of architects, consultants, property management agents, and business owners. The vast majority were honest, hardworking professionals - and often great fun to be around. But I did bump into one or two whom I suspect may have bent the rules and blurred the legal lines - coming second wasn't acceptable to some of them.

Modern-day open cast mining for rare earth metals is a huge global industry, and in many countries, it is riddled with corruption and slave labour. You only need to look at some of the South American, or African countries like the Democratic Republic of Congo, where mining cobalt for electric vehicles, or other rare earth minerals, gems, and precious metals, is the modern-day version of the awful conditions once endured by my ancestors in the colliery.

VALLEY NOIR VALLEY BLANC – JM BAYLISS

An anthology of short stories, combining historical, adventure, mystery, darkness, paranormal, 'not of this planet' and some fun. Inspired by Wales. The collection includes the Henshaw International 2020 short story prize winner - 'Taste the Darkness'.

Available as paperback or e-book.

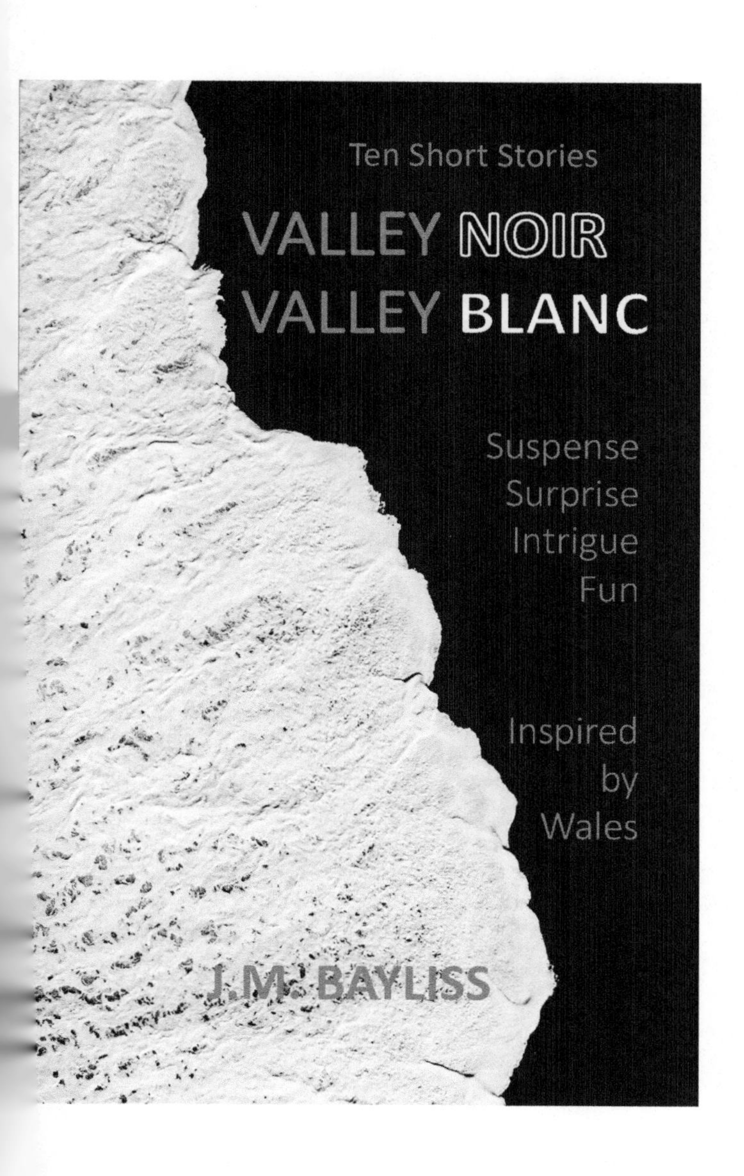
Ten Short Stories
VALLEY NOIR
VALLEY BLANC
Suspense
Surprise
Intrigue
Fun
Inspired
by
Wales
J.M. BAYLISS

The Lucidity Programme – JM Bayliss

The past has found its voice.

An incredible 74-year-old scientific mystery suddenly re-emerges. The British government is running out of ideas and time to solve a major threat to national security. Two elderly sisters in an Oxfordshire nursing home decide to 'put their affairs in order'. They pass a dangerous family secret to the government, a secret that could potentially leave the world defenceless to unstable or hostile governments. Wil is an unassuming farmer whose lucid dreams are being hijacked by voices from the past. He is inadvertently led into a series of exploits before coming to the attention of Government Communications HQ. He becomes their last hope in the search for the scientific discovery of the century. Naively, he steps up, not realising the full extent of the sacrifices he may have to make.

Available as paperback or e-book.

The past has
found its voice
THE
LUCIDITY
PROGRAMME
J.M. BAYLISS

The Lucidity Programme

Chapter 1 – Change the Dynamic

Review Meeting, Cheltenham - May 2019

"How long before *they* beat us to it, and find it, Phil? The PM will ask me later. What's your best guess?"

"Three months? Six if we're lucky. Unthinkable. *Unthinkable.* We'll get there - we must." Chalk replied.

"Christ." The Defence Secretary ended the call.

One hour earlier. Phil Chalk had entered the second-floor meeting room. He was neither military nor ministerial, but commanded huge respect - they all stood.

Seated inside the room, which overlooked a manicured inner courtyard garden, were five women and three men. All, silent, other than for a distracting fizz caused by the filling of some glasses with Buxton's finest. Blank faces, deep in thought, as they struggled to present positive facades. Some made last-minute checks on laptops and tablets of inadequate facts or figures that didn't add up. An emotive meeting agenda confronted them - a serious threat to British national security, and global peace.

On the south-west edge of Cheltenham sits an eye-catching, ring-shaped building. Six-hundred feet in diameter, seventy feet high, set on one-hundred-and-seventy-six acres, surrounded by dedicated car parks and the highest security imaginable. This modern, spectacular piece of architecture is GCHQ – the UK government's General Communications Headquarters, affectionately known as 'The Doughnut' or 'Eavesdropping Central' to the locals.

Often working in collaboration with the military, security services, police forces and friendly foreign governments, GCHQ keeps the UK safe from all kinds of problems within our own country and abroad.

Employed inside are an eclectic mix of over four thousand well-organised, highly-focused academics – linguists, mathematicians, cryptologists, analysts, and researchers. GCHQ also advertises to recruit hackers and mavericks, to address the growth industry of cybercrime.

Today, GCHQ hosted some regular visitors from DSTL - Defence Science and Technology Laboratory the government's famous scientific department based in Porton Down near Salisbury.

Together, they strived for answers for weeks after someone had passed DSTL some astonishing, technological information that needed GCHQ assistance to validate its authenticity and help solve a puzzle. Something, if genuine, would be a serious and dangerous threat to NATO forces and defence systems.

The team of senior people had reached an impasse and were getting nowhere. They suspected other interested parties around the world had become aware of the information and might be trying to solve the same conundrum. The obvious concern focused on their competitor's progress. Did *they* have better intelligence than DSTL?

Chalk, of DSTL, concluded, "Guys, we will find the answers – as always. We have excellent resources, support from Westminster, and the best people - all working together. We don't stop. We keep going. We continue searching for something or someone to help us – we do not give up."

He remained confident, defiant, that they would find the answers and a solution – at some point – but when. The risk associated with losing the race to a hostile or unstable foreign government was unthinkable.

Their pool of ideas needed refreshing and topping up. So far, all of their usual impeccable standards and successful investigation methods had failed to resolve the situation confronting them. They needed a fresh approach, something special to happen to change the dynamic.

Printed in Great Britain
by Amazon